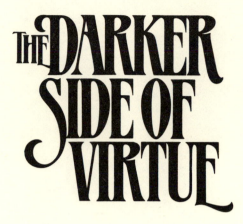

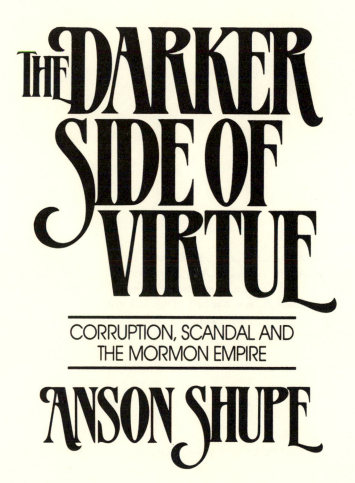

THE DARKER SIDE OF VIRTUE

CORRUPTION, SCANDAL AND
THE MORMON EMPIRE

ANSON SHUPE

PROMETHEUS BOOKS • BUFFALO, NY

95 94 93 92 91   5 4 3 2 1

Library of Congress Cataloging-in-Publication Data

Shupe, Anson D.
    The darker side of virtue : corruption, scandal, and the Mormon empire /
Anson Shupe.
        p.   cm.
    Includes bibliographical references and index.
    ISBN 0-87975-654-3
    1. Church of Jesus Christ of Latter-day Saints—Controversial literature.
2. Mormon Church—Controversial literature. I. Title.
BX8645.S57   1991
289.3—dc20   90-26060
                                                                      CIP

Printed in the United States of America on acid-free paper.

Contents

Acknowledgments

Giving thanks to people who have provided information and assistance to the author of a book on Mormonism can be a touchy issue if the LDS Church does not cast a fully favorable eye on the project. Therefore, this short list of acknowledgments may make me appear less grateful than I really am to many members of that religious body and others who collaborated in information-gathering efforts and the reviewing of evidence.

Furthermore, over the past few years I have benefited from discussing this research with numerous scholars and journalists, not to mention interviews with trial attorneys, district attorneys, regulatory agency investigators, law enforcement officials, sociologists, physicians, and psychologists. Whenever possible their contributions are cited in the notes found at the end of this volume. In particular I wish to thank Dr. O. Kendall White, Jr., of Washington and Lee University; Arlene Burraston-White of Lexington, Kentucky; Dr. David G. Bromley of Virginia Commonwealth University; Glen Silber of CBS News; William Broad of the *New York Times;* Kathy Trische of the *Seattle Times;* Teresa Kramer of the *El Paso Herald Post;* science writer Malcolm McConnell; Bernardo Matias Perez and several other law enforcement agents with the FBI; Jeffrey H. Herman, who swam against the current and believed in this project; and my criminologist colleague Dr. Peter Iadicola of Indiana-Purdue University at Fort Wayne. Many other professionals offered indirect service as sounding boards for ideas and findings presented here. Not all agreed with my conclusions. But to each I extend my appreciation for his or her cooperation, support, and reflections.

1

The Darker Side of Virtue

Norman Rockwell painted the Mormons. Not literally, of course, for his artistry depicted Americans from all walks of life. But at least his well-loved covers for the *Saturday Evening Post* captured the essence of Mormon virtues.

Families were a mainstay among Rockwell's themes. So was respect for authority, for the flag and country, for God and community.

These same virtues are famously important to Mormons. Members of the Church of Jesus Christ of Latter-day Saints, as Mormons are officially known, are often admired as a hard-working, clean-living, family-oriented people. This reputation, plus their Western pioneer heritage, makes them classic Norman Rockwell *Americana*.

Founded in Palmyra, New York, in 1830, this new religion—as different from Christianity as Christianity itself is from Judaism—resulted in a phenomenal success story. From its frontier origins, the Church rapidly attracted converts both in the United States and Europe. Throughout the 1840s Mormons experienced vicious persecution that martyred their founder/prophet Joseph Smith and drove thousands of them halfway across North America to establish a thriving foothold in the rugged Great Salt Basin of Utah.

Today the LDS Church is *the* fastest growing religion, not just in this country but in the world. Far from being persecuted, the Mormon faith and its adherents today enjoy one of the most positive, wholesome images in American religion. Once considered a threat to society with their "heretical" scriptures, communal economy, and polygamous marriages, Mormons are now known for their low rates of many current social ills that plague American families. Indeed, President Ronald Reagan, no small champion of conservative America, wrote to the son of Utah's U.S. Senator Jake Garn shortly before the young man left for a missionary stint in England: "I have such great respect for your Church. Although I am not a Mormon, I very much respect your Mormon values."[1]

Reagan was referring, of course, to those qualities that Mormons have come to exemplify; such qualities range from faithful tithing to their Church, obedience to Church elders, and abstention from tobacco and alcohol, to raising large families with low incidences of divorce and juvenile delinquency. Beyond these, all that most Americans know of the LDS Church is the Mormon Tabernacle Choir and its splendid Christmas record albums, the impressive complex of LDS temple and tourist buildings in the heart of Salt Lake City, and the conservatively dressed pairs of well-scrubbed young men (and, with increasing frequency, women) trekking door to door in suburbs to witness for their faith. Indeed, that is the public relations *persona* of Mormon faith and life indelibly impressed on non-Mormons, who know by reputation the LDS virtues of strong families, thrift, industriousness, self-reliance, honesty, patriotism, and a special reverence for the LDS Church's own history.

These days that reputation counts for something. In this era of ethical expediency in American business and government, Mormonism understandably commands a certain respect from the rest of the country. "Me-firstism" may have taken over much of American culture, but Mormons still stand for civic responsibility above hedonism. While the larger society has become mired in a moral decline of corrupt Wall Street traders, Washington politicians who line the pockets of their friends with lush consulting fees, and crooked philandering television preachers, it is comforting to many to know that somewhere there is at least one American-born faith still upholding traditional values. Mormonism represents a moral beacon anchored firmly to bedrock in a sea of relative values and situation morality. Even the faith's theological opponents in other denominations give it that much in grudging admiration.

But all is not as it seems.

There is a darker side to many of these well-known Mormon virtues. They can be two-edged swords, destructive as well as constructive to those who unquestionably take them for granted. For example, in mid-April 1983 a late snowfall in the Wasatch and Uinta Mountains resulted in the worst flooding in Utah's history, causing more than two thousand persons to flee their homes. Within hours thousands of Mormon volunteers, alerted through the Church's "telephone tree" communications network, came forward to fill sandbags, build makeshift levees, and remove mud. Millions of dollars in damages were averted. It was a triumph of community spirit and cooperation in the best American tradition.

Yet that same effective Church authority and the larger "official" Mormon community have sometimes reacted with intolerant, even repressive attitudes toward dissent among members. Dallin Oaks, a member of the Church's Council of the Twelve Apostles, told a Utah audience several years ago that Church members should under no circumstances *ever* criticize any leaders above them because these are "the Lord's annointed." "It does not matter that the criticism is true," he added, thus demanding a mindset of uncritical conformity.[2] Since the early 1980s the same LDS Church hierarchy that mobilized the 1983 flood fighters has been busy excommunicating about twenty thousand members a year, most frequently for criticizing Church leaders and professing "false doctrine."

There are other instances of touted virtues that possess a negative flip side:

—Those pairs of earnest young Mormon missionaries who knock on doors to share their faith are mere window dressing for recruitment. Their success rates at conversion are abysmally low. The LDS Church's real missionizing accomplishments in recent years have been the results of low-key, even covert (and sometimes illegal) campaigns in Moslem countries as well as "special deals" made with communist regimes, in Eastern Europe and the Soviet Union; such deals keep Mormon converts submissive to authorities. With the downfall of many communist governments, Mormon missionizing prospects are better than ever.

—Stereotypes of Mormons' legendary thrift and industriousness aside, federal and state law enforcement officials consider Utah the get-rich-quick scheme/fraud capital of the United States. They blame the epidemic problem on Mormons' drive for financial security and their gullibility for high-profit/no-risk promises made by con-artists.

—The LDS Church's acknowledged love of history and genealogy really extends only to historical evidence if it supports official dogma. Otherwise, LDS leaders have been busy buying up documents that challenge its orthodox account of its origins and have tried more than once to repress or cover up the existence off these documents. The Church's obsession with good public relations rather than a respect for truth now determines admissible history.

—The noticeable Mormon presence in the U.S. intelligence communities (FBI, CIA) is not simply a factor of patriotism. A "Mormon mafia"

in the FBI has systematically discriminated against non-Mormon mi-
nority-group agents who have been unwilling to convert, meanwhile
promoting the careers of Mormon agents at the others' expense.

—A strong emphasis on the family, backed by the dense LDS Church
network of contacts and activities, helped to produce a horrifying
sexual-abuse scare in Lehi, Utah; here Mormon children in 1985
began reporting how they had been sodomized and violated *by their
own parents in Satanic rings.* Families were split apart, and the courts
stepped in to remove children from their parents as rumors of Satanic
cult activity spread.

—The LDS Church stresses high ethical standards and competitive
business practices to its rank-and-file members. Yet in the early 1970s
LDS Church leaders mounted a no-holds-barred illegal pressure
campaign on Mormon politicians and the Mormon head of NASA
to have the U.S. space shuttle solid booster rockets built by a Utah
company, despite the fact that the rocket's engineering design was
known to be flawed by both engineers *and* the U.S. Government
Accounting Office.

These examples span a considerable range: politics, economics, international
relations, history, family, even outer space. What else could be expected
of a rapidly expanding religion so aggressively involved in the secular world?
Some religions have made their peace with the status quo and are content
to compartmentalize themselves within the world. Not so the Mormons.

And the temptations of that worldly involvement can bring out the
negative aspects of the very virtues for which the LDS religion is praised.
Faith is perverted into fanaticism, self-confidence into arrogance, and
ambition into ruthlessness. Respect and reverence for leaders can become
blind obedience. Patriotism can degenerate into jingoism or simply become
a dodge to justify self-interest.

An American Dilemma—A Mormon Solution?

In recent years many persons have tried to account for the causes underlying
so many scandals involving America's highest leaders in business, politics,
and even religion. It has become fashionable to pinpoint the blame on
a so-called moral vacuum afflicting the entire country. Preachers cry out
their jeremiads and warn how far we have strayed from the absolutes of
the Bible. Sociologists write of our uprootedness and alienation. Psycholo-

gists lecture on our narcissism and against a generation of affluent baby-boomers raised to idolize materialism.

After investigations revealed that the October 19, 1987, "Black Monday" stock market crash on Wall Street had been caused in part by shenanigans such as those of convicted insider-trader Ivan Boesky and junk bond manipulator Michael Milken, an issue of *Time* magazine devoted its lead story to business and political dirty dealing. Its cover title was "What Ever Happened to Ethics?"[3] Prominent theologians were quoted as claiming that our post-Watergate, post-Boesky, even post-Bakker-Swaggart nation is in a climate of moral disarray and ethical confusion. The editors of *Time* strongly suggested that Americans have drifted morally, that we need to look again to our spiritual roots to rebuild a national structure of values.

In different ways all such observers have basically arrived at the same end point. And, often, the same cure. America, the experts have concluded, is short on good old-fashioned virtues. They say we need a healthy infusion of revived traditional values. Discipline, hard work, self-restraint, and respect for authority make up the prescription. Without such qualities restored, our communities will continue to fall apart, our youth will acknowledge nothing greater than their own urges, and our leaders will fear nothing greater than disclosure of their misdeeds.

Alas, it should be so cut and dried.

Much of such pop-wisdom, whatever its commonsense appeal, is made up of equal parts nostalgia and naiveté. The truth is that ethical anarchy is not as simple an explanation of any ethics problem in this country as it might first appear. Put bluntly, submission to the rules of religious dogma offers no sure-fire cure.

That is what this book is about. It is a story of virtue gone astray, of how admirable traits can turn inward and become obsessions. I focus on one highly visible religious group, the Mormons, my purpose not to encourage bigotry or religion bashing but to follow the trail of best intentions turning into calamity. For all their well-publicized virtues, Mormons are no more insulated from the dangers of materialism, fraud, hysteria, or power than anyone else. Ironically, their own best qualities sometimes set them up for horrible confrontations with their worst. There is a lesson in the Mormon experience for all Americans.

At the same time, it may be that many readers are only vaguely familiar with the beliefs and structures of Mormonism. These points are important to grasp at least generally because they are so intimately linked to the unpleasant facts to follow. Therefore, a brief introduction to this Utah-based faith may provide some useful background to later chapters.

The World of the Latter-day Saints

All observers, scholars and journalists alike, agree that Mormon subculture is unique. Probably the closest comparison could be made to the individual colonies of religious sects that fled Old World persecution to settle on the Eastern seaboard of North America in the seventeenth and eighteenth centuries. Each possessed its own distinctive theology and civic style, consciously keeping itself different from others.

Likewise, non-Mormons who have lived in Utah and other western Mountain States with high concentrations of LDS members, former Mormons who have left the Church, and those still loyal to the Salt Lake City "Brethren" would all agree that the LDS subculture is a world apart. It has its own heroes and icons, holidays, and traditions, and even its own vocabulary. In many ways Mormonism is still a colony marking time in modern America.

Here are the most important dimensions of this phenomenon:

Mormon leaders' claims to special charisma and revelations. Joseph Smith was raised in a region of New York State which historians call the "burned-over district" because of the repeated waves of religious revivalism and sect hysteria which caught up town folk and rural citizens alike. As a youth, Smith prayed for divine guidance as to which of the various denominations and churches was the one "true" church. Around 1820 the teenage Smith experienced a vision in which God and Jesus Christ revealed to him not only that the Almighty was angry at the ungodliness and hypocrisy of the various Christians and their competing churches but that Jesus Christ was soon to return to earth.

Smith had been chosen, he was told, for his sincerity, and he was commissioned to restore the true Church of Christ on earth. He learned how the legitimate succession, from Israel's King David through Jesus's earthly family lineage, and then down through Christ's original apostles, had been corrupted. It began when the sun-worshipping Roman Emperor Constantine made Christianity the nominal Imperial religion in the early fourth century. The Roman Catholic Church and later Protestants only compounded the errors. Joseph Smith was charged by the visionary Christ with restoring the authority of apostolic succession; that is, he was instructed to found the one true church and gather a new set of apostles just as Christ had done.

Later visions revealed to Smith a fantastic lost history of the Americas, starting about 600 B.C. when a courageous band of Hebrews left Jerusalem just ahead of a conquering Babylonian army. While the Babylonians sacked Israel's cities and enslaved its people, the Hebrew refugees sailed across the Atlantic Ocean in desperate flight. Their adventures, and the details of the mighty civilization they founded and subsequently lost in a gigantic civil war, were eventually translated by Smith from previously hidden special gold tablets into what became the Book of Mormon.

This is the official LDS Church version of the events leading up to the beginning of Mormonism. My purpose here is neither to defend nor criticize it. The important point is that millions of Mormons believe it. They also accept the current LDS Church president with even more sanctity than Roman Catholics regard the Pope. The LDS Church president is a living prophet and the receiver of Almighty God's revelations. He is, to Mormons, "prophet, seer, and revelator." His true apostleship flows from the restoration of Christ's authority which Joseph Smith was commissioned to begin.

By extention, that authority trickles down the LDS ecclesiastical hierarchy in pyramid fashion, touching even the local ward bishops. As one 1981 LDS leader asserted in an editorial in a Church newspaper:

> God will do nothing regarding His work except through His own duly anointed prophets! They are His servants. They are the watchmen on the towers of Zion.
>
> They will give us the Lord's word in no uncertain terms as God makes it known. That is why He has His prophets on earth. They are for the edification of the Saints and to protect us from every wind of doctrine. Let us follow them and avoid being led astray.[4]

The result is that leaders, not followers, are considered to be in much better positions to see the extended picture because of revelations. From their earliest years Mormons are taught to obey Church doctrines and to regard their leaders' decisions as inspired by God. Therefore rank-and-file members should be careful lest they criticize or fail to trust completely in their leaders' wisdom.

How many Mormons actually depart from this "party line" is unknown. As in many religious traditions, many individual members undoubtedly pick and choose the limits of their obedience to dogma. However, the pressures to conform are obvious.

Mormonism's millennial sense of election. Jesus Christ revealed to Joseph Smith that the end of the world, his Second Coming, and his subsequent one thousand year reign (or millennium) were imminent. Accordingly, those who would follow Smith in restoring the true Church would therefore be living in the last days (thus their designation as the *Latter-day* Saints).

But while most conservative Christian groups in America are *premillennial,* the Mormons were and to a certain extent still are *postmillennial.* Premillennialists expect a sudden return of Christ, without warning. They only know that his return will be preceded by a period of wars, misery, chaos, and widespread social breakdown. They believe they can do nothing to hurry or prevent the Second Coming and its preliminary tribulations. Their duty is to convert as many to Christ while they hunker down to await the event.

Postmillennialists, on the other hand, share the belief that a coming time of trouble will occur before Christ's return, but they also hold to the idea that they must actively prepare the way before the return. Establishing the Kingdom of God for Christ to head as temporal, political, and corporate leader is their responsibility. This entails constructing a financial and political foundation, in terms of worldly power and influence, to be held by those believed to be Christ's stewards.

According to this view the LDS Church has a special mission to accomplish for Christ. The Church believes that its Restored Gospel, complete with the Bible, Book of Mormon, and other revealed truths (such as Doctrine and Covenants), is superior to past Christianity in the same way that most Chrirtians see their gospel message as superior to that of Judaism. Mormonism, in this sense, is "completed" Christianity. Mormons are the "elect." Their own theology declares them a special people (the "New Israel," as they are told). Moreover, if they keep their covenant with God they each will evolve after death into gods themselves, ruling worlds without end much as Jehovah now does.

Many scholars believe that modern Mormonism has softened its original millennialism. Most agree that the emphasis on living in the last days began to decline around the turn of the century after the Church banned the practice of polygamy, Utah gained statehood, and the first Mormon was elected to the U.S. Senate. The LDS Church and its people began to accommodate to American culture, appearing less odd and increasingly less concerned about the coming millennium.

When Mormons were persecuted with beatings, lynchings, and shootings, hounded as an antisocial cult from New York to Ohio to Missouri to Illinois to a desolate Western wilderness, they understandably felt pessimism and looked to the wrath of God to destroy their enemies. But now Mormons are glorified, not vilified, by the mass media. According to this current view, the average Mormon not only has made his or her peace with mainstream American society but is as "home" in it as anyone else, perhaps more so.

However, it is still an open question as to whether the postmillennialism of the LDS Church has passed entirely or still might play an important role, even indirectly. There are many indications that postmillennialism is alive and well in the LDS Church, if not so much among many rank-and-file members, then among the upper echelons of its leadership. Books on millennialism sell very well in Utah. Moreover, the expectation of an imminent time of political and social chaos still guides the LDS Church, Inc.'s investment strategies. Church leaders talk about it in their speeches to the faithful. A number of official Church publications (judging by their frequent editorials on the subject) seem to take millennialism for granted. Even if the average Mormon may not be as preoccupied with a coming time of tribulation as he or she once might have been, nevertheless traditional expectations about the millennium still have a definite (if indirect) impact.

Mormonism's tension with larger society. Hostility between Mormons and their gentile persecutors during the nineteenth century promoted a garrison mentality among the Utah Saints. Such a defensive oppositional worldview was only strengthened by later events, such as the Utah War of 1857 when almost two thousand federal troops were sent to wrest control of the territorial government from the LDS Church and impose martial law. Men and boys built barricades to block mountain passes and formed raiding parties to harrass the soldiers when they camped at night on the way to Utah. The later arrests of Mormon leaders for polygamy and the Mormons' own underground railroad for hiding the fugitives also kept the tension alive.

These animosities have largely disappeared except in predominantly Mormon areas in the West where non-Mormons now feel that *they* are the ones considered outsiders. But the years of conflict left marks on the LDS faith. Persecution and the sense of being an elect group provided Mormons with the sure knowledge that they were different. A sense of pride arose from such feelings. One Mormon historian has even suggested that these sentiments were so important to the young LDS movement that when the Church started becoming more "respectable" in the eyes of larger American society, its leaders deliberately began to emphasize certain "taboos" for members to recreate a consciousness of Mormon/non-Mormon boundaries. These taboos are, of course, the now familiar restrictions against consuming coffee, tea, liquor, and tobacco; such taboos are to be found in a body of sacred LDS teachings called the Word of Wisdom.[5]

Aside from health advantages, these taboos on practices otherwise so common in larger American society have helped modern Mormons retain some sense of their own distinctiveness. Likewise, while those pairs of enthusiastic, clean-cut young Mormons canvassing neighborhoods produce questionable conversion results, the many doors slammed in their missionaries' faces and the general public disinterest reinforces to Mormons that they *are* different, that ultimately at the Second Coming Judgment the apathetic non-Mormon world will get what it deserves.

The creation of a special Mormon worldview. The years of persecution and hostility during the nineteenth century threw Mormons back on their own resources. They were isolated in the Utah wilderness and had to rely only on one another. They also developed a lifestyle of general self-reliance around their theology, which encouraged the development of a unique worldview. From practicing theocratic politics to writing new hymns, from experimenting in communal farms and factories to the well-known practice of taking plural wives, Mormons created their own world with its own ways of thinking. Parts of this world *were* given up very reluctantly as the Church entered the twentieth century, but some parts remain completely intact. In a cold world of religious intolerance and frontier dangers, it was no accident that Mormon men and women held (and still use) the titles "brother" and "sister."

An important part of this worldview is a sense of family—that Mormons share a special heritage and destiny, that while on this earth they may expect something more from one another than they can at the hands of Gentiles. This "something more" is what any family member takes for granted from a brother or sister: openness, warmth, friendliness, goodwill. Mormonism in many ways makes all Mormons part of an extended family, a sense which has been lost in many other contemporary Christian churches.

That faith in Mormon reliability is doubly reinforced by the religion's overall sense of special election in God's eyes and by the presumed protection or reward in the here and now that comes from such acts as tithing to the Church and going to the local temple. The most important negative result of this worldview for Mormons is that it makes them vulnerable to someone who would betray or abuse their trust. Mormons, in other words, are potentially more gullible (in a way non-Mormons generally would not be) to a "come-on" proposed by someone claiming also to be a Mormon. On the other hand, Mormons also may feel they have a special claim on fellow religionists when they seek professional and other allies in the largely non-Mormon world.

Mormon networks of kin and church. Mormons, like everyone else, are parts of family networks; there are many generations, many in-laws, many blood relatives. The Mormon penchant for large families makes this even more true.

But Mormons are also embedded in the dense network of the LDS Church. At the lowest level is the *ward,* composed of approximately 400 to 500 people or the equivalent of a modest Protestant congregation. The ward is overseen by a bishop (a nonprofessional part-time clergyman) and his two counselors. The *stake,* equivalent to a Roman Catholic diocese, is composed of five to seven wards (or approximately three thousand people). The stake president (also a nonprofessional clergyman) has not only two counselors but also a stake high council made up of twelve councilmen to help him administer the wards under his jurisdiction. Stakes are in turn parts of larger *regions* (administered by regional representatives) which are supervised by the First Council of the Seventy. Above the First Council of the Seventy is the Council of the Twelve Apostles and the First Presidency, which consists of the President and his two counselors, each of whom carries the title "President" as well.

This pyramid structure was designed to allow an efficient downward flow of information and directives as well as to mobilize members for action in the event of trouble. Such communication was often used in the past, and Church leaders who cling to postmillennial beliefs expect to use it again in the near future.

In addition, there are two orders of priesthood (the Higher, or Melchizedek, and the Lower, or Aronic) which involve most active Mormon men. Thus the LDS Church can claim that it has no paid clergy. *All* Mormon males in good standing are clergy. Various charitable and cultural groups also exist for women and youths, though there is no priesthood for women.

If one were to tally all the paid employees in LDS Church offices, all the employees of LDS Church-owned companies and their subsidiaries, and the vast grass-roots army of voluntary workers at all levels of the Church, they would easily number in the many hundreds of thousands. For example, two Mormon historians have estimated that just in the average ward (of which there are thousands) there exist about two hundred administrative positions including clerks and lay persons in charge of monitoring financial, membership, and conversion statistics.[6]

This complex ecclesiastical bureaucracy, with its multiple levels, combined with a complex honeycomb of other women's, men's, and youth groups, from Boy Scout troops to numerous welfare societies, constitutes an extremely dense interpersonal network. It can communicate messages with amazing speed through each ward's "telephone tree." When Florida Mormons mobilized to block their state's ratification of the Equal Rights Amendment, one Church leader there boasted, "The structure exists where I can make sixteen calls, and by the end of the day 2,700 people will know something."[7]

Mormonism is the Protestant Ethic. The Protestant Ethic came from the Calvinists, early followers of the stern Protestant Reformation theologian John Calvin. Its basic ideas, in the terms that Joseph Smith undoubtedly understood them, were that hard work is a virtue in itself, that riches or good fortune attained without such labor are immoral, and that one's employment is more than a job—it is a sacred calling.

In many ways Mormons are good Calvinists (though not thought of as such by most theologians). They seek to excel at whatever they do, rising to the top of the professions they pursue. In industry, commerce, the military, government, and mass media they work hard and believe in material success as a sign that they are blessed for something special.

Their Church corporation is a testimony to this success ethic. Financed by generous contributions from its members and an extensive portfolio of investments, LDS, Inc., is a mammoth conglomerate diversified into insurance, broadcasting, real estate, agriculture, and many other business avenues. In *The Mormon Corporate Empire,* published in 1985, my co-author and I conservatively estimated from a detailed breakdown its total wealth at approximately $8 billion.[8] We now know from additional information that we placed far too low a figure on its assets. In fact, the Church corporation's total wealth was likely somewhere near twice that amount at that time, and today even that estimate may be far too low.

Sometimes this success has led to an overglorification of material success, even at the expense of ignoring the Protestant Ethic's point about the immorality of wealth not gained by hard work. The pattern is similar to the "Gospel of Prosperity" preached by various televangelists who proclaim that the message of Christianity is one of good health, prosperity, and fortune to the exclusion of sacrifice, pain, and discomfort. Earthly rewards are believed to be returns on investments made in the name of God, and losses are simply not calculated into the formulae of giving.

As I will show, Mormons themselves have recently become aware of the perils of identifying too closely with the secular world and are their own best critics. Some Church observers are concerned that believers will think that faithful tithing or regular temple attendance will automatically shield them against fraud and harm. These observers see a flipside to the work ethic, one that elevates success over the virtue of fulfilling one's calling. They warn that any worldview that leads believers to expect special blessings because of their faith and good works alone unwittingly prepares them for tragedies sooner or later.

A Cautionary Preface

Those with firmly planted stereotypes should be forewarned. Six of the following seven chapters examine virtues for which Mormonism is popularly known: straightforward missionizing, industriousness, a reverance for history, strong family values, conservative patriotism, and ethical economic behavior. Yet, the flipsides these chapters also explore may prove disconcerting to many readers. Certainly none of the findings confirms the flattering, squeaky-clean public-relations image of the LDS Church. Many are shocking.

There are those in the LDS Church, particularly its gatekeepers and leaders, who would prefer not to acknowledge these topics. These sorts of discussions, after all, are indelicate, embarrassing, and damaging to the Church's reputation. Certainly they are not, as Mormons say, "faith-promoting."

But they present realities. And in most instances they affect non-Mormons as well as Mormons.

It will do no good for Church spokespersons to ignore these issues or to blame the messenger for the message. No one knows better than the many LDS Church members who helped with the research of this project how serious and widespread many of the problems described here have become.

Finally, this book's investigative approach may trouble many persons, from liberals who anticipate bigotry and dislike criticisms of religious groups to conservatives who defend them. But all are obliged to deal with the facts presented.

Various faiths make exclusive claims to revelation of the Truth, but these are transcendent things, not subject to empirical proofs. (Otherwise we would all be the same Believers in the face of obvious evidence.) The actions of courts, police, and even believers, however, are verifiable in ways that lend themselves to legal and scientific proofs. I make no claim that the situations in the following pages could not, or do not, occur from time to time in other religions. Obviously we need more research in other religions on similar themes, no matter whose oxen are gored. However, it is with the dark side of conspicuous Mormon virtues that I will be concerned here. The Church of Jesus Christ of Latter-day Saints in this sense is a case study, one that will hopefully inspire comparable examinations in other modern religious groups.

2

The Myth of Mormon Missionizing: Where the Real Conversions Have Happened

In 1987 the Church of Jesus Christ of Latter-day Saints proudly announced the largest membership increase in its 158 year history. The number of the faithful had risen to over six and one-half million worldwide. Such growth was accompanied by a record-breaking legion of thirty-five thousand active LDS missionaries in the field.

More than through any other agency, Americans have encountered the Church as those clean-cut polite young men, each dressed in a conservative uniform of white shirt, tie, and dark pants. They travel by bicycle and canvass suburbia door to door on foot. Each young male (though increasingly females as well) is encouraged by the Church to go on a two-year mission at his family's expense. A Mormon speaks of his mission like a red badge of courage, for during that time a missionary endures months of rejection, apathy, and loneliness. Yet the individual missionary's overall enthusiasm for his faith, with all his directness and grass-roots simplicity, is the power driving Mormondom's phenomenal growth.

Most people, including Mormons, prefer to think of conversion as an intensely personal, spiritual event. An energetic witness and a searching soul are the essential human ingredients. The rest is God's will.

That is the myth behind Mormonism's expanding membership.

The reality is far more worldly. International diplomacy, political compromise, deception, and subtle salesmanship, aided by an expensive public-relations machine, are the real reasons why Mormonism is the fastest growing religion on earth.

Mormon missionizing is a complicated and extensive enterprise. No other religious group invests so heavily in this activity. Mormon missionizing uses face-to-face efforts, print media, and telecommunications as well as motion pictures, television, and radio. It involves complex multi-stage outreach strategies on a worldwide basis. It mobilizes Church members already working in all kinds of ecclesiastical and secular positions.

Nor are its directors above using subterfuge and moral compromise if such measures seem to further mission successes. Numbers are important to the Church. Converts, missionaries, baptisms, tithes, temples, new stake headquarters: the statistics grow and are pursued as if statistics alone validate the LDS faith no matter how they are achieved.

One LDS Apostle predicted that by the Church's bicentennial in 2030 there could be as many as ninety million Mormons on the planet.[1] While perhaps grandiose in the face of so many other competing Christian and non-Christian faiths, the Apostle's estimate is not utter fantasy. But to understand why such growth is possible, one has to see the many faces of Mormon missionizing as it is being conducted today throughout the world. The truth is that the conversion effort is far more than those pairs of earnest young men trekking door to door to proclaim their faith.

The Great Commission—Mormon-Style

The first half of the nineteenth century in America was the era of the first great Bible and missionary societies among Protestant Christians. Hopes were high to evangelize the world from Asia to Africa. Denominations pooled their resources to realize Christ's Great Commission to his apostles: "Go, then, to all peoples everywhere and make them my disciples: baptize them in the name of the Father, the Son, and the Holy Spirit, and teach them to obey everything I have commanded you" (Matt. 28: 19–20).

When Joseph Smith founded the LDS Church in 1830 he gave his followers the same charge. Within a few years Smith had sent missionaries to England, Scandinavia, and throughout Europe. The response to this new sect was astounding. In its first fourteen years the Church gathered in approximately thirty-five thousand members. After the Prophet Smith's death, Church leaders even set up the Perpetual Emigrating Company to help converts with the expenses of crossing the Atlantic and journeying to Utah. By 1887 more than eighty-five thousand European converts had made their way to Zion.[2]

Publication and dissemination of the Book of Mormon, then and now, has always been the most basic LDS witnessing activity. This "Newer" Testament's first printing of five thousand copies in 1830, an enormous press run for that time, quickly caused a sensation. Though it was vehemently denounced by other clergymen and theologians and ridiculed by historians, its message of a lost but reclaimed Christian heritage touched many persons. Volumes are still turned out in huge printings of as many as three million or more copies a year, in languages as different as Korean, Samoan, Hebrew, Norwegian, and Polish. Along with the Bible and the Koran, the Book of Mormon is one of the mort widely distributed books in history. The LDS Church long ago lost count of how many copies have been issued, but the total has to be in the many tens, if not hundreds, of millions.

The other well-known strategy for witnessing has been personal encounters with missionaries. Certainly the front-door ritual between household residents and courteous young LDS elders has created the impression that this highly visible activity is behind the impressive, steadily rising numbers of Mormon conversions.

Yet things are not as they appear. In fact, the expanding Church size creates a larger missionary corps, not vice versa. Much missionary experience is largely a symbolic exercise for young Mormons, some of whom will go on to take leadership roles in their Church and must prove their devotion through rites of passage, but the plain fact is that it fails to win many converts.

One of the mission programs that *is* effective is largely invisible to the general public. It is the Church's home mission program. Sociologists Rodney Stark and William Sims Bainbridge analyzed this low-key strategy and concluded:

[Door-to-door] missionaries do not serve as the primary instrument of recruitment to the Mormon faith. Instead, recruitment is accomplished primarily by the rank and file of the church as they construct intimate interpersonal ties with non-Mormons and thus link them into a Mormon social network.[3]

Using the LDS Church's own statistics from the state of Washington for 1976-77, Stark and Bainbridge discovered that the success rate for door-to-door approaches was a meager nine-tenths of 1 percent. That means 991 out of 1,000 attempts resulted in failure!

Then the two sociologists turned to the home mission program. This strategy was outlined clearly in the June 1974 issue of the Church magazine *Ensign* in a "how-to" article on conversions written for grass-roots Mormons by the president of the Oregon mission. The article offered a thirteen-step method by which Saints could gradually ingratiate themselves with their neighbors and associates (by doing minor favors such as babysitting, running errands, and lending yard tools), selectively reveal bits of Mormon lifestyle and faith, and eventually build bonds of familiarity with prospective converts long before the proselytizing became overt.

Like Mormons, dvout believers in other faiths and brands of Christianity naturally want to share their faith and may even feel compelled to do so. There is nothing remarkable about such desires. But typically such sharing is not done so deliberately, with its motives kept hidden for so long. Indirectness is the key to home missions' success. Advancing at roughly one phase of the sequence per month, the end stage—if reached—would result in a baptized convert within a year. Stark and Bainbridge summed up this manipulative strategy when they wrote that "the important thing about the instructions is that they are directed toward building close personal ties and at many points specifically admonish Mormons to avoid or downplay discussions of religion."

In contrast to the dismal conversion rates recorded for door-to-door witnessing attempts, Stark and Bainbridge found that the home mission conversion method succeeded in one out of every two cases. Moreover, while the Church goal for home missions is that each member bring one new person into the Church each year, conscientious Mormons can be simultaneously working on various neighbors and acquaintances at different stages of the conversion process. And when adults join they usually bring their spouses and children with them. Thus the conversion rate can be significantly accelerated beyond one person per member per year.

The home mission program in the United States dwarfs the loudly touted but mostly window-dressing door-to-door mission strategy and is second only to the famously high Mormon birthrate in producing new members. The program's subtle strategy is well understood by social scientists who have studied conversion routines among other religious movements such as the Unification Church.[4] Personal and emotional relations have always been used effectively by people trying to convert others, however deceptive the method may seem to outsiders. For a time this approach helped transform the Moonies from an obscure Oriental Christian sect into a household word during the 1970s. For many years it also has been building the base of Mormonism.

Though no single person can take credit for this successful missionizing technique, the late LDS President David O. McKay played an important role in encouraging it. "Every member a missionary!" McKay proclaimed to the Saints. "You may bring your mother into the Church, or it may be your father; perhaps your fellow companion in the workshop." McKay spoke those words in 1959; over the next ten years convert baptisms swelled from 33,330 to 70,010 each month.[5] The number of field missionaries also dramatically increased during that time, but research suggests that they were more an effect than a cause of the increasing conversion rate. This does not mean that LDS missionaries are totally ineffective but that their real role in Church growth is often exaggerated. Such tactics were merely face to face.

In recent years the LDS Church has turned to infusing the Great Commission with electronic broadcasting and space-age technology. Bonneville International, established in 1962 as the broadcast arm of the Church, is a powerful, well-financed, and rapidly growing communications conglomerate. Linked directly to the Church's Corporation of the President (the apex of its extensive financial empire) through the Deseret Management Corporation, Bonneville in turn controls nine other Church-owned corporations, all in one way or another managing, producing, and distributing broadcasts that carry the Restored Gospel to the world. Besides owning several television stations and twelve radio stations in larger viewer/listener markets around the United States, the Church is the second-largest stock holder in the influential Times-Mirror Corporation, which itself controls many more radio/television stations and newspapers. Bonneville International also owns a number of thriving related businesses. These include a movie production studio in Hollywood, a full-time Washington, D.C. news bureau, and a growing network of cable/satellite and telecommunication systems.

Since the early 1980s, the LDS Church has accelerated its integration of electronics with its mission efforts. In 1981 Bonneville ordered five hundred satellite receiver dish antennae (bringing its total number at that time to seven hundred), thereby creating the world's largest television network based on a satellite. Bonneville International also appropriated more than $75 million toward purchasing new equipment by 1990, including new receiver dishes for Canada and Mexico. The goal is to place hundreds of such dishes in all stakes of both nations, then to locate more in South America, Europe, Asia, and the Philippines. During the mid-1980s plans were even drawn up for a Church-owned commercial satellite.[6]

The foot soldiers of Mormon witnessing—the door-to-door troopers and the less obvious home mission folks—are finding electronics increasingly incorporated into their strategies. Videos and films with first-class production values as well as satellite transmissions are providing a more sophisticated introduction to Mormonism for "investigators," as prospective converts are called.[7]

Such high technology also presents a way to reach billions of persons (many of them illiterate) much faster than by personal contact. Media image construction sets up conducive public relations which often can be a prerequisite for winning new converts and sometimes even government approval to evangelize.

A good example is the LDS Church's public service programming. Many Americans have seen on television or heard on radio the Church's "Homefront" series of brief uplifting messages. All deal with basic family and moral issues encouraging parental communication with children, traditional maternal roles for women, and community involvement. Essentially geared toward white, middle-class North America, these spots are nevertheless expertly produced and edited, and most importantly, religiously low-key. The Church is identified only at the end of each segment as a sponsor.

In various countries the Church has used the Homefront series to project a flattering image of itself in advance of seeking official permission (where needed) to send in its missionaries. This media resource has been particularly important since 1978 when LDS President Spencer W. Kimball announced his revelation from Almighty God that black males could now be admitted to the Mormon priesthood. (Virtually all Mormon men in good standing are members of a Church priesthood.) That new policy opened up Africa and much of Central and South America to LDS missionaries, but in such places Mormons as a group were either unknown or had a reputation as racists. The Homefront series helped support the massive public relations task.

In some Third World countries Homefront themes focus on health and hygiene. In others, the emphasis may shift to patriarchal values or appeals for law–and–order and obedience to authority. But in many instances Homefront media messages serve as advertisements that cast the Church favorably in the public eye. For example, Bonneville Media began supplying programming to television and radio stations in the Dominican Republic during the 1970s before the Church officially organized a mission there in 1981. Church research (which is extensive on missionizing) credited the first one thousand conversion baptisms mainly to the effects of the advance media publicity.

Likewise, during the 1970s, Bonneville began an intensive campaign to have broadcast stations carry Homefront spots free of charge to Chile, the fastest growing source of South American LDS converts. Many stations agreed, and within five years, five separate missions were established. Chile now ranks fourth among countries with the most stakes with a total of thirty-seven.[8]

The Church downplays any theological content in Homefront ads. As the vice-president of international public relations at Bonneville Media Productions said in an interview:

We work very hard at building good, solid relationships with these international broadcasters. It requires great skill and a lot of effort to gain their confidence, to win them over to our side. They like our materials on the family and health-related subjects. In new areas, especially, we have to be very careful what we provide so that the local broadcasters don't think it's propaganda we're supplying them.[9]

A document circulated internally within Bonneville Media shows that, like the home mission program, different media targets are not all at the same stage of cultivation. Some countries are at what Bonneville considers the starting phase, meaning that neither their leaders nor their citizens are generally aware that the Church is setting up to proselytize them. Their broadcasters are approached by Bonneville's subsidiaries for possible business arrangements that are ostensibly unrelated to any religious groups. At this stage, Bonneville and its branches are in fact unannounced fronts for Church missionizing.

A prosaic example was the early broadcasting of tapes of Brigham Young University basketball games, provided free by the Church to stations in countries such as Chile, Peru, and Uruguay. Missionaries working in these countries took advantage of those free broadcasts to get their message heard more often. In Puerto Montt, Chile missionaries looked for those homes with television antennae to call on. They would then ask the people answering doors if they had seen the American basketball game the previous week. In many cases people had. The missionaries then introduced themselves as students from the same school. "This proved to be a real door-opening approach for them," Bonneville Media executive Walter Cannells boasted.[10]

As relations improve the progression of media missionizing reaches the moderate phase. Here an increased effort is made with broadcasters to air specially prepared Homefront spots dubbed in native languages or even produced especially for different cultures. But other than Church sponsorship mentioned at the closing of the messages, religion plays no explicit part in them.

In the third, or intensive, stage of relations, pressure from the Church is exerted to show more than simply Homefront spots. By now missionaries are active in the society and need a stronger Church media presence. Bonneville's various departments furnish film-tape footage, background information, and other media materials favorable to Mormonism. News stories that highlight anything positive about the faith are encouraged.

By 1985 Bonneville Media Productions alone was working with sixty-eight countries. Of them, seventeen were in a starting relationship, fourteen had reached the moderate phase, and thirty-seven had advanced to intensive pressures for exposure. Though international events in the past few years (particularly in Eastern European communist societies) may have shifted one or more countries from one phase to another, the overall scheme of Church media influence is basically the same:

1. Starting Relations: Bangladesh, Brunei, the Figi Islands, Kenya, Libya, Malta, Micronesia, Nepal, People's Republic of China, Saudi Arabia, Solomon's Islands, South Africa, Tanzania, Thailand, Turkey, Western Samoa, and Yugoslavia.

2. Moderate Relations: Egypt, Finland, India, Luxemborg, New Guinea, Norway, Pakistan, Singapore, Sri Lanka, South Korea, the Soviet Union, Sweden, and Taiwan.

3. Intensive Relations: Argentina, Australia, Bolivia, Brazil, British Guinea, British Honduras, Chile, Columbia, Costa Rica, East Germany, Ecuador, El Salvador, England, France, French Guinea, Guatemala, Hong Kong, Hungary, Indonesia, Israel, Italy, Japan, Jordan, Malaysia, Mexico, Monaco, the Netherlands, New Zealand, Panama, Paraguay, Peru, Portugal, Spain, Surinam, Switzerland, Uruguay, and Venezuela.[11]

Many of these countries are not particularly hospitable to missionaries in general or Mormons in particular. Some are Islamic, communist, or for other reasons hostile to missionizing. But the LDS Church is there, in one presence or another, and electronics are paving the way.

In The Mormon Corporate Empire my co-author and I conservatively estimated the LDS Church's investment in electronic communications at half a billion dollars, which far outspends the more publicized televangelists of the "electronic church" such as Jerry Falwell, Oral Roberts, Jimmy Swaggart, and Pat Robertson. Since the publication of that book, we have received subsequent information on the value of various Church media assets, from the market prices of radio and television stations to satellite-launching costs, which indicates that our estimate was far too low. Through its numerous subsidiaries, the Church is likely investing far more —perhaps twice as much, or $1 billion!

And the leaders at the Church helm believe that they have a sacred calling in harnessing all these high-tech resources. For them, it is a matter of faith that God, as a former president of Bonneville International assured LDS readers of a magazine, "in His wisdom has given us television and radio to assist Him in His great purposes. May we be blessed and ever diligent in the use of all communications media to hasten the day of His Kingdom."[12]

But Mormon missionary successes abroad are not only matters of slick Madison Avenue-style public relations or sophisticated electronics. Particularly in societies that restrict religious freedom, the Church must tread carefully. In certain instances it must disguise its presence, denying it is active as an evangelizing faith or has any such intentions. In other contexts it must bargain for toleration, proclaiming support for the status quo even if the regimes are undemocratic, atheistic, or oppressive.

That is what has been happening in recent years as Mormonism makes unique inroads into predominantly non-Christian cultures. In an era when the missionaries of other Christian groups have often encountered exclusion or repression, the Mormons seem largely the exception. With occasional setbacks they are challenging both monolithic devotion to Allah as well as the state-god of atheistic Marxism. The Mormon missionizing effort is pushing ahead at full steam, overcoming hurdles that handicap many other denominations' strategies.

Saints Underground: Mormons and Islam

"Where missionary work is against the law, we don't do it," flatly declared LDS Church spokesman L. Don LeFevre. It was 1985 and he was responding to the furor in Jerusalem over Brigham Young University planning to build a $15 million Center for Near Eastern Studies on the Mount of Olives. More than seven thousand Orthodox Jews protested noisily in a rally at the Wailing Wall, convinced that the LDS Church's real purpose for the Center was to secure a foothold for missionizing Jews. All missionizing is forbidden by law in Israel, but it has not been unknown. Now some Israelis suspected the Mormons.

The Church hastened to deny harboring any such interest in mission work within Israel's borders. The Center, it asserted, was intended strictly for academic purposes. BYU students attending it would even be required to sign a statement that they would not participate in proselytizing activities. As spokesman LeFevre reiterated, Mormons did not evangelize where they were not wanted.

The Orthodox Jews held a different view. They protested the fact that the Book of Mormon had already been translated into Hebrew and were afraid that copies would be imported. One leader denounced the Church's $1 million gift to Mayor Teddy Kolleck's Jerusalem Foundation as a blatant bribe to smooth over the red tape holding up construction of the Center's buildings.[13] And conservative Jews in Israel made contact with their American counterparts who for years have encountered Mormon attempts to convert them to the Reformed Gospel.[14] Most compelling, however, was what the Israelis had learned about Mormon missions in some neighboring Moslem countries where missionizing was just as illegal.

The Problem of Entry

Mission work by individuals, however secretive, in Islamic countries has often jumped ahead of media-generated official good will for the LDS Church. This has happened not only because many Islamic countries have strict prohibitions against proselytizing of any sort, but also because the Homefront series is generally less effective in non-Western settings. And, without some minimal acknowledgment in the media spots that they were produced by the Church, their public-relations value would be nil.

Saudi Arabia has been an especially intense target of LDS mission work since 1980, thanks in part to the assistance of the international arms–dealing Khashoggi family. The head of this family, Mohammed, was once a personal physician to the Saudi king; in addition, he cultivated many important contacts in the government. One of his sons, Adnan, attended college in California and found that he could receive sizable commissions by representing American companies' interests in his homeland. He later founded the corporation Al Nasr ("Victorious," in Arabic) to handle foreign requests to do business in "the Kingdom." Many of these "requests" came from American weapons producers, including Lockheed, Litton, Northrop, Raytheon, and dozens more.[15] Adnan Khashoggi became a multi-millionaire. Since then he has become better known to Americans for his role in helping Colonel Oliver North funnel money from the sale of weapons to Iran (at considerable profit to Khashoggi) to Nicaragua Contra guerillas in the Irangate scandal.

The Khashoggi family's tie to the LDS Church came through Triad America, a family real estate holding company. Initially they were contacted by Bill Gay—a top Mormon official in the corporate empire of paranoid millionaire Howard Hughes—about the joint financing of land to develop industrial parks in Salt Lake City and Houston. The partnership deal with Hughes eventually fell through, but in the end the Khashoggis owned hundreds of acres of land in the Southwestern United States and still wanted to develop it.

The family negotiated with LDS leaders via Zion Securities Corporation, the Church's real estate arm, to build the Triad Project. This ambitious venture involved restoration of historically valuable sites and construction of office buildings (including a nine–story building to accommodate Bonneville International—a plum for the Church) and industrial complexes in Utah's capital. The Church in turn helped the wealthy Khashoggi family obtain a federal HUD grant of $1.5 million with the help of Utah Senator Jake Garn. When Adnan Khashoggi's brother Essam visited Salt Lake City in the spring of 1982 for the groundbreaking ceremonies of the Salt Lake International Center, he also met with members of the First

Presidency as well as with several Apostles.[16]

What was the Church's interest in becoming so cordial to foreign investors, at least one of whom was an international arms dealer? The answer lies in the influential Saudi contacts that the Khashoggis shared with LDS leaders. These were to become extremely useful in the course of mission events in Saudi Arabia.

The Unfolding Saudi Mission

The LDS strategy for witnessing to the Saudis was vintage home mission. Mormons typically entered the country as employees of ARAMCO (the Arabian-American Oil Corporation) and had been given permission by the government to practice whatever religion they wished on a limited basis, and in private. First contacts by home missionaries were made in casual conversations or by innocuous tactics such as leaving an English edition of the Book of Mormon out on a table at home where visitors might see it. (Several blatant attempts to smuggle copies printed in Arabic past Saudi customs officials resulted in immediate deportation.)

Baptisms first occurred among other foreigners working in the country on construction and oil–related projects: Koreans, Filipinos, Sri Lankans, and so forth. Then Saudies became involved.

And as has happened elsewhere, the home mission approach began to show results. By 1984 the Church had an estimated 1,200-1,600 members in Saudi Arabia located in sixteen wards and branches in areas such as Riyadh, Jeddah, Al Khorar, Ras Tanur, and Dhahran. In April of that year Mormon employees of ARAMCO obtained necessary entry documents for Church Apostle Boyd K. Packer and another elder in the First Quorum of the Seventy who officially (and falsely) entered the country as "consultants" to the oil company. Unknown to the Saudis, the Mormon leaders had really come to dedicate the first stake in that country.[17]

Success Breeds Overconfidence

As in the American home mission program, detailed records of contacts were kept by Mormons. As converts were baptized and assumed ward responsibilities, organizational charts were drawn up.

But over time conversion success began to promote carelessness. Local leaders had been warned by high Church officials back in Utah to keep such documents carefully hidden, but they sometimes failed to do so. Worse, some Mormons in Saudi Arabia began holding meetings in their homes for as many as fifteen to twenty-five non-Americans at a time, thus attracting attention to the mission effort. An enthused missionary even began openly baptizing converts in the Red Sea.

One counselor to a branch presidency in Saudi Arabia described the home mission mood:

> We couldn't help ourselves. With golden opportunities all around, many of our local leaders went all out to get new converts. I had more missionary success in two years there than I had during my entire [mission] time in San Francisco.[18]

The reactions of stake leaders bordered on the cavalier. A bishop there recalled: "We were told by them that the Brethren in Salt Lake City took the attitude, 'What the Saudis don't find out, won't hurt them.' "[19]

But the Saudis did find out. They learned about the home meetings, and then they discovered the records. A counselor in one branch presidency heard a knock at his door one day in 1985 and found five Saudi secret police on his front step. He was abruptly arrested and his home searched. At the branch president's home the police took possession of an organizational chart of the entire stake leadership down to the ward and branch officers. With that they proceeded to track down every man on the list.

Entire families were arrested, the men separated from their wives and children. Police interrogations of these fathers and husbands were none too gentle. Meanwhile, many family members often had little idea where their other loved ones were. The Saudis relentlessly pursued every person touched by the home mission program as if they were health inspectors trying to contain a disease epidemic.

After roughing up some of the American men—things likely went no better for the Asians involved—and incarcerating them for several days, the Saudis began unceremoniously deporting dozens of missionary leaders back to the United States and other countries.

It was a diplomatic mess, considering the importance of the skills of some departing Mormons to ARAMCO and the embarrassing fact that the Church had been methodically breaking Saudi law for several years. But the Khashoggi contacts were resources to be drawn upon for just such a crisis.

In 1986 the Church dispatched David Kennedy, former Secretary of the Treasury under Richard Nixon and roving troubler-shooter for the LDS hierarchy, to meet with Saudi government officials. Kennedy technically went to Saudi Arabia as a representative of a group called the American-Arab Council (of which the LDS Church is a strong supporter). But his real task was to smooth out the Church's jeopardized relations with the Saudis and see what could be salvaged of the mission in that country. Kennedy was ultimately successful, but ever after both Arabs and Mormons were more cautious about each other.

A similar home mission fiasco, though physically less trying on the Mormons involved, occurred in Somalia. Like Saudi Arabia, Somalia forbids proselytizing. In 1981 Utah State University sent twelve Mormon agricultural experts to that country to establish an extension service. Church mission officials, aware of Islamic sentiments about witnessing, asked some of the departing Utahns to carry religious materials, such as the Book of Mormon and religious tracts on various subjects, in their baggage. The twelve experts were instructed to keep a very low profile but to do whatever they could to generate an interest in the Church among Somalians.

The home mission effort had moderate success before being discovered just as it had been in Saudi Arabia. The result was the same: the Mormons were deported.[20]

Dancing with the Devil: Mormon Missions and Communism

The LDS emphasis on conversion numbers brought down the Saudi Arabian and Somalian missions. Records to keep track of who contacted whom, who performed baptisms when, and who filled what office allowed police to pinpoint pivotal local leaders.

Furthermore, if every home mission effort is ultimately based on some degree of deception, then the missions in Islamic countries are doubly so. Heroic though the individual missionaries may be, their underground activities remain a kind of hypocrisy in light of Church claims to be "up front" about its missions operations.

Communism has presented the Church with a problem different from Islam, however. Marxist regimes have been in principle atheistic and at best minimally tolerant of religion. Mormonism, for its part, has had little good to say about Marxism and its followers since World War II. Church leaders have consistently equated communism with Satanism. In 1942 LDS President David O. McKay, together with other members of the First Presidency, officially declared that

> Communism destroys man's God-given free agency . . . . Latter-day Saints cannot be true to their faith and lend aid, encouragement or sympathy to any of these false philosophies. They will prove snares to their feet.[21]

Succeeding Church presidents reaffirmed this condemnation of communism. Current President Ezra Taft Benson, unquestionably the Church's premier anticommunist, even suggested in 1977 as an Apostle that not only the teaching but also the very discussion of Marxism be banned at Brigham Young University.

How then could the Church hope to gain official approval for its missionaries to enter countries controlled by the very political systems it so vehemently opposed for many years *and* convert persons who would still have to remain loyal citizens of those societies? The answer: unlike the totally surreptitious strategy employed in Islamic cultures, to penetrate communism the Mormons chose a high-profile public relations approach.

And on the Church's past anticommunist policy for rank-and-file members, its leaders did a sudden about-face.

The Marxist Mandate

The LDS Church actually has had its eye on missionizing the vast populations living under communist rule for some time. As early as 1945 Church President George Albert Smith said:

> I look upon Russia as one of the most fruitful fields for the teaching of the gospel of Jesus Christ. And if I am not mistaken, it will not be long before the people who are there will desire to know something about this work which has reformed the lives of so many people.[22]

A decade later President David O. McKay, who inspired so much post-World War II mission growth, hosted a Soviet delegation in Salt Lake City and used the opportunity to press (unsuccessfully) for purchasing land for the Church in the Soviet Union.[23]

But a major campaign to open up communist nations for missionizing had to wait until the 1970s. On many occasions the Council of the Twelve Apostles met and discussed the matter of a "best strategy" for tackling such a formidable undertaking. The problem was whether one single strategy could serve their purposes. Governmental attitudes toward organized religion varied widely across communist regimes; fairly liberal toleration existed in Yugoslavia and East Germany, while uneasy toleration had to be countered in countries like Poland, Hungary, and Romania. More difficult still was unremitting Stalinist-style hostility in Czechoslovakia and tiny Albania, not to mention repressive policies in the People's Republic of China.

After much deliberation, the Apostles decided on Brigham Young University, their cultural and educational flagship centered at Provo, Utah, as the vehicle by which to launch their "communist strategy." Specifically, they planned to work through the school's many music and dance groups that regularly perform internationally. Bright, colorful, and entertaining corps of wholesome young adults would become the missionary vanguard.

What the Apostles actually decided was to adopt a version of the home mission program, but one that would target *whole cultures* rather than individuals. The format was still to cultivate good will and positive public relations with friendly overtures devoid of outward religious messages, then gradually reveal selected bits about the LDS faith and its interest in permanently settling in the host society. Finally, in a Machiavellian twist, the staunchly conservative, anticommunist Church would "cut deals" with regimes, assuring them of converts' submission and "good citizenship" in exchange for toleration.

Cultural tours by the singing, dancing Mormon students thus became the means of entry through both Iron and Bamboo curtains. These trips presented various Church leaders and representatives with opportunities to visit and plan missions in countries that would otherwise have denied them visas if they tried to enter simply on their Church credentials. Several years after the plan was first implemented, the chairperson of the BYU Dance Department sized it up:

> Getting into places like this [a communist country] is hard enough, let alone for an Apostle. The Brethren are able to take advantage of the situation here at the Y because we are always invited as an educational and cultural institution, *not* as a religious one. By accompanying our groups, the Brethren can act as official representatives for the religious organization behind the school. You'd be surprised how many doors this has opened for us in Iron Curtain bloc countries, where the Church could never have gone otherwise except for our song-and-dance groups from the Y. We are known throughout all of Europe as being *the* popular university from America when it comes to folk dancing and folk singing. We've capitalized on our popularity there and especially in Asia to create an enormous amount of good will for the Church and its leaders.[24]

By having the Church's International Mission office work closely with the BYU Office of Performance Scheduling, the plan was implemented in the late 1970s and early 1980s. During this time many Protestant and Roman Catholic groups under communist rule had to smuggle religious literature, from Bibles to prayer books, into communist countries while their adherents were forced to worship underground. The LDS Church, however, strode spectacularly through the front doors of, and at the invitation of, the same authoritarian governments.

Tearing the Iron Curtain

The Apostles' variation on the home mission strategy was a colossal success. Between 1977 and 1981 five touring musical groups from BYU performed in Poland alone. In 1977 the Church President himself, Spencer W. Kimball, visited Warsaw and in a little–publicized ceremony dedicated Poland for the preaching of the Restored Gospel.

But nothing could compare to the exposure the Church received in 1979 alone. BYU's American Folk Dancers performed before large audiences in Romania, Czechoslovakia, Hungary, Poland, and the Soviet Union. They were filmed for ninety-minute national network television specials in Bucharest and Moscow. In Romania a special on the dancers was aired three separate times on the same day. Meanwhile, Central Soviet Television aired its documentary on the entertaining Mormon students across eleven time zones to an estimated 150 million viewers in the U.S.S.R.[25]

The communist reactions were encouraging, and wholesome, uplifting cultural exports from BYU, minus any religious overtones, continued.

In 1981 Elder Gordon B. Hinckley, Second Counselor in the First Presidency, accompanied the Young Ambassadors, a BYU music/dance ensemble, on a tour that swept across Eastern Europe like a rock group on triumphant tour. The Ambassadors performed at cities such as Belgrade and Zogreb in Yugoslavia, Bucharest in Romania, and Moscow, Kiev, and Leningrad in the U.S.S.R., always to cheering standing-room-only crowds. Once again these media Americans were featured on Central Soviet Television in their own half–hour program. In addition, they were interviewed by Radio Moscow and Young Communist Radio. A flattering photo spread was done on both the Young Ambassadors and BYU in *Soviet Life* magazine. Douglas Tobler, a BYU history professor who served as tour manager, ecstatically proclaimed that the students had acted in "a John the Baptist function in preparing these nations for the message of the gospel"[26]

However, by now Church leaders who traveled with the troupes under the guise of being chaperons or counselors began their own politicking. On the 1981 Young Ambassadors' tour, for example, Gordon B. Hinckley met privately with several Soviet government officials. Out of that initial discussion came another critical meeting one year later between Apostle Thomas S. Monson and communist leaders in East Germany.

The agenda and conversations in these meetings were confidential, of course, but it was no secret that Church leaders wished to set up missions in the countries where the university folk artists were performing.

Some sense of how Church leaders bargained is revealed by remarks made in a radio interview by David Kennedy, the Church's ambassador-at-large who was later to salvage the Saudi Arabia mission debacle. Kennedy described in candid detail the "delicate negotiations" that took place with the Polish government in 1977. That year Kennedy and President Spencer W. Kimball visited Warsaw and obtained permission to establish an LDS mission. The Mormons promised that their future members would stay out of opposition politics and would support the communist regime. Polish officials were told by Kennedy that Polish Mormons would be taught to be "good citizens," to uphold the government, and to follow the country's socialist work ethic. In short, Mormons wouldn't provoke political trouble.

This willingness to accommodate, even to the point of encouraging LDS Church members to support authoritarian governments, was the secret to the Church winning entry into communist societies. "We must find a way to spread the Gospel of Jesus Christ without confronting particular governments," Kennedy told a Brigham Young University audience the year after the Polish negotiations.[27]

Certainly communist regimes appreciated that conservative political stance. In countries with unstable economies and frustrated yearnings for democracy, any religious group that makes its peace with the status quo and exhorts its members to comply with the government would be an asset for beleaguered political elites. The Mormons could even become a showcase group to which governments accused of violating human rights and religious liberties could point to "prove" that the stories of repression were really groundless. It would be an unlikely symbiosis, Mormons and communists, but the relationship made political sense.

Mormon scriptures could even be used to justify this pragmatic course, no matter how much anticommunist rhetoric emanated from previous Church leaders. One passage sometimes cited can be interpreted as encouraging pragmatic acceptance of nearly any ruling order, communist or not:

> We believe that all men are bound to sustain and uphold the respective governments in which they reside . . . and that all governments have a right to enact such laws as in their own judgements are best calculated to secure the public interest; at the same time, however, holding sacred the freedom of conscience. (Doctrine and Convenants 134: 5)

Mormon theology is essentially postmillennial, and the theme of a coming time of troubles (including civil strife and social unrest) prior to Christ's return to earth is popular among both LDS leaders and believers. Democratic government, and particularly religious freedom, are regarded as divine gifts provided for the cultivation of the Restored Gospel, but they are only temporary even if useful. Christ's return will usher in a theocracy that will render all other ideologies irrelevant. Thus no government or ideology can command ultimate loyalty, for in the near future they will all disappear.

As a result, Mormonism has now become synonymous with patriotism, conservatism, civility, and good citizenship, not only in the United States but also in the other cultures in which it happens to locate, including communist ones. Mormonism has the chameleon's ability to adapt to various political systems without making waves and "render unto Caesar what is Caesar's" because it so fully respects its own prophecies of doom for the Gentile world. That is why during World War II, when American Mormons might have found themselves in foxholes shooting at Axis-nation Mormons, the Church issued a statement releasing them from any onus if they killed a fellow Latter-day Saint. As sociologist O. Kendall White, Jr. summed up the wartime policy:

> The implication, which the First Presidency even made explicit, is that a young man has an obligation to do whatever his government orders. If he is drafted into military service, he must go regardless of whether his government is Fascist, Communist, or Democratic. If his government orders him to kill, even a fellow Latter-day Saint whom it has defined as the enemy, he is under obligation to execute its commands. However, the young man is absolved from any moral responsibility because the government officials, who supposedly are responsible for the war, must bear the judgement of God for each individual's actions who is following their command.[28]

The Fruits of the Communist Mission

After a decade of subtle mission work and quiet diplomacy in Eastern Europe, the first harvest is being reaped. Having established a mission in Poland in 1977, missionaries struggled to attract a minimal membership base. By 1988 they obtained permission from the Polish government to establish the first Mormon chapel. In 1985 the first LDS temple and stake headquarters in Europe were completed in Freiburg, East Germany with a membership of five thousand Saints.

In July 1988 the Church received full recognition from Budapest, Hungary, which meant it had permission to conduct worship services, missionary activites, educational classes, and baptisms. Then in September of the same year the big news came: the Church was openly negotiating with Mikhail Gorbachev's administration to set up mission operations in the Soviet Union. The Church Translation Department hurried to complete a Russian version of the Book of Mormon as the Soviets lifted a ban on shipping religious literature into the country. Soon it was confirmed that missionaries were being prepared and called up for a Soviet mission.

Church members were elated but also slightly puzzled at the prospect of having to reconcile traditional anticommunist tirades from their President Ezra Taft Benson with the notion of a Soviet Saint. Church spokesperson Jerry Cahill assured the faithful that there was no problem, claiming that there was no Church policy precluding a member from being a communist.[29]

A communist Mormon may seem an impossibility, but it is a growing reality. In November 1988 the East German government announced that it had agreed both to permit the LDS Church to import missionaries from other countries and to allow Church members from East Germany to travel on missions abroad. It seems the East German government bought the concept that conservative Mormon Germans would make fewer waves for the government. Thomas S. Monson, Second Counselor in the First Presidency, met in Berlin with several officials to finalize the missionary arrangement. Afterwards he issued a statement quoting the state secretary for religious affairs to the effect that the East German government respects the Latter-day Saints because they are law-abiding citizens.[30]

The earthshaking events of 1990 in Eastern Europe—the repudiation of exclusive Communist Party control in East Berlin, Hungary, Estonia, Poland, Lithuania, Czechoslovakia, and even by factions within the Soviet Union—have only multiplied the LDS Church's chances of spreading its Restored Gospel message in these formerly closed societies. For one thing, the Mormons have already established footholds under the worst of conditions, giving them an advantage over other missionizing denominations previously prevented from starting churches or even sending Bibles. For another, along with a repudiation of one–party rule has come a general relaxation of restrictions on religious liberty. Indeed, Czechoslovakia's newly elected playwright-poet-turned-president, Vaclav Havel, gave encouragement to a new era of religious *laissez-faire* when he stated in his 1990 New Year's Day speech:

> A man is never a product of the external world only, but is always capable of relating himself to something beyond, despite a systematic attempt to eradicate this capacity by the external world. . . . We are a small country, but despite that we used to be the spiritual crossroads of Europe. Why should we not become this crossroads again?[31]

Certainly evangelical Christians, who expect to benefit from the removal of religious repression, anticipate greater opportunities for Christian missionaries to be active in Eastern Europe. At the same time, they worry that their most active competitors—the persistent Mormons—will likewise take advantage of the new political mood. A 1990 article in *Christianity Today* warned that the "down side" of religious freedom in the new Eastern Europe would also mean expanded opportunites for "false" religions and cults, categories into which Mormonism has always been thrown by its theological opponents and rivals.[32]

A Coming Crisis In Mormon Missions?

A scenario identical to that of the Eastern European mission effort has been played out in the People's Republic of China. In 1976 the Church began a concerted effort to mobilize its diplomats as well as the Young Ambassadors, the Lamanite Generation, and other BYU musical/dance groups to build cordial relations with the world's largest nation. The results of repeated goodwill visits by BYU students and LDS General Authorities to China are not yet clear, but there have been high points, such as the 1984 visit by premier Zhao Ziyang with Mormon officials at the LDS-owned village of Laie, on the island of Oahu. That Ziyang was on his way to confer with President Ronald Reagan marks the event as even more significant.[33]

Recent events in China, particularly the military's brutal repression of students protesting for democratic rights in Tiananmen Square in 1989, would seem to jeopardize—at least for the near future—the LDS Church's opportunites for mission inroads. For the past three decades Chinese Christianity has been struggling to assume a national identity yet retain its universal roots with mainstream Christendom. Mormonism in China is now caught up in what could be a new evolutionary push to new under-standings of religion in this "peasant Marxist" society. Less optimistically, Mormonism might instead be involved in a replaying of the Maoist 1960s with organized religion driven underground in an intellectual dark ages.

Ultimately the Church's more obvious successes in Eastern Europe are also held hostage by powerful economic and political currents of change. While Mikhail Gorbachev's twin liberating ideals of perestroika and glasnost are sweeping the post–World War II Eastern bloc nation by nation, they may be raising hopes unrealistic in the face of many socialistic states' moribund economies and dismal political options. Declining living stan-dards may turn the heady excitement of experimental democracy into sour cynicism. Mormonism, which is a foreign capitalist creed in the eyes of many socialist Europeans, may not fare well in an even more depressed, failed communist climate.

There are other precedents for rejection:

—When its rulers were in danger of losing control of economic and political forces and required immediate scapegoats, Iran saw fit to pro-ject the blame for its internal troubles onto Westerners and non-Muslims, even executing young adolescent Bahai women as enemies of the state.

—In the spring of 1989, to the horror of Latter-day Saints worldwide, terrorists with machine-guns killed two young LDS missionaries at the door of their apartment in Bolivia. Police there turned out a massive manhunt and apprehended the murderer who pulled the trigger, a Neo-Maoist "liberationist" whose group was named after a nineteenth-century Indian who raised a peasant army against Europeans.[34]

—About the same time in volatile Ghana the president accused both Mormons and Jehovah's Witnesses of disturbing public order and threatening that West African nation's sovereignty, giving missionaries only a week to leave the country.

The high visibility for which Mormon missionaries are so well known could contribute to their victimization in a world hypersensitized to colonialization and wary of ideologies that claim to have the answers to all of life's complex problems. Perhaps the future for various Mormon missions in troubled Eastern Europe may not be as sanguine as the Church optimistically predicts.

But meanwhile Church missionizing has more immediate problems to resolve.

For example, it has long been a suspicion among Mormons that some unknown percentage of foreign female converts are really only seeking mates among the handsome young male missionaries they encounter overseas; obviously, the motive here is immigration to the United States. Many young male missionaries are fresh out of high school, with little worldly experience. Even more disturbing is the fact that almost half of returning missionaries reportedly become "Jack Mormons," or inactive or backsliding members. And the Church is embarrassed about another controversial aspect of mission work: rumors have surfaced about homosexual incidents among healthy, lonely young men thrown together in pairs for long periods of time.[35]

Meanwhile, surveys have shown that for every five converts to Mormonism living in Utah during the early 1980s, two subsequently left the Church.[36] There has been no single reason offered for defections, but the Church is vitally aware of the problem. In the fall of 1988 a committee was formed by the First Presidency to figure out how to stem "membership slippage" among converts. The consensus was that new members were not being integrated into the round of Church activities quickly enough and thus fell out of faith due to feelings of isolation.

The situation is analogous to the "baseball missionizing" in Britain by LDS missionaries during the 1960s. In a two-year period (1962-1963), baptisms of new members shot up an average *40 percent* a year but then abruptly declined. The reason: Mormon missionaries created softball teams to lure athletic young men into token baptisms that were forgotten soon after warm weather faded. Meanwhile, precious little of the Reformed Gospel was ever explained to them.[37]

Aggressive missionizing continues to be the hallmark of Mormonism. But as the home-mission experiences overseas reveal, means do have a way of shaping ends. Tools of witnessing for faith are neither morally neutral nor always uplifting. Whether deception and moral pragmatism will become the tail that wags the dog or be kept in check as merely useful strategies for new missions is a question the LDS Church must confront in the future.

3

Wolves Among the Fold:
Scams and Schemes in Zion

The Mormon penchant for hard work is legendary. The first generation of Saints pioneered a barren, arid wilderness and transformed it into a thriving, populous territory, later to become a proud state. They did this by no magic formula; rather, it required heroic effort, sacrifice, and determination. Self-reliant and industrious, these early Mormons kept no place for slackards who did not contribute labor to the community. The Mormons built an empire for a purpose, for they expected Jesus Christ to return soon, and he would need the foundation of a kingdom from which to rule.

Their descendents have continued this tradition, preferring to earn their rewards by honest sweat rather than accept handouts. Modern Mormons often make tough businessmen, probably because the LDS subculture encourages sobriety, thrift, prudence, integrity, and the Protestant Ethic.

The great state of Utah has a serious problem. Mormon Zion is overrun with a host of scams, swindles, and business rip-offs that cost citizens *hundreds of millions of dollars every year.*

According to a number of law enforcement officials, every conceivable con is involved: shares of stock sold in phony diamond/uranium/silver mines; phantom mineral futures and fake high-tech companies; chain letters and pyramid-plan hustles; "guaranteed" gimmicks revolving around worthless land deals; forged documents supposedly surviving from the early days of Mormonism. There was even a bogus plan to raise investments to finance a salvage operation in which divers would bring up lost caches of Hitler's gold from the bottoms of Europe's lakes, and one nuttier still in which several hundred people invested in a scheme to convert plain dirt into gold.

The con-games run the gamut from the transparently loony to the seemingly respectable. But they all point to the fact that Utah provides fertile soil for economic crime. And Mormons more often than not are the victims.

What is happening is that a remarkable number of persons who are or claim to be members of the LDS Church make their way to Utah, or seek out Mormons elsewhere, to finance illegal quick-buck money-making schemes. Moreover, these grifters frequently try to win endorsements for their operations from LDS Church officials and then use these to reassure investors that the ventures have the approval of the LDS hierarchy and are thus "blessed" in some special way. Like wolves loose among a fold of unsuspecting sheep, these individuals prey on the religious trust of Mormons.

Mormons, despite their reputation for having hard-nosed economic sense, seem particularly gullible to these come-ons. The con-artist's spiel can include a casual remark about a nephew on a Church mission, a high Church authority who is "a good friend," or even the deliberate wearing of thin clothing to reveal temple garments underneath. [Such garments, which must be worn at all times, resemble long underwear and are a sign of a Mormon's worthiness to enter the temple.] Insignificant to non-Mormons, such subtle cues can be important to Mormons in deciding to trust someone otherwise a stranger.

How extensive are these crooked activities? One Salt Lake City investigative television reporter described the situation by saying, "Utah is likely *the* white-collar crime capital of America."[1]

This is not an isolated opinion among experts on the Utah crime scene. U.S. Attorney Brent Ward, who as a (Mormon) government prosecutor has helped investigate and convict swindlers in Utah for years, concurred. "We (in Utah) are becoming the fraud capital of the nation." In his view Utah has been turned into a virtual "testing ground" for con-artists' unscrupulous scams. "If it works here, they take it on the road," he said.[2] Ward once told an "NBC Nightly News" reporter that fraud in the state of Utah had become worse than any other single crime.

Likewise, Jeffrey Oritt, consumer fraud specialist for the Utah Attorney General's office, agreed that Utah "has become a national test market for fraud."[3] Many professionals in law enforcement see the state as the hub of such activities in North America. A San Francisco agent for the U.S. Postal Service, after investigating a Utah man who had single-handedly defrauded investors of $137,000 within nine months' time in a sham silver and gold purchase-storage plan, said:

> The Salt Lake City region is most unique for frauds. It's a thriving place for things such as gold and silver schemes, worthless uranium fields, and penny stocks. There's simply more of that in Utah than anywhere else. You couldn't have these things thriving in California like they do in Utah![4]

What does the damage from all this chicanery cost the public? Precise figures on the money lost are not available. There are simply too many rip-offs taking place, investigated by too many agencies in too many jurisdictions, to make a comprehensive tally. But all estimates are high. One consumer education specialist for the Utah Attorney General's office estimated that between 1980 and 1983, nine thousand persons had lost about $200 million to "shady business deals, including diamond and real estate fraud." In 1982 alone there were more than 120 active fraud cases in the Utah Attorney General's office involving losses of an estimated one billion dollars.[5] Whatever the real total dollar amount, the costs of such crimes are staggering. And they continue year after year, fueled by basic aspects of the Mormon subculture itself.

In a state where the LDS Church is the largest employer and therefore a mighty economic presence in its own right, how aware are its leaders of this problem?

The LDS Church has indeed acknowledged the problem as one especially involving its members. For example, Elder Hugh W. Pinnock of the Church's First Quorum of the Seventy (an LDS upper administrative eschelon) has deplored Utah's notoriety as the "scam capital of the world." Pinnock called the situation an overwhelming embarrassment. In a magazine article he noted that Utah ranks third in the nation for business defaults and in 1981 alone witnessed eleven major business frauds.[6]

In a unique admission of the extent of the scandal among Mormons, an official LDS Church publication, the *General Handbook of Instruction,* warned in a section entitled "Business Schemes and Political Causes":

> Individuals and groups who are promoting business schemes or political or social welfare causes sometimes take advantage by quoting from Church books and Church leaders and by arguing in Church gatherings to support their propositions. Church officers and members should not become involved in such schemes and causes, and should not allow their names to be used in connection with them.[7]

LDS Church officials are appalled at this problem, and with good reason. The existence of so much criminal fraud and the victimization of so many LDS Church members (including some of its leaders) are stains on the public image of a religion otherwise known for so many positive qualities. Yet the official statement above has no parallel in any other American denomination or church. Mormonism seems to attract and feed a surprising amount of economic crime, despite adamant warnings from LDS leaders.

This ugly underbelly of Utah's economic success was ignored until recently. It seemed too inconceivably sordid in light of Mormonism's reputation for financial integrity. Then, following the mounting outcries of angry citizens who had been bilked, often through LDS Church-related contacts, the subject began to be openly discussed. For example, a Salt Lake City television program in 1983, entitled "Civil Dialogue," hosted a blue-chip panel of consumer fraud experts who discussed the underlying factors behind the enormous number of fraudulent businesses in Utah. The panel represented a Who's Who on the subject: the Director of Utah's Division of Consumer Protection, the Coordinator of Investigations for the State Department of Business Regulation, the Deputy Director of the Department of Business Regulation, and a representative from the Division of Consumer Protection for the Utah Attorney General's office.[8]

One year prior to this television program, a special 1982 issue of *Exchange* magazine (published by the Brigham Young University School of Management) was devoted entirely to the theme of "business integrity." One article by the director of the Master's in Business Administration program at BYU lamented the fact that "state officials have recently reported that in Utah alone investors have lost $165 million to phony deals." And *Exchange*'s editor noted in an introduction to the same issue that "According to investigators for consumer and government agencies, fraud and general dishonesty within the Utah business community appear to be running rampant."[9]

After years of politely ignoring the problem, Utahns now face an epidemic of white-collar crime. Mormons and non-Mormons alike increasingly speak about it and speculate why it is happening. At the 1989 Sunstone Symposium held in Salt Lake City, an annual event which provides a forum for more liberal, free-thinking LDS Saints to come together and share their ideas and writings, a panel of distinguished economists discussed the topic "Mormon Financial Scams." There was a standing-room-only crowd.

Thus the fraud issue is no longer a question of "Does it exist?" or "How much of it exists?" but "How can we contain the growing problem?"

Mormonism, Greed, and Gullibility

Mormons are not inherently more avaricious than other folks in America. However, their subculture's intense emphasis on material success and their trust in their fellow Mormons, which can sometimes border on the naive, frequently set them up to be duped. When coupled with members' expectations that personal prosperity will flow from faithful tithing, regular attendance at temple rituals, and other Church practices, the distinction between economic success and religious virtue can become blurred.

Noted LDS historian Hugh Nibley has criticized this easy slide into materialism:

> The Economy, once the most important thing in our materialistic lives, has become the *only* thing. We have been swept up in a total dedication to the Economy which, like the massive mudslides of our Wasatch Front, is rapidly engulfing and suffocating everything.[10]

More to the point, financial success *per se* has become more important than how it is attained. The Protestant Ethic has been turned on its head for many Mormons. There is a growing urgency to capture financial security and wealth, cutting corners if need be. LDS historian Marden Clark recognized the ultimate danger of the prosperity obsession that Nibley warned against when Clark wrote to Mormons:

> Our emphasis on welfare, food storage, staying out of debt, and so forth has made many of us hyper-conscious of the role of money in our lives. We have placed a good deal of emphasis on success, both monetary and otherwise. It is no accident that some of the best known of the new breed of financial advisors are Mormons. All these hundreds of talks on success are both symptom and cause. So is our intense preoccupation with and honoring of the wealthy, the famous, the champion. We almost cannonize our Willard Marriotts, our Johnny Millers, our Danny Ainges, our Osmonds. . . . I can't help wondering if some of the things we glory in most don't get twisted to support the easy-money hunger.[11]

This "easy-money hunger" is at the heart of much Mormon gullibility. For example:

—A diamond scheme in Centerville, Utah, strongly promoted by a Mormon bishop to friends and neighbors in his ward, promised a 2,000 percent return on investors' money.

—An attorney described one fraud in an interview: "Few of the victims really understood the details of how the scam was supposed to work. But they did understand the $84 per $1,000 their investment was supposed to pay them *every month*. That's 104 percent annually!"

—A Mormon couple was persuaded to put up $500,000 in stock shares as collateral for a bogus firm. They were promised the money returned within a year plus a 100 percent profit on their investment.

—A young man who invested $500 in a Salt Lake City diamond scam recalled later: "I was promised that if I was in the business nineteen months, I would get a return of $292,000."

Characteristic of such scams is the promise of high, even astronomical, returns within a fairly brief period. The four cases above are real. For the last young man, turning $500 into $292,000 in nineteen months' time would entail a promised return of over 1,300 percent per year. Not bad at all. In theory, if the lucky fellow could remain patient for another nineteen months, one could project that the original $500 would be worth one and one-half trillion dollars!

Many schemes appeal rather blatantly to investors' greed. A "sure thing" proposition allows the con-artist to form a pseudo-alliance with the investor and easily exploit that dishonest streak that wants something spectacular in exchange for very little. Prudence rarely has a place in the psychology of con-game victims. It is the quick pay-off that attracts takers.

But the shortcut to lucrative rewards is not the only attraction. Investors are also drawn by the fact that the proposed scheme is nothing so mundane as a certificate of deposit or a U.S. Savings Bond. It's the glamour that sells these schemes: the drama of lost Nazi gold, uranium and diamond mines, or exotic inventions that will change the world.

Yet not all victims are particularly greedy. Some Utah investment frauds have involved respectable citizens looking only for reliable returns on their money. They weren't necessarily lured by glitter and extravagant claims. Such investors believed they were making safe purchases. The trick for those operating such plans was to take money from many people even though each may have paid a relatively small amount.

There is one additional technique used to entice victims: credible assurances of a "safe" investment. A good con-artist must therefore accomplish a difficult task. Investors need to be convinced that a high-risk/high-profit venture has had the high risk removed. There are various ways to do this. In sophisticated con-games there are often many players, including *shills*. Shills appear to be initially cautious, skeptical persons similar to the victim who are visibly rewarded for trying their hand at playing the scam. But they are really actors in the game. Their role is to convince the potential victim that the scheme is capable of working.

In some schemes, endorsements are sought from sincere high-profile persons of impeccable reputations who obviously would not be in cahoots with anything underhanded. For Mormons such persons would best be Church officials, and the higher up the better since such individuals ought to be closer to sources of revelation and discernment. These people invest as directed and indeed receive the promised rewards. To potential victims they seem living proof of the con-artist's claims. To the schemers, however, they are merely overhead costs spent to convince other naive people that the deal is legitimate.

But there are ironies to such frauds. One is that victims are not always certain that they have been truly ripped off. This is especially true when even the most fly-by-night companies can take many months and even years to declare bankruptcy, obscuring their records in red tape and complicated court proceedings. Even if con-artists choose not to disappear altogether, it may require a considerable length of time for victims to figure out that the repeatedly "delayed" dividend check from the bogus corporation is never coming.

Another irony is that, however incredible it may seem to observers, many conned victims are unwilling to press charges against those who have exploited them, and they sometimes will not even complain. This fact is one of the strangest yet most recurrent aspects of economic crime. Victims of a fraud are often embarrassed or guilt-ridden that they became involved in the whole affair. Hence they remain silent. In his extensive study of con-artists, David W. Maurer remarked that "once a victim is fleeced he often proves to be the most reluctant and even untruthful witness against the men who have taken his money."[12]

Victims' reactions in the examples of fraud in the remainder of this chapter were mixed. Some Mormons howled with outrage. Others who invested in a fraudulent scheme on the basis of a fellow Saint's endorsement felt acutely in a bind. To point fingers at their associates, friends, relatives, and perhaps even a bishop or stake president would be more than socially awkward. Denouncing them might not only expose their own "money hunger" but also threaten Church leaders. This ambivalence was as painful as the loss of their money.

The Ponzi Model

Utah crime authorities have good reason to regret that an Italian immigrant named Charles Ponzi ever lived. Charles Bianchi, alias Charles Ponzi, settled in Boston during the 1920s. He was the father of the classic pyramid hustle that bears his name and became the prototype for many contemporary thefts, including some of the biggest in Mormondom.

Ponzi latched onto the gimmick of buying international stamps in Europe for a penny or so and then purportedly selling them in this country for five times or more their value. He excited investors with the prospect of lucrative returns on modest investments.

Starting cautiously, Ponzi did indeed provide initial investors with their promised returns. But the "returns" came from the initial investments of additional new participants, not from any stamp sales. As word spread, the small investments turned into larger ones. Within a few months Ponzi no longer took in nickel-and-dime amounts but hundreds of thousands of dollars per month. The plan was to pay off some, but not nearly all, of the growing number of investors. Interest and credibility in the scheme had to be maintained to keep new investors coming, but not at the expense of a large profit for Ponzi. It is estimated that within nine months' time Ponzi had taken in somewhere near $15 million.

Ponzi eventually was arrested and convicted of fraud, but he was to have a mixed destiny. After a prison stint he was deported to Italy where eventually the dictator Benito Mussolini appointed him to a post in the government's Finance Ministry. Ponzi died penniless, but with his pyramid plan he left a significant legacy to the criminal world (apart from his achievements in the Italian Fascist regime).

Ponzi pyramid frauds are the bane of Utah law enforcement and regulatory officials' existence. Such schemes are insidiously credible in their early stages because they seem to work as promised. Enough believable people do receive the expected extravagant pay-off and pass the good news of the venture on to enough of their friends and contacts that the pyramid base of further investors widens. Unfortunately, the base expands far beyond any possibility of paying off all investors, and the pyramid invariably collapses. Pyramid schemes raise a lot of cash, most of which is never intended for investment or investors. A little circulates back but only long enough to keep the myth of great profits alive. The rest is collected by one or a more shrewd individuals . . . at the apex of the pyramid.

Most illegal schemes duping Mormons have been "Ponzis," including several of the ones to be described here. In all cases, however, they make a mockery of the Mormon virtues of hard work and honest earnings and illustrate how the pursuit of success can be twisted by easy-money hunger.

Ponzi Lives! The Independent Clearing House/ Universal Clearing House Scandal

The concept was legal: Independent Clearing House and Universal Clearing House, along with several subsidiaries, would collect (or "factor") accounts payable on behalf of various companies. In turn, the clearing houses would keep the money briefly, shifting funds among bank accounts to earn maximum interest. Investors were invited to make minimum investments of $1,000 and were told that amount would earn 8.4 percent interest each month, or 104 percent per year.

What *was* illegal was that the clearing houses did very little collecting of accounts payable. Instead, the real money to be made was off the investors. Their monies (one investor put up $500,000) were illegally channelled to oil and gas companies and used to purchase gold and silver coins, mining stock, automobiles, precious metals, oil leases, real estate (including luxurious homes), and trading commodities. Nine different oil companies, for instance, received over $1 million from the clearing houses. The con-artists also set up three separate insurance companies and five other businesses with the investments.

In March 1981 the Federal Bureau of Investigation received its first complaint about the clearing house operation. And these complaints began to mount. Dividends were not being paid as promised. Other than a few early investors, who were used to broadcast what a "sweet deal" this investment opportunity was, most investors had not seen any returns worth mentioning. Thereafter began an exhaustive eighteen-month investigation involving forty special agents, including ten FBI accountants and seven postal investigators. Eventually more than eleven hundred interviews were conducted by Salt Lake FBI investigators working with agents from thirty-seven field divisions.[13]

What emerged was a complicated scheme of investment fraud that took in over $32 million from nearly four thousand investors, or "undertakers," as they were called by the con-men who masterminded the twin clearing house idea. Attorneys for the Salt Lake Bankruptcy Court trustee and other investigators doubted that much of the money would ever be recovered, and their pessimistic expectations were born out.

One obstacle to tracking down the money was that the con-artists had created a paper labyrinth of shifting investments in which much of the money went into what area accountants term "suspense." In "suspense" the paper trail of funds hits a brick wall, ending without a trace. For example, International Clearing House took in $17,506,432 from "undertakers." Investigators could trace approximately $13 million of it through accounts of subsidiary companies, but almost $4.5 million disappeared into "suspense." The case was the same for Universal Clearing House. Bookkeeping was atrocious. Investigators believed it was kept so deliberately.[14]

Another factor complicating any hope of recovering investors' monies was that these clearing house companies were set up as offshore trusts in such glamorous but remote areas as the Grand Caymon Islands in the Caribbean or Belize off the eastern coast of Central America. Offshore company records could not be seized by U.S. government agents.

And the legal mess resulting when the companies' founders declared Chapter 11 (reorganizational) bankruptcy also insured that most investors would never see their money again. More than a dozen lawsuits arose over the bankruptcy, not to mention criminal suits, and each required a jury trial, thus stretching litigation into the indeterminate future.

What was significant about the ICH-UCH scandal, besides its classic Ponzi style, was its use of the Mormon subculture to lure investors. All four of the principal company officials were LDS, two of them conspicuously active church members. The clearing houses used Church officials, bishops, and stake presidents as a promotional medium to entice other Church members to invest. Said one attorney involved with the Salt Lake City Bankruptcy Court trustee office:

> One of the greatest selling pitches that these shysters can use is to get Church leaders associated with their scams. The higher the leaders they can get, the more legitimate their scams seem. Of course, if that fails then they'll try for second or third-level leaders. But chances are they'll always wind up with a bunch of bishops and maybe even a few stake presidents. Here you're dealing with leaders that the people have easy access to at least twice a week. Such a scam is possible because the Church has taught the members to have implicit faith in their leaders. So even if something doesn't seem logical, they will set aside common sense and good judgement in preference to that complete faith in their leaders.[15]

Recruitment followed along networks of Church contacts. Many investors later told investigators. "Oh, my Elders' Quorum President told me it was a good deal," or "I heard my bishop say how much interest he was getting," or "My bishop told my uncle that this was a sure thing." One legal investigator saw how the investment scam had spread in a frenzy among many LDS families:

> Some family members even quit their jobs and made their livelihoods by recruiting everyone else in their family, their wife's family, their kids, their aunts and uncles. It went through families like some sort of disease. I know of some families who even planned their entire Family Home

Evenings around listening to the sales pitches made for these investments.
[Family Home Evening is a special program encouraged by the LDS
Church for all family members to set aside Monday night of every week
to spend together in some form of recreational, educational, or spiritual
activities.][16]

Early investors were not only recruited for their prestige and credibility
but also given returns as guaranteed by the con-game. The early investors
became the clearing houses' most enthusiastic supporters. They would tell
their friends and associates, "Look at what has happened to me. This is
a sure thing. You'd better get in while the getting is good!"

Church officials and upstanding citizens alike—in fact, virtually everyone
except the early "demonstration" investors—lost their investments in the
clearing house scandal. Even a brother-in-law of Spencer W. Kimball, then
the LDS Church President, became caught up in the fever of this seemingly
lucrative business opportunity and lost $150,000.[17]

The reaction of victims was sometimes one of rage. One angry man
shrieked at bankruptcy attorneys, demanding his money be returned to
him *in the name of Jesus Christ*. Often, however, the reaction was shock,
and not simply because the plan had seemed such a sure thing. Some
Mormons' stunned reaction was: "Why, I pay my tithing. I've lived the
Word of Wisdom [an LDS sacred book of revelations that includes a code
of health norms]. I've gone to the temple. I just can't figure out why on
earth this should have happened to me!"

Despite their losses, some victims predictably cast their sympathies with
the perpetrators of the scam rather than with law enforcement officials.
This is a classic example of what psychologists term *cognitive dissonance*.
In order to reconcile the contradiction between their original high expectations and the undeniable fact that they'd been suckered, some victims
steadfastly held to a renewed faith in the investment. Something else must
have gone wrong, they maintained, perhaps even because law enforcement
officials interfered. This reaction was a shock to bankruptcy court attorneys.
Said one:

You'd think they would be supportive of the government people and
attorneys like us who are trying to work our tails off for their benefit
in solving this complicated scheme. But instead we've found a very definite
phenomenon of overt hostility towards us and an overwhelming supporting for those who defrauded them.[18]

In fact, one member of a committee representing the clearing-house
creditors attempted to convince the judge to lower the amount of bail for

one defendent, testifying to the defendent's integrity even after the committee member had already been fleeced! The judge, for his part, then doubled the bail in disgust!

The ICH–UCH scandal was an enormous embarrassment to thousands of respectable LDS members, victims or not, and it was one of the largest single scams in modern American. Certainly it was the most extensive in the history of the Church. One year later, Elder Hugh W. Pinnock of the First Quorum of the Seventy penned advice shaped out of tragedies caused by the easy-money hunger:

> I believe a big part of our problem lies in the reward system we have been taught. The mistaken belief that we will constantly receive earthly rewards for being Mormons and having worthy goals can lead us to make a number of unfortunate decisions. This belief can convince Church members that we can get high returns with low risk and little effort or that we will be rewarded regardless of the viability of the investment or venture.[19]

But even at the time Pinnock wrote, another massive con was in progress, and a well-known Church official was one of its directors.

The Land Flips Racket

On September 3, 1983, Grant C. Affleck, principal owner of AFCO Enterprises, Inc., was arrested after a federal grand jury in Salt Lake County decided that he had defrauded some 650 Utahns of between $20 and $50 million dollars in a resort development investment scheme. He was indicted on eleven counts of mail fraud, eight counts of securities fraud, one count of transporting people in interstate commerce to defraud, and two counts of bankruptcy fraud. His victims were mostly Mormons living along the Wasatch Front.[20] His scheme involved selling land with other people's money: the *same* land, which was "sold" over and over.

The idea was to persuade investors to use the equity in their homes or personal property as collateral to obtain loans which they then turned over to AFCO for "sure-fire, high-return" investments in land. Affleck and AFCO returned a small part of each loan immediately as an incentive to investors. Then the "land flips," as the practice is known, began. Here's how a land flip scheme works:

A developer buys a piece of property for a housing subdivision, apartment complex, or condominiums. With the help of unscrupulous confederates in real estate appraisal offices and banking, the developer then "flips," or sells and later repurchases, the same property, often several times within the space of a day or two. Each time the land is flipped its price increases so that in the end it can be artificially inflated to four or five times what the land was originally worth.

The investor's money is then used to purchase the land, thus clearing a tidy profit for the developer. There is one catch to the scheme, however: enough customers have to be found to pay the inflated price of land or buildings or else the investors become the suckers.

AFCO managed two Utah properties: Glenmoor Village, a real estate development in Salt Lake County, and Sherwood Hills, a resort in Sardine Canyon, Cache County. The population in the state of Utah has consistently grown during this century, not just because of Mormons' traditionally high birth rates but also due to expanding industry and commerce in the state. Affleck figured he could easily overcome the problem of locating customers, given the demographics and robust business climate. But he didn't. During the late 1970s sales were disappointing. In fact, AFCO never earned a profit in any year of its existence.[21]

Meanwhile, Affleck owed the Deseret Savings and Loan Corporation over $5 million on the Sherwood Hills resort and was required to pay $140,000 each month on the principal and interest. As the 1980s approached he was a man with financial woes. Through AFCO, Affleck began pledging Glenmoor Village building lots as security on the Sherwood Hills loan. As a grand jury and the bank were to learn, in some instances Affleck pledged *the same lot* as many as five times to cover his loan.

All the while, Affleck continued to hustle new investors in a desperate attempt to keep AFCO afloat. Complaints began to arrive from investors who wanted their unsent dividend checks. Affleck sent letters pleading for patience and reassuring investors. He even cut the salaries of AFCO workers. In 1982, however, the scheme collapsed with AFCO in bankruptcy, the bank foreclosing, and angry lawsuits mounting.

AFCO's pitch to woo Mormon investors was similar to the one in the clearing house scandals. Elder Paul H. Dunn of the LDS Church's General Authorities was an AFCO director as well as a close friend of Affleck, and his face and name were important parts of AFCO's sales presentations. Affleck, himself a Mormon, prominently displayed a photograph of Dunn in the prospectus material shown to potential investors. Dunn's image was used to guarantee the company's integrity. The effect was to convince many Mormons that the company had some sort of implicit imprimatur of respectability from the LDS Church itself.

Dunn resigned the AFCO directorship in 1978, he later claimed, because AFCO was exploiting his position in the Church. Nevertheless, as *The Wall Street Journal* reported, AFCO continued to provide Dunn with a new car every year, including several Cadillacs, until 1982 when the company finally went bankrupt. Dunn also continued regularly to attend AFCO board meetings and counsel directors until the end. (In a sworn deposition Dunn said his only role at such times was to deliver prayers and "inspirational" messages.)[22]

However, at Affleck's trial evidence emerged to show that Dunn had backdated his resignation from AFCO. While the company's fortunes continued to sink lower in the early 1980s, Dunn himself continued to help put Affleck in touch with more new investors and even made telephone calls from his Church office trying to prevent creditors from foreclosing on AFCO's assets.[23]

After a five-week trial Affleck was convicted on eight counts of fraud and sentenced to ten years in a federal prison.[24] His lawyer sought a probated (no imprisonment) sentence, claiming that Affleck had never meant to hurt anyone and that he presented no risk to the community. He was, after all, a Mormon in good standing.

However, in sentencing Affleck the judge brushed aside such assurances, saying, "In virtually all of the fraud schemes that I have seen or read about, the perpetrators or the promoters of those schemes do not intend to hurt anybody." The judge declared that considering the length of time of Affleck's fraud and the enormous harm he had caused to so many people it "would be totally unappropriate to grant probation.[25]

Meanwhile, Affleck's lawyer (at Affleck's request) never subpoenaed Dunn to testify; clearly, Affleck was hoping to save this LDS General Authority and the Church further possible embarrassment. It was not, however, the end of the legacy of AFCO.

The Memorial Estates Debacle

In August 1960, at least two decades or more before any of these previously mentioned scams were envisioned, Elder Bruce R. McConkie, together with a group of prominent Mormon businessmen, organized the Memorial Estates Security Corporation. According to the prospectus issued for investors, MESC was to be a Utah "cemetery organization desiring to facilitate the construction of beautiful memorial parks" for the benefit of "loved ones" on a prepaid basis. It offered two hundred thousand shares of stock at $1.00 a share and an additional sixteen thousand $50 bonds with a maturity date of ten years from the date they were issued. Investors were guaranteed an earning of 7 percent per year (tempting interest at the time) to be paid in cash installments on December 1 and June 1 of each year.[26]

This prospectus proved to be an important factor in why many Mormons felt confident investing their money in MESC, for it prominently displayed pictures of Mormon directors, including Bruce R. McConkie (MESC's vice-president), four stake presidents, three stake high councilmen, one bishop, and a number of members from the LDS Church Welfare Committee. Their Church affiliations were conspicuously touted.

Later that same year MESC consolidated its stock with that of another cemetery company, Redwood Memorial Estates, Inc. One Salt Lake City attorney, who was also a major MESC stockholder, sensed too much official LDS presence in what was ostensibly a public option and warned the president of Redwood in a letter:

> I believe that the "church" is much too intimately involved in this entire operation. I do not in any way mean it to infer that we should divorce ourselves from the church. However, it seems doubtful that it is sound business policy to be so closely tied. There is definitely, in my opinion, too much chance that the church will suffer because of this close tie.[27]

The attorney's misgivings proved valid. By September of 1964, MESC was in serious financial trouble. At one board-of-directors meeting an officer suggested to McConkie that they buy back the stock of investors at the original price, to be paid out over three years, yet he also wondered aloud where they could find the collateral to back up such payments. There was also a suggestion of ineptitude in the managing of MESC, perhaps the leading reason MESC got into financial trouble. The same officer suggested that they should either sell the cemetery or hire an executive familiar with the cemetery business.[28]

By November things had deteriorated further. The directors filed a petition in the federal district court to have MESC declared bankrupt and placed in receivership.[29] At that point it appeared to be simply a business venture that had not panned out.

Two years later an elderly couple named James and Caroline Cottam from Veyo, Utah sued Bruce R. McConkie and fourteen other MESC officials on behalf of the more than 270 stockholders and bondholders of the company. The Cottams claimed they were misled into investing in MESC by certain "misstatements" in the prospectus and by MESC's withholding of certain information. The "misstatements" amounted to (1) the impression conveyed by the pictures and descriptions of Mormon Church officials that MESC was either Church-related or Church-approved, and (2) the number of building projects in the first cemetery, portrayed by an artist in the prospectus, that in fact were never built. (Represented in the prospectus were a pagoda-style bird sanctuary over 30 feet high, a belltower standing in a fountain, a "chapel of meditation," and a "bridge of memories" over another fountain.)

The majority of investors, according to court records, were elderly couples living in small rural communities. Did they, too, feel misled as did the Cottams? Many said yes. In January, 1969, attorneys representing the investors sent copies of a questionnaire to all 270-plus investors. This survey asked specific questions about why the people had invested in MESC, what their understandings of the returns of the investment were to be, their experiences of payments of dividends, and so forth. Their replies provide a clear example of many faithful LDS Church members trusting in the board of directors simply because so many were Mormon Church leaders.

A total of 210 questionnaires were returned. Two-thirds of the investors were elderly (ages sixty to seventy-five), another 10 percent middle-aged (forty-five to fifty-nine), and only 19 percent younger. (A professional handwriting expert was employed and confirmed that awkward printing and visibly "shaky" handwriting belied pooor health.) Moreover, the elderly had invested fifteen times as much as persons thirty years and under and four times as much as middle-aged persons. In fact the elderly contributed two-thirds of all monies ever invested into MESC!

Asked what factors played a role in their decisions to invest in MESC, the answers were vintage scam-victim responses. *Close to half* made specific references to individual Mormon Church officers and/or specifically Bruce McConkie shown in the prospectus as directors. Wrote one middle-aged woman: "Knowing some of these men personally made me feel my money would be invested well and bring me back some security for my future retirement."[30] One Price, Utah, investor laid out the situation in his deposition to lawyers:

> The salesman made quite a pitch for the officers of the company as he went down the list of the officers. He told me their positions (in the Church) and how important they were in the community. And this seemed to be a strong point in his sales pitch, and very frankly it made an impression on me because people who are doing pretty well are normally the people who are in on the successful investments.[31]

Investors' reactions to promotional materials were the same. The highly visible advertisement of LDS officials in the corporation convinced them that the investment was sound: "We relied upon the integrity of corporate officers shown in the Prospectus. . . ." "We relied heavily on the name of Bruce McConkie because we were sure that anything he was connected with would be completely reliable and honest. . . ." "Our main reason for buying was our faith in the officers and directors. . . ."[32]

Despite such confidence, it is clear now that MESC reneged on paying dividends long before its collapse. Moreover, the directors and officers made no attempt to inform investors of its growing insolvency. It is not known where the investors' money went, although it most certainly did not go for cemetery development. Many investors, because of their veneration for the LDS Church and the fact that MESC officers were their leaders in the Church, did not pursue the scheduled dividends until a lawsuit began. Among Mormons victimized by scams there is sometimes a reluctance to "rock the boat" and cause trouble when Church leaders are concerned. Perhaps the directors of MESC in their silence were counting on that factor.

One Mormon with the gumption to pursue the dividend matter was a Cedar City, Utah, attorney named Morris A. Shirts. In June 1965 Shirts wrote directly to McConkie (at that time in the First Quorum of the Seventy) since McConkie had been listed in the prospectus along with seventeen other persons holding high positions in the Church. Shirts noted, "It was primarily because of this affiliation that we decided it would be a good place to invest money for a missionary fund for our children." His grievance to McConkie explained that at first he had received interest on his bonds with no trouble, but for several years he had to write to the company and ask for it to be paid. The most recent letters had not even been answered. When he retained his own attorney, the lawyer's letters also received no response.

Shirts argued that according to the terms of the bonds, the principal and interest would be immediately paid by the company in case of a default in the payment of the interest. Technically speaking, he had not bought ownership in the company but merely loaned it money. Now he wanted what was his. He wrote McConkie as graciously as he could but appealed rather directly to their common LDS affiliation:

> Before considering the possibility of filing suit against the company, I thought as a member of the Cedar West Stake Presidency, I might solicit your suggestion in the matter and possibly keep it out of the courts. We should like the $800, plus interest, we paid for the bonds returned immediately. Could you please help me?[33]

McConkie never answered the letter.

The rest of the story became a maze of lawyers, court hassles and red tape, back-room deals, and the loss to many elderly persons of their lifetime savings. The case came up for final pretrial conference before a United States district judge in March 1969. The investors' suit raised the prospect of further trouble for MESC and its officers because of certain "irregularities" in their business practices. According to the Securities Exchange Act of 1934 and the Investment Company Act of 1940, the common stock and the bonds issued by MESC constituted "securities." By law, therefore, MESC should have registered as an investment company with the U.S. Securities and Exchange Commission.

But it never had. MESC was supposedly a company dealing in cemeteries, not using other people's money for other investment purposes. That fact, plus the securities laws violated, would have proven highly embarrassing for a number of Church officials if the case had gone to trial. Investment fraud, rather than simply bankruptcy, had become the issue.

There was a flurry of closed-door meetings by the attorneys of both parties on April 25, 1969, just three days before the case was set for jury trial. Abruptly the attorneys for the MESC defendents made a last minute attempt to settle out of court with the investors. The sum proposed was $113,500 in cash. The investors' attorneys accepted the proposal without having time to consult their clients. However, after their own legal fees were paid—one-third of the amount—only $76,045 was left to be distributed among 193 surviving investors.

It was a shameful pittance. The total amount originally invested by those 193 persons was $193,579, or an average of $1,003 each (though many had invested considerably more). Left to divide only $76,045 among themselves, the average investor recouped only $394. In some cases elderly investors lost virtually their entire savings.[34]

More than one of MESC's officers went on to betters things after the bankruptcy and out-of-court settlement. Three years later, for instance, Elder Bruce R. McConkie was ordained an Apostle to the Council of the Twelve, just below the First Presidency, while J. Thomas Fyans, one of MESC's directors and later president of the company, was sustained to the Presidency of the First Quorum of the Seventy.

Others touched by the MESC's demise could not so easily put the affair behind them.

Babies for Sale

Since 1979 the LDS Church has maintained an official policy encouraging its members to adopt children only through licensed agencies. Past problems with private adoptions pointed to the potential for serious abuse, and the Church wanted to avoid irresponsible or shady adoption practices affecting its members. After 1984, however, LDS officials decided to tighten Church adoption standards.

It was in that year that news broke of a cruel scam, operated by Mormons primarily exploiting Mormons, over undoubtedly the most sensitive issue in a famously family-oriented religion: persons collecting cash from adopting parents for children who often were never delivered. What was worse, in some cases the children were tricked away from their real mothers.

The con started innocently enough, seemingly without anyone intending to defraud. But then someone realized how the illegal act could be repeated over time on a systematic basis for profit. And then a baby-selling racket began.

The pivotal figure in this fraud was Debbie Tanner, a Mormon housewife in Arizona. During the late 1970s she and her husband, Terry, had three adopted children plus a natural child of their own. That same year a Mexico City court awarded them custody of two little boys. One the Tanners had intended to adopt; the other was to go to an Oklahoma couple.

But at the last minute the Oklahomans changed their minds. The Tanners, who had lost a five-year-old son to a rare blood disease not long before, decided to keep this second boy for obvious emotional reasons. Many Mexican children who are unsuccessfully put up for adoption ultimately find themselves illegitimate, unwanted, homeless, and poverty-stricken. The Tanners knew this and made him a family member.

Yet, if the Tanners' decision was humanitarian, it also hatched an idea that Debbie and others were to develop into a lucrative practice. She figured there were many couples who were either unable to conceive children or interested in providing a home for orphans and unwanted children. Mormon families who for some reason could have no children of their own would especially want to bring another soul to the knowledge of the Restored Gospel of the LDS Church.

Debbie Tanner learned how to import Mexican children, successfully overcoming legal obstacles by using cooperative lawyers, forged birth certificates, and eager North American would-be parents. In 1977 she met up with Walter Turley, a Mormon living in Mexico who had failed in the export pottery business and had started into gold and silver mining. Turley knew legal details of adoption on both sides of the border as well as Mexican informants who could act as baby-locators.

Ordinary foreign adoptions processed through the U.S. Immigration and Naturalization Service as well as the courts could take as long as one year or more, and costs often started at $5,000. Turley knew ways to "arrange" adoptions with Mexican lawyers that short-circuited the bureaucracy, turning the paperwork around in months and sometimes weeks. In the beginning he and Tanner used a Mexican lawyer named Prospero to forge birth certificates and other documents. Under Turley Debbie Tanner served an apprenticeship in learning the techniques of illegally smuggling Mexican children into the United States.

One of these techniques was to play on Mormons' trust in Mormons. Walter Turley, it seems, had been a ward bishop in Guadalajara's Third Ward for two years. (Mexico hosts a number of large Mormon communities dating from the late nineteenth century when the Church banned polygamy and many Saints headed south of the border in protest.) After he moved to Durango, Turley became a branch president within a larger ward.

Tanner put Turley's Church titles up front in her assurances to Mormon couples (the majority of all couples she approached) that the adoption operation could be trusted. Jerri Start, a Mormon employee of the Holt Adoption Agency in Eugene, Oregon, remembered: "That was the sole issue in the beginning because Mormon people were involved. . . . She [Tanner] would say, 'There are Church leaders in Mexico that say it's ok.' "[35] One Ogden, Utah, Mormon, who paid $2,500 to Tanner in 1980 and never saw a promised child for adoption, similarly recalled: "These people did come on as having LDS background." The wife of a Washington state physician referred to the religious factor: "That's why I trusted her explicitly."[36]

Initially Debbie Tanner's motives seem to have been merely to subsidize her own adoption costs. When she first found babies for other couples in 1977 she placed them for a time with the Turley family. The Turleys usually asked several thousand dollars for their expenses, but Tanner rarely accepted any. But gradually she escalated the price of locating children, from less than $100 to $400 to as much as $7,500.

Walter Turley became uneasy as he saw her charging far more than the costs of locating children and pocketing the difference. He had helped her with as many as twenty adoptions, but in his opinion the money issue began to get out of hand. In 1979 he broke off completely with Tanner.

Tanner struck up a new partnership, moving her adoption organization from Durango (where Turley lived) to Juarez and changing lawyers. She enlisted new baby-finders and dealt increasingly with an El Paso man who owned a topless bar called The One-Eyed Jack Cantina. His name was Bryan Martin Hall, and with him the adoption scam escalated to the big-money level.

Investigators from the FBI, the Internal Revenue Service, and the Immigration and Naturalization Service eventually learned that between 1980 and 1983 Hall had collected $1.25 million from couples paying Tanner for promised adoptions ($610,000 belonged to couples who never saw any children materialize).[37] Eventually, as the network (and demand for babies) grew, Hall also dropped out of the picture. Tanner moved the operation to Agua Prieta, directly across the border from Douglas, Arizona, and obtained yet another lawyer to help with the doctored birth certificates. She used to refer to the early days in Juarez, Guadalajara, and El Paso as "Mexico I." "Mexico II" was her expanded business in Agua Prieta. In late 1982 she expanded Mexico II by creating the base of an unlicensed adoption mill in Willcox, Arizona, named *Casa Para los Ninos* (House for Children).

How did Tanner locate Mexican children for North American couples eager to adopt? She had various sources. In time her methods became increasingly sophisticated. Initially Turley's Mormon contacts in Mexico suggested abundant names of unfortunate pregnant and poverty-stricken young women who were willing to part with their children. For a while in Torrean, south of Juarez, Dr. Pablo Lopes and his wife Sonia operated a baby pipeline for Tanner. The Lopes couple convinced unwed mothers seeking abortions to give birth and immediately hand the babies over to Tanner for adoption.[38]

Tanner also had baby locators in the field, such as Fannie Hatch, a Mormon woman and former resident of Mexico. Hatch reportedly paid pregnant Mexican mothers to promise to put their newborn infants up for adoption in Tanner's care.[39] Far into the operation Tanner and a lawyer friend began attending adoption "seminars" for couples in Arizona and California, recruiting potential parents for their own business. By late 1983 Tanner's prices had soared past $7,000 per infant.

But Debbie Tanner had started running into problems. Demand for adoptions had always exceeded supply, yet Tanner continued to recruit parents, promise babies, and take money for them in advance. Asked why she kept adding earnest couples to the congested adoption list, Tanner once replied, "We just have so many people. I just hate to turn them down."[40]

In the end the adoption network scam fell apart for several reasons. Angry couples and parents on both sides of the adoption fence realized they had been conned and went to the authorities. At least two Mexican mothers claimed they had been tricked into signing away their children. One woman, Ermila Hernandez, accused Tanner's agents of taking advantage of her ignorance of English. Her understanding had been that her four little girls were to be taken into U.S. homes temporarily while she looked for work in this country and sought permanent legal residence. When she discovered that she had unknowingly surrendered them to Tanner, she obtained a lawyer.

On the American side, complaints of impatient couples began to simmer and then boil over. Tanner had used a tactic of delivering what several states' attorney generals termed "show babies" to selected parents. Similar to con–artists whose pyramid schemes let a few early investors receive the promised returns in order to let them serve as enthusiastic endorsements, Tanner targeted some couples as early recipients of babies to encourage others.

For example, one woman in Pennsylvania received a child after only a few weeks' time while other couples had been on a waiting list for months. But that woman's friends were impressed. As a result, five couples wanting to adopt sent $3,800 each to Tanner's partner Bryan Martin Hall in El

Paso. (The "show baby" ploy was also used in Iowa, Utah, and Massachusetts.) However, two years later, exasperated by no children and no signs of action from Tanner, couples in the Mormon network, which Tanner had so shrewdly cultivated, began contacting the FBI as a group. Shortly after, the investigations began and the indictments were formed.[41]

What was the extent of the damage? In emotional terms it is impossible to compute. On the monetary scale, as with most scams, there are clear dollar estimates. Tanner claimed she had helped four hundred couples receive Mexican children, though her records were sloppy and unreliable. Investigators found, however, that approximately two hundred couples in forty states paid over $1 million total, often in amounts of five or six thousand dollars, to Tanner. *Two-thirds* of the couples never saw the children they expected to adopt, and most of these victims were Mormons.[42]

Tanner's adoption racket was a bizarre variant of a pyramid scam, using children as dividends, but the principle of fleecing investors was the same. Those in early stood a better chance of realizing returns; those in later were only likely to see their expected reward if they were useful as successful "examples" to keep others investing. Almost everyone else got nothing.

The Consummate Grifter

Snellen Maurice Johnson had charisma.

A physically large man who operated Intermountain Bronze Casting in Heber City, Utah, Johnson had curly hair, a large nose, and rough features far from handsome. But he possessed flair and a folksy grin, and the sum total of his appearance plus his enthusiasm for his projects created an appealing "good old boy" aura that inspired confidence. Once he posed for a public relations photograph with television and motion picture cowboy star Roy Rogers standing before a specially commissioned bronze sculpture of Rogers on his famed horse Trigger. Wearing a cowboy hat alongside Rogers, Snellen Johnson looked every bit the model of rugged frontier integrity.

Snellen Johnson was also outwardly a proper Mormon, a family man, and an upstanding citizen. After all, he held a temple "recommends," which is only given out by Church officials after lengthy inquiry into a member's background. He regularly paid his tithing, ward budget, and fast offerings.[43] If his local ward ever needed donations for some particular project, the good elders knew they could always turn to Brother Johnson.

Moreover, Snellen Johnson seemed to have influential connections in the upper echelons of the LDS Church hierarchy. He was on cordial speaking terms with one of the two counselors in the First Presidency office, not to mention others on an impressive list of General Authorities and stake presidents in addition to ward bishops and branch presidents.

But the fame, the public rectitude, and the high-level LDS contacts were parts of a mask. True, Johnson was generous with money, but it usually belonged to somebody else. His claims of personal friendships with LDS Church elites ranged from the frighteningly authentic to the totally fabricated. At times he was what psychologists would undoubtedly label a pathological liar.

His propriety was also questionable: out of the public eye Johnson was a wife-batterer, an adulterer, and a defaulter of loans. Most importantly, the affably persuasive Snellen was a consummate grifter and con-artist. He possessed a criminal past of unsavory business deals long before he put together his last and greatest fraud.

Johnson was, figuratively speaking, a wolf among a fold of sheep. In time he even went after some of the shepherds.

A Man with a Shady Past

Snellen Johnson had all the attributes of a supersalesman. Shortly after his final fraud conviction, his wife, Kathryn, remembered:

> Snell is so smart, has so much charm and salesmanship about himself. His power and charisma are unmatched by anyone I've ever met. He can get anyone to believe what he wants them to believe. That's the kind of spell he holds over them.[44]

But Snellen Johnson did not actually work his scam magic like some hypnotic Svengali. His was an interpersonal strategy that involved cultivating influential contacts whom he then worked for further contacts. One contact was Sterling W. Sill, a Mormon co-worker of his going back to 1964 when they worked together at the New York Life Insurance Company. Sill eventually became a prominent businessman and media personality in Utah. For many years, he was a speaker on *Sunday Evening From Temple Square,* a popular program of the LDS Church-owned radio station KSL. A prolific author who claimed almost two dozen books to his credit, Sill wrote *How To Personally Profit from the Laws of Success.* He was also a member of the LDS Church's First Quorum of the Seventy and, after his retirement, became an emeritus member.

Sill frequently loaned money to his old pal Snellen Johnson. But Johnson cynically regarded the loans less as the results of Sill's generosity than as the fruits of Johnson's cunning. Recalled Kathryn Johnson:

Sterling Sill used to give Snell money all the time. Whenever Snell would need some, he'd just phone up Sterling. It was unbelievable . . . the people he could get to do things for him and have confidence in him. Snell once told me, "I know just how to manipulate Sterling to get what I want out of him."[45]

At one time Johnson owed Sill over one million dollars. But Sill trusted Johnson. And Johnson even named his oldest son Snellen Sterling, which flattered Sill.

Johnson tried various business ventures, not many of which turned a profit. His bronze casting business advertised that it had cast commemorative statues of Roy Rogers' wife, Dale Evans; Kentucky Fried Chicken's legendary Colonel Sanders; famous race horses; and even the entire National Football League's teams. But he was constantly taking out loans. All the while he maintained a high profile for supporting Church projects with donations. He and Kathryn had been married in a Mormon temple, and his temple recommends remained valid for years despite his legal problems. Hardly anyone knew of his verbal and physical abuse toward his wife or of his affairs with other women, including his secretary.[46]

Snellen Johnson's first criminal conviction attracted little notice. He was a loner then and not milking networks of Mormons. In 1974 he pleaded guilty in a U.S. District Court to conspiracy and violations of the Federal Securities Act for making false statements to a bank in order to obtain loans.[47] He and his brother, Lyle, almost came to the attention of many Utahns when they tried unsuccessfully in the mid-1970s to buy the "Utah Stars" professional basketball team. The "Pinpoint Team," a group of investigative journalists at the LDS Church-owned *Deseret News,* learned that Snellen, who with his brother made a $650,000 down-payment on the "Stars," had a criminal record. Both brothers, investigators discovered, also had abysmal decade-long credit ratings and histories of lawsuits.

Curiously, the Pinpoint Team was prevented from blowing the whistle on the Johnson brothers' questionable financial affairs. Only months later was the basketball bid even given brief, sanitized mention by the *Deseret News.* The reason is that an unnamed, high-level Church official telephoned the newspaper and vouched for the Johnson brothers' credibility and integrity. The Johnsons, their lawyers, members of the Pinpoint Team, and the *Deseret News'* editor, William B. Smart, met to discuss coverage on the purchase of the basketball team. Later Smart met once more with the Johnsons and their lawyers in the absence of the Pinpoint investigative reporters. A bargain was struck: news stories on the Johnsons' personal histories were killed. In turn, Church pressure on the *Deseret News* ceased.[48]

Not long after, however, the Johnson brothers were found to have written bad checks totalling $160,000, and the basketball team went out of business.[49] But a pattern was set: Church contacts proved useful, in this case for extricating Snellen Johnson from publicity about his dubious financial affairs.

It Helps to Have Friends

Probably the most important Mormon contact cultivated by Snellen Johnson was Victor L. Brown, Presiding Bishop of the LDS Church. To appreciate the significance of such a relationship, one has to realize that the Office of the Presiding Bishopric handles all tithing and other monies paid into the LDS Church by members. As such, Brown had enormous financial responsibilities ranging in the billions of dollars that put him in touch with high Church officials throughout the country but especially in Salt Lake City. Brown was to be the unwitting linchpin in a scheme that made good use of his high office and public image.

Around 1980 Brown and Johnson became involved together in various art businesses inspired by Johnson. Most were spinoffs of his bronze casting, with names like American Arts Foundation and Prairie Pacific Marketing.

About that same time Snellen Johnson and Sterling Sill had a falling out, with Johnson owing Sill close to $2 million on past loans. Sill owned the mortgage on Johnson's expensive Heber City home and went to court to foreclose on it in order to retrieve at least some of his money. Even so, Johnson still owed Sill over $1 million. Sill finally worked out an arrangement with Johnson to reduce the balance owed to $500,000 and allow Johnson to repay it in ten annual payments of $50,000 each.[50] It was a bittersweet compromise that lost Sill hundreds of thousands of dollars and let Johnson rather smoothly contain and even reduce his debts.

Meanwhile, Johnson went back to making false statements in attempts to secure bank loans, and again he ended up in a federal court. Unlike the first time six years earlier, however, it did not look like he was going to be let off on probation. Johnson was convicted on six counts of fraud and sentenced to two years in prison.

Johnson's lawyer filed an affidavit for reduction of his sentence to probation without incarceration. The grounds were that Johnson's misrepresentation to the bank was not intentional or malicious, that he was otherwise a responsible businessman and corporate executive (through his bronze casting enterprises), and that imprisoning him would substantially impoverish many other people. Portrayed as a pillar of the business community as well as a solid Mormon family man, Johnson claimed to be the employer of forty-three persons who would have to be discharged if he went to jail and the sole supporter of his mother, wife, five children, a sister, and five nieces and nephews as well as partial supporter of two other sisters. In the affidavit he claimed that probation would allow him to conduct his business profitably (the employees would keep their jobs) and provide for the welfare of his family—which had suddenly expanded on paper *after* his conviction.[51]

Johnson also drew on his Church contacts. His lawyer obtained letters of support for Johnson's probation from Victor Brown and, incredibly, the still-embittered Sterling Sill. It is likely that Sill figured he could never hope to see any of the remaining $500,000 Johnson still owed him if Johnson faced a prison sentence and economic ruin. Perhaps Sill still had a lingering affection for the affable Johnson despite the way Johnson had used him. At any rate, Sill may have choked on the words but nevertheless wrote Johnson's attorney:

> It is my hope that Mr. Johnson may be permitted by the Federal Court for Utah to remain out of prison in order that he can comply with the compromise arrangements [on the money owed Sill] we have made. My personal acquaintance with Mr. Johnson over the years leads me to believe that he has the ability to pay his personal indebtedness and maintain his family in a comfortable way if he is able to proceed with his current business venture.[52]

Brown, who held a much more visible and prestigious office in the Church compared to Sill, likewise wrote to the lawyer:

> At your request, I am pleased to write this letter on behalf of Snellen J. Johnson. I understand that you may use this letter to advise the Federal District Court on Mr. Johnson's present situation.
> I have known Snellen for a number of years and am aware of the criminal actions pending against him.
> On numerous occasions during the last few years, I have had the opportunity to counsel with Snellen. I personally believe that he is remorseful and is presently conducting himself honorably in the community. His present business venture is providing him with a means to pay back debtors in Utah and throughout the country. I believe the affirmative effort on his part is evidence of his sincerity and of his desire to make things right. I hope Snellen will be given an opportunity to remain in the community as a productive citizen.[53]

The appeal was persuasive. In August 1981 the judge placed Johnson on four years' probation instead of sending him to prison.[54]

But Victor Brown's hopes that a Snellen Johnson allowed to stay free of jail would "remain in the community as a productive citizen" were to be disappointed. Within the year Johnson was back with a multimillion-dollar investment scam that reached into the highest level of the LDS Church for its victims and exploited his friendships with trusting Mormons.

The NAVSAT Affair

Snellen Johnson retained his charm and persuasiveness after the second fraud conviction, but despite having escaped going to prison, his ego was hurt. Those closest to him saw his desire for success accelerate. Recalled his wife:

> His ego was so big and inflated, it would not permit him to accept defeat or failure when he got those second convictions. No, he had to go out and prove to himself and the world that he was better than that.[55]

The bronze casting business which figured so importantly in his appeal for probation was largely forgotten. It was too slow, too conventional for making big money. Johnson drifted into selling tax shelters. Soon the cash came in quickly enough to buy a new home and fancier cars.

Then Johnson developed a new scheme. He became partners with a man named Spencer S. Hooper, and together they resurrected an idea that Johnson first had in the late 1960s: NAVSAT. NAVSAT, an acronym for Navigation Satellite, Inc., was to provide computerized services for ships at sea involving satellite communications between ship and shore computers. In reality NAVSAT never did any such thing, for the hardware was never installed. At the later trial, evidence submitted showed that no NAVSAT system was ever installed on any ship nor was it ever fully tested nor ever fully operational. But the idea sounded good. It had the flavor of space-age technology. The late N. Eldon Tanner, one of two counselors to the LDS president in the First Presidency, had heard of Johnson's NAVSAT concept and wrote about it in a late 1970s article appearing in the Church's *Ensign* magazine. Tanner's point was allegorical: he compared the idea of NAVSAT to an individual's journey through the rough seas of life, the need to communicate with God periodically for stability, and so forth.

Johnson photocopied the article, underlining the parts referring to NAVSAT, and used it in his sales pitch for investing in NAVSAT. He audaciously claimed that Elder N. Eldon Tanner had given NAVSAT his personal endorsement. Said the trial attorney for the Security and Exchange Commission in Salt Lake City who helped investigate the case: "A lot of people invested money just on the strength of that claim."[56]

Elder Tanner learned of Johnson's specious claim that he had endorsed NAVSAT and was furious. He repeatedly telephoned Johnson. Finally, Presiding Bishop Victor Brown arranged a meeting at Church Headquarters in Salt Lake City between Tanner and Snellen Johnson with Brown present. By this time Johnson had already persuaded Brown himself to invest close to $50,000 in NAVSAT. It would be difficult for Brown to come down too hard on the company.

For some time Tanner questioned Johnson closely about NAVSAT and the investment process. Finally even Brown joined in. Johnson became evasive and uncomfortable under their grilling, then eventually angry at their persistent inquiries. Finally he stormed out of Tanner's office declaring, "I don't have to take this from anyone, not even the First Presidency!" Yet it was a measure of Johnson's persuasive power that, in spite of this emotional performance in the high Churchman's office, Elder Tanner went on soon after to invest in NAVSAT.[57]

Johnson continued to claim Tanner's endorsement of NAVSAT with the *Ensign* article as evidence. He also claimed (falsely) that NAVSAT had agreements with firms such as IBM, Sperry-Univac, Union Oil, Exxon, and Comsat.[58] The NAVSAT system, he assured mostly Mormon investors, was already fully operational and being installed.

At the same time, Johnson's partner, Spencer Hooper, was working a scam selling promissory notes for International Resources, Inc. The notes were allegedly secured by the pledge of common stock of NAVSAT Systems, Inc. Hooper told investors that the U.S. Congress had passed a law requiring ocean-going ships to be equipped with such communication systems by 1984. In reality, Congress had done no such thing.[59]

Johnson's wife recalled of her husband's activities: "Just go through a list of the Church officials, and it almost reads like a *Who's Who* of those who were a party to his investments."[60] For example, J. Thomas Fyans, one of seven Presidents of the Quorum of Seventy and a General Authority of the Church, was at one time president of NAVSAT. (Fyans was also a director and later president of the defunct Memorial Estates Security Corporation discussed earlier.) Presiding Bishop Victor L. Brown became a NAVSAT director. Brown, in fact, became a prominent endorser of NAVSAT, adding his prestige to Johnson's promotion of the scheme.

And the scheme utilized the LDS Church's hierarchical structure to maximum advantage. Stake presidents who learned of NAVSAT as a lucrative opportunity from Salt Lake City Church officials endorsed the project to their local bishops who in turn sold the idea to ward members. In two years' time the network eventually spread from Salt Lake City to Las Vegas to San Francisco, Chula Vista, and San Diego. Hundreds of Mormons gave NAVSAT "short-term loans" in exchange for the company's worthless stock. In San Diego alone Johnson brought in over $2 million. One California bishop who was cited in the indictments against Johnson (but not prosecuted) raised about $260,000 just by himself. (He later became a member of the Chula Vista stake high council.)

The sequence frequently proceeded as it did when one Chula Vista bishop called Victor Brown for a personal assessment of Johnson and NAVSAT. Brown gave Johnson glowing character references. The Chula Vista bishop in turn used that recommendation from a top Church leader to recruit dozens of other investors into the NAVSAT scheme. The trial attorney for the Security and Exchange Commission in Salt Lake City reported. "There was a saying floating around the Chula Vista stake for quite awhile, that 'An investment in NAVSAT is safer than an investment in food storage!' "[61] (The comment about food storage refers to the practice of many Mormons storing enough food, water, and other necessities to last one year or longer for the expected time of major social disorder and tribulation prior to Jesus Christ's second coming.)

But the inevitable doubts began to arise. Suspicions were voiced that Snellen Johnson was actually selling memberships in NAVSAT (as a pyramid scheme) rather than ship-to-shore satellite communications systems. Predictably, investors began wondering when their windfall profits were going to arrive. Bishop Victor L. Brown finally pulled out and quietly made arrangements with Johnson to be compensated for his investment.[62]

Brown never publicly told what he knew about NAVSAT. Meanwhile, Johnson and Hooper continued their confident spiel about this sure-fire investment in the technology of tomorrow, repeating their claims of important Church leaders' support.

When the bubble finally burst in late 1982 Snellen Johnson was put on trial, along with co-defendant Spencer Hooper, for thirty counts of mail, wire, and securities fraud. Together Johnson and Hooper had swindled at least $7 million from hundreds of people, most of them LDS faithful, who believed in Johnson's grandiose promises and trusted in his purported endorsements by respected Church leaders. At his trial Johnson explained with a straight face that he had needed a constant cash flow of incoming loans to develop his struggling company. Like most pyramid con-artists he blamed the scheme's failure on everything but the fact that his operation was essentially built on sand, with no real service or product to market. His protestations were less than convincing to the jury, especially when one witness testified that during the same time when investments were pouring in Johnson had opened a bank account in Liechtenstein.

After a thirty-seven-day trial, Snellen Johnson was convicted of all thirty counts (Hooper of 25 after a forty-one-day trial) and sentenced to five consecutive five-year prison terms. It was the stiffest sentence ever handed out in San Diego for a white-collar crime.[63] For obvious reasons the trial was not held in Utah. It would have been too embarrassing to the Church.

The Aftermath of Fraud

While the early 1980s was a time when public awareness about the plague of scams involving Mormons reached an all-time high, eruption of such scandals has in no way dropped off. Utah newspapers still regularly report fresh schemes at large among the Saints, some that have been operating for years. Such was the case of Granada, Inc., a bankrupt investment brokerage firm which bilked thousands of investors of over $48 million in real estate transactions. Its owner, C. Dean Larson, is a former LDS bishop and once served as an attorney for the Church. Though Church officials requested the court not to indict Larson "for the sake of his reputation," in May 1989 he was charged by the Utah Attorney General's office with forty-four counts of unlawful dealing of property, offering and selling unregistered securities, and theft and securities fraud. In August 1990, he was convicted on eighteen of those counts and sentenced to nine years in the Utah State Prison.[64]

Utah is also gaining a new distinction as the hub of telemarketing fraud. As telephone soliciting has become big business across the country, so has misrepresentation. Some states, such as California, have passed legislation to curb flagrant abuses in telemarketing, thus driving crooks elsewhere. Many have settled in Utah. Image Plus International, a classic "boiler room" telemarketing operation, was chased out or left just ahead of law enforcement authorities in three states before it settled in Toquerville, Utah, in early 1989.

Initially local citizens were pleased: the company would hire townfolk to operate the telephones and new tax revenues would be gained. But within six weeks the Utah Division of Investigations closed down Image Plus International. It had been generating over $5,000 a day with fraudulent promises over the telephone—not up to the daily $10,000 to $30,000 it was capable of doing, but enough to concern investigators.[65]

And some cons have an ancestry that continues to plague Zion. Two Salt Lake City men had an international telemarketing scam broken up in 1989 after they were charged with defrauding investors from Los Angeles to Switzerland of more than $500 million. Their strategy was to manipulate the stock of dormant Utah public corporations without real assets by conducting sham transactions that inflated the value of the shares; then they sold the stock to the public through high-pressure telephone sales pitches. The con spread to Europe where a share of stock originally worth fifteen cents was sold for three dollars. French, Swiss, and West German police raided the scam's branches in their respective countries in 1988, but it took longer for the trail to lead back to the headquarters in Salt Lake City. It is no coincidence that the stock manipulation bore a striking resemblence to the AFCO "land flips" scandal of a few years earlier. One of the two men who set up this stock hustle was Michael Drew Wright, former assistant vice-president of AFCO Enterprises, Inc.[66]

There are familiar elements in all these frauds: rank-and-file Mormons' uncritical acceptance of various LDS Church leaders' glowing endorsements of supposedly lucrative investment plans, the sense of urgency that possesses believers and leaders alike not to be left out of a "good thing," and the mindset of gullibility that thinks exorbitant returns on investments can be made overnight and still be perfectly legal.

Even the Church is occasionally culpable for not discouraging the scandals more strongly. Several times, for example, Church officials intervened to protect grifter Snellen Johnson when reporters tried to expose his rotten business record and illegal past. In fact, several years before the NAVSAT scandal, a Mormon stake high councilman from the Los Angeles area had been an investor-victim in one of Johnson's smaller but similar schemes. Outraged, the man contacted Church officials in Salt Lake City to press for excommunication proceedings against Johnson. (The LDS Church's *General Handbook of Instruction* states that Church courts may be convened to consider excommunication for theft, embezzlement of Church funds, and misuse or embezzlement of other people's funds.) But, as investigators of NAVSAT learned, he was advised through upper Church channels to "back off and leave Johnson alone."[67]

It is shocking how far into the hierarchy of the LDS Church crooks like Snellen Johnson have been able to reach for endorsements and how widely and rapidly schemes have spread among grass roots Mormons. That is embarrassing enough to Church leaders. But there is a subtle corrosive aftermath to these scandals which is less openly admitted: accompanying members' grief is a shaken faith in those leaders.

The reason is that Latter-day Saints are expected to "sustain" their leaders in the belief that these men share in the chain of revelation from the Holy Spirit that descends from the First Presidency down to ward and branch bishops. They are admonished to obey, not question, the wisdom of those "called" to Church leadership. As one anonymous Securities and Exchange Commission investigator who had "lost his testimony" over the NAVSAT scandal bitterly exclaimed, "If these men are called by inspiration, then why can't they see what's going on? If they're supposed to have the Spirit of the Lord with them, why have they become involved with such crooks? Where are the revelations that they're supposed to be getting?"[68]

Non-Mormon investors, too, have been shaken in their opinion of Mormonism. When the Securities and Exchange Commission in Salt Lake City was pursuing its investigation of NAVSAT, attorneys asked several California "Gentile" investors who belonged to the Church of Christ denomination why they had decided to put their life savings into the venture. The answer: "Because we've always had confidence in the Mormons as being an honest and hard-working people."

Scams like NAVSAT have been a public-relations catastrophe for Mormons and non-Mormons alike who are bilked and then tell their woes to others. One attorney in the NAVSAT investigation summed up the long-term harmful effects of such scandals to the LDS Church: "Can you imagine how many hundreds and hundreds of missionaries it would take to repair such damage? I doubt if anything could ever be done to have them think well of the Church again."[69]

4

The Tales of Hofmann:
Forgery, Deceit, and Murder

Deep within the granite rock of Little Cottonwood Canyon, twenty miles southeast of Salt Lake City, the Mormon Church stores its genealogical files in subterranean caverns designed to withstand major catastrophes like floods and earthquakes, even nuclear war. Huge ten- and fourteen-ton steel vault doors and blast locks seal out contaminated air and provide access to the six vaults which are actually chiseled-out semicircles lined with white corrugated steel several hundred feet long. The Church's genealogical information is recorded on one-hundred-foot rolls of microfilm, constantly being added to at the rate of sixty thousand rolls a year. Eventually the Church hopes to record over six billion names in its archives.

Church members believe they can vicariously baptize deceased non-Mormon relatives in temple rituals to assure them the chance of heaven. As a result they are constantly scouring old Bibles and family trees throughout the United States and Europe in search of more ancestors' names. This commendable genealogical effort is part of a Mormon reverence for history. No other religion has ever possessed a more vital sense of its own history as the unfolding of God's special design in human events. Mormons are fascinated with their own religion's roots, believing the recent historical record of Mormonism offers examples of God in action. Thus they are often persistent collectors of artifacts, letters, and diaries of early members.

There are always deals pending among some of Utah's most prominent Mormon residents, deals involving purchases of valuable historical documents relating to the LDS Church's origins. On occasion, agents of the Church as well as private collectors engage in playing out the roles of sellers and recipients of these documents. Salt Lake City, the heart of Mormonism, is often the scene for such deals.

For a time during the mid-1980s the main seller of such goods was the *Wunderkind* of LDS document finders: a former LDS missionary and Utah State University pre-medical school dropout named Mark Hofmann. No one had quite the knack for discovering rare Mormon books and letters, even if many of the lost documents seemed to call into question orthodox versions of how the LDS Church had been founded. Hofmann kept coming up with the choicest, most controversial finds of critical historical significance. He had turned his antiquarian skills into a lucrative business that brought him into frequent contact with various luminaries in the Church hierarchy, even the First Presidency.

But Hofmann's fortunes were to change dramatically. In 1985 Salt Lake City experienced a series of three terrorist-style bombings, one of them almost killing Hofmann himself. At first he was seen as a sympathetic victim. However, by the end of his sensational trial he was revealed to be deeply involved in a shocking story of fraud and murder.

The Bombings

Around 8:00 A.M., Steve Christensen, a businessman and avid collector of Mormon historical documents, had gone as usual to his office in Salt Lake City's downtown Judge Building. As he went to open his door he noticed on the floor a box wrapped in plain brown paper with his name scrawled on it. Stooping to lift it, he unwittingly triggered a simple but devastatingly effective pipe bomb. The explosion shattered windows, destroyed an adjacent wall, and drove dozens of carpentry nails taped to the steel pipe into Christensen's body and brain. Several fingers, an eye, and part of a foot were immediately blown away. He lived a few moments but no more. Later, during the autopsy, the state's chief medical examiner removed the nails, pieces of wire and battery, and one nine-inch shard of pipe from Christensen's badly riddled chest cavity. At a later preliminary hearing one police officer called that piece of metal the ugliest looking weapon he had ever seen.

That same morning, not long after the downtown explosion, housewife Kathy Webb Sheets had just returned from joining a neighbor on a morning walk. Kathy was the wife of well-known Mormon business consultant Gary Sheets, whose investment firm had fallen on hard times and who had bankrolled a team of experts to examine one of Steven Christensen's recent manuscript purchases. Like Christensen, Kathy Sheets noticed a curious box wrapped in brown paper sitting in the driveway near her garage door. She picked it up under one arm to take it inside, unknowingly activating the detonation device of a second pipe bomb. The blast severed her arm and several fingers, simultaneously disemboweling her and splitting her open from chest to abdomen.

Salt Lake City was immediately seized by fear. In a part of the Southwest where renegade polygamous Mormon sects (such as those started by the infamous brothers Ervil and Joel LeBaron) still feuded and assassinated rival leaders and their families, fanatic hit squads were more than a remote possibility. Concerns were also fueled by the possibility that, at a time when the LDS Church hierarchy had become especially touchy about critical "historical research" by scholars, some rogue squad of LDS Security enforcers might be running amok, marking victims it considered dangerous to Church interests.

Then the media picked up on the fact that Christensen had been the former president of Coordinated Financial Services, the same troubled Utah investment firm owned by Kathy Sheets's husband, Gary. Sheets's bankrupt firm had between twenty-five hundred and three thousand unhappy investors across the country, some possibly linked to organized crime, when it lost tens of millions of dollars. Mafia revenge suddenly became a credible motive, so much so that the day after these two bombings one Salt Lake County sheriff's detective waved a computer printout of CFS's investors before reporters and prematurely boasted, "These are our suspects."[1]

But that theory was short-lived. A third bomb exploded the next afternoon, seriously injuring but not killing a different kind of businessman —Mark Hofmann, finder of rare historical documents, particularly of those relating to the LDS Church. He was halfway into his car in a parking lot not far from Temple Square when a pipe-bomb package on the front seat detonated, hurling him into the air as the automobile burst into flames. Hofmann lived, but barely.

With at least two of the three victims directly active in serious Church-document collecting, a new element of fear akin to hysteria spread throughout the Salt Lake valley and beyond. In a religious subculture mightily preoccupied with studying its past, many Mormons were document collectors. Many others studied and wrote about them. And all were aware that documents can be either buttresses or undercut the Church's "official" storyline on its relatively recent origins. If some ruthless, eccentric defender of the faith was bent on trying to eliminate possible faith-threatening collectors, then the net of potential victims had suddenly expanded on an alarming scale. For who knew what might ultimately be considered "faith-threatening?"

Calls to the police requesting protection immediately skyrocketed, and some scholars at Provo's Brigham Young University as well as at the city's University of Utah began car-pooling and deliberately varying where they parked their automobiles. Uneasiness about who directed the bombings was widespread as Mormons waited to see who might be the next victim and what clues the next explosion might give about the bomber's identity.

But there were no further bombings. Hofmann, as it turned out, was the last victim, and for good reason. It took more than a year for the full story to unfold. Robert Lindsey, in *A Gathering of Saints*, called it "the largest criminal investigation in the history of Utah,"[2] but in the end the police found their man. It was Mark Hofmann, the spectacularly successful locator of Mormon historical documents, who was himself almost killed by a bomb—a bomb, it turned out, that he himself had made, as he had the others. Hofmann at first maintained that he had no idea about the origins of this third bomb; then, under interrogation, he intimated that he had intended it to be the means of his suicide swan song. Later, by his own admission, it became clear that he had intended a third victim high in the hierarchy of the LDS Church. Initially Hofmann protested his innocence, but he eventually admitted his guilt as part of a plea bargain worked out between his lawyers and prosecutors. Thanks to Hofmann's confession, we now know his methods, his motives, and his clearly amoral, sociopathic character.

Actually, the violence of the bombings was the endpoint of a larger story of elaborate forgeries and fraud, double-dealing, and extortion. It is easy, in the face of the carnage Hofmann created, to lose sight of how otherwise characteristic were his cons on other Mormons. Unique in this case was the fact that Hofmann turned to murder as a decoy to draw attention away from the extensive trail of his document-finding scams.

Three books have been written detailing the sensational 1985 bombings in Salt Lake City.[3] The author of one of these even sold the movie rights to Twentieth-Century Fox studios. Meanwhile, in the summer of 1988, CBS announced it was developing—what else—a mini-series about the bombings for television. Yet all these treatments largely missed the true significance of the Hofmann story. They treated the Hofmann scams as if they were a set of freak occurrences, only briefly acknowledging or totally skipping over a widely prevalent problem in Utah.

In fact, the Hofmann forgery scams, apart from the violent bombings, were vintage Mormon white-collar crimes. It was a classic case of an unscrupulous Mormon preying on other Mormons, in ways particularly seductive to them as fellow religionists. The frauds were facilitated by the

LDS subculture's widespread obsession with its own historical navel-gazing and (as so often is found in cases of fraud) a reluctance by victims to report the cons to authorities. Hofmann lured his victims from both ends of Mormondom; he deceived the grass-roots membership while reaching into the stratosphere of the Church hierarchy, even duping the LDS President and his most able counselors and experts.

Thus, Hofmann's crimes of fraud, however much they spilled over into murder, were no anomalies. The modern conditions of Mormonism, every bit as much as his skill, duplicity, and ruthlessness, enabled him to commit his deceit.

A Man with a Rare Talent

Mark S. Hofmann, by his early thirties, was a troubled man with a rare talent. He was a self-taught master forger with a knife out for the LDS Church tradition in which he had been reared and taught to love.

Hofmann had admired Mormon history since he was a boy—so much so, in fact, that he stopped merely collecting church artifacts and began creating them out of whole cloth using materials at hand and his imagination. Hofmann's forgery career began when he was a teenager. At the age of thirteen he made his first legitimate purchase of Mormon memorabilia: a five-dollar note from Joseph Smith's failed Kirtland (Ohio) Safety Society; the note cost young Hofmann the considerable sum of $250. Two years later, however, he showed he could be innovative enough to affect history. By crude electroplating he changed the date on a rare dime and sent it to the American Numismatic Association in Colorado Springs for authentication. Surprisingly, the coin association proclaimed it genuine. Later asked by a friend about the altered coin, Hofmann's reply previewed his adult career as a con-artist. If the American Numismatic Association certified the coin as genuine, he said, then it was. Authenticity lay in the minds of the experts, not in the items themselves.[4]

Mark Hofmann was a sixth-generation Mormon, but as he entered into young manhood he became disillusioned with his LDS faith. The experience is not unusual for Mormons who read beyond the narrow Church-approved reading lists on their own history and who learn of the inconsistencies that scholars and other writers have sometimes found in the historical record and official church dogma. The orthodox LDS story of Joseph Smith discovering and translating "lost" golden tablets that were "lost" again as soon as the religion was founded seemed contrived to Hofmann. He went to England on the standard two-year missionary stint expected of young Mormon men, and by all accounts he threw himself energetically into winning converts. But Hofmann's questions about the basic tenets of Mormon faith increased in number and scope.

After his mission work Hofmann became a pre-med student at Utah State University, but found himself increasingly drawn to the history of Mormondom. Perhaps after two years of pushing the faith so energetically to Gentiles in England, yet secretly harboring serious doubts about its validity, he felt compelled to sort things out for himself. In any event, he became a regular fixture in the university's Special Collections area.

In particular, Hofmann was struck by *No Man Knows My History*, a controversial account of Joseph Smith by Mormon historian Fawn Brodie. Brodie drew on Smith's contemporaries and a wealth of early members' diaries and letters to argue that the Book of Mormon and Smith's claims of divine revelations were essentially frauds. (Brodie was excommunicated for writing it.) While Brodie's debunking of Mormonism satisfied many of Hofmann's spiritual questions, he reportedly was impressed by her description of Smith's deception. It seemed the ultimate con: a new religion that brought to its founder wealth, prestige, power, and, in those straight-laced Victorian times, all the women he wanted once he introduced polygamy. Smith's Book of Mormon had created a mythic history and then allowed him to make real history based on those myths.[5]

Hofmann's spiritual doubts found no sympathy at home. The Hofmann house had always held an unquestioning Mormon fundamentalist obedience to Church dogma and the inspired pronouncements of the "Brethren" (i.e., the First Presidency and the Councils of the Twelve Apostles). Hofmann's father, in particular, did not approve of questioning the faith. In fact, his son was sternly scolded for even daring to ask questions, whether they dealt with the Church's historical record or broader issues, such as Darwin's theory of evolution. The inquiring mind, young Hofmann learned, was the devil's tool as much as God's gift. Doubts had to be squelched. His father's typical reaction was an anti-intellectual warning that young Hofmann's "testimony" must be weak if he asked about such things. Prayer and submission, not further study or dialogue, were the cures.

But the doubts continued. Then came cynicism, followed by agnosticism and bitterness.

Hofmann's feelings about his family powerfully influenced the deeds he would commit. Even later, at a preliminary hearing into the bombings, when his guilt for forgeries and murders rapidly became transparent, he could not bring himself to speak the words "I did it" to his domineering father. To admit to a betrayal or rejection of the Church was the same as symbolic patricide. His love/hate ambivalence toward his parent/church approached deep Freudian dimensions. He hated and resented both, but felt irresistibly caught up in their worlds of influence and authority. Concluded one Salt Lake City psychologist:

> I think he's real ambivalent about his dad. I think that, if anything, his effort was probably to destroy something in the long run that was of tremendous value to his dad, to discredit the church, that is, and thereby to shake his [the father's] dogmatic beliefs. And also to assume the dominant position in their relationship.[6]

But Mark Hofmann had another reason to be angry at his Church. He had discovered a nasty family secret: his mother had been born into a polygamous family, not some breakaway sect living in the hills but a prominent family headed by a respected member of the mainline church. Polygamy was a practice supposedly banned by the church in 1890 as the result of special revelation to LDS President Wilford Woodruff (and in response to pressure from Gentile public opinion outside Utah, including the U.S. Congress). But in reality it lived on for many years, practiced underground by many respected Church leaders. While it was theologically (but secretly) justified, it was publicly taboo and increasingly denounced by the Church as immoral.

Hofmann's mother had been forced into a childhood existence of lying to strangers about her family and harboring the difficult knowledge that there was something at once sacred as well as illegitimate about her parentage. The sheer duplicitousness of this church-sanctioned practice, and how it troubled his own family, infuriated Hofmann when he learned of it. He was strongly protective of his nurturing mother, who seemed the opposite of his gruff father. She did not blame him for asking his questions about religious faith. Indeed, he was even able to discuss his religious doubts openly with her without recriminations. He was angered at her shame and the pain caused by growing up with a double standard. It was a hypocrisy, historical sources told him, very much perpetuated by the Church, but officially and sanctimoniously denied.

Hofmann's strict Mormon family was the crucible within which his anger toward the Church *and* his sociopathic tendencies were forged. Behavioral scientists distinguish psychopaths from sociopaths by one important dimension. Psychopaths and sociopaths are just as capable of destructive and antisocial acts, but psychopaths tend to have no long-range vision of what they do. They are impulsive and less attuned to the world around them. They act for the moment. Their mental worlds, in other words, turn inward more readily.

Sociopaths, on the other hand, can plan elaborately for the future. Their character defect is not one of lack of alertness or limited perspective as much as one of skewed perspective: sociopaths lack the ability to fully empathize, to imaginatively take the place of another person in a situation and sense what what he or she feels, and then react to that emotion. This primary defect may be subtly cloaked, but it is primarily interpersonal. And callous, even ruthless, behavior may be the result as others can become objects standing in the way of goals rather than feeling human beings. Thus they can be disposed of as objects in the sociopath's eyes, without remorse. A key problem, as early accounts of journalistic and professional interviews with Hofmann showed, is that sociopaths can also lie convincingly, without conscience.

One prison psychologist tested Hofmann and found that he had an IQ of 137 (certainly above average, but sociopathology has nothing to do with intelligence). The same psychologist determined that Hofmann had a narcissistic, self-centered personality (consistent with most sociopaths), but not sociopathic.[7]

But a Salt Lake City police psychologist, Eric Nielsen, independently concluded that Hofmann definitely demonstrated sociopathic symptoms, combined with paranoid delusions that told him he could easily fool and connive the people around him.[8] Certainly, recorded episodes in Hofmann's youth and early adulthood—practicing deception and fraud on playmates and adults, repeated experiments with explosions and firearms (including one explosion that scarred his chin), cruelty toward animals, and physical violence against women—were consistent with a sociopathic diagnosis.

The result was the existence of two Mark Hofmanns—a Jekyll and a Hyde. To all outward appearances the loyal Mormon Hofmann was a faithful Church supporter and happily active in his ward affairs; this appearance was made all the more believable by his disarmingly affable, toothsome smile. Inside, however, he seethed with hostility toward both his Church tradition and his father's knee-jerk defense of its authority. He entertained at home with hot-tub parties, lived high on the hog at expensive restaurants and hotels when out of town, and in other ways acted out the private life of a fallen-from-faith "Jack Mormon."[9]

Mark Hofmann was not the first disillusioned casualty of an authoritarian religion who felt used and misled. During the 1970s and 1980s newspapers were full of accounts of ex-Moonies, ex-Hare Krishnas, and ex-fundamentalist Christians whose personal adventures in exotic cults and rigid sects had born bitter fruit. In fact, Mormonism itself had indirectly produced a rich literary tradition of disgruntled ex-members. Yet no one could have foreseen how the rebellious Hofmann youth who had lost his faith would creatively channel that rage.

But there is more to the equation than possible Oedipal dilemmas and anger redirected at a religious tradition.

The Mormon Underground

Hofmann's personal history was to be only one element in the explanation of how he pulled off his chain of forgeries. He also needed an economic environment which would eagerly, sometimes uncritically, accept them. This gaggle of scholars, collectors, hobbyists, and religious enthusiasts makes up what is loosely called the "Mormon Underground" or the "Historical Underground." Members of the Underground collect, share, swap, and study Mormon historical documents with a relish unfettered by Church pronouncements that sometimes suggest group-think obedience is more important than independent rational inquiry. Research takes place in an intellectually open climate of honesty and exploration, as it did in the early 1980s when Mark Hofmann was at large. Most important, the Underground is a specialized marketplace eagerly consuming documents, pertaining to early Mormonism, whether these be letters, rare editions of books, newly discovered diaries, or notes.

This Mormon Underground still exists and still runs in counterpoint to the official LDS historians' bureaucracy. This ecclesiastical monolith has been tight-fisted with the sources of its history, even acting heavy-handedly toward member-scholars who do not "toe the mark" in their writings to fit the Church bureaucrats' narrow definition of "promoting" the faith. Original documents are now locked away in vaults. Access to various others is restricted to those defined as theologically or ideologically "safe." "Faith-promoting history" alone is a "legitimate" outcome of inquiry into Mormon history by Mormons. In truly Orwellian fashion, LDS President Ezra Taft Benson and various apostles regularly lambaste "humanistic" and "contextual" histories of the faith. Apostle Dallin Oaks, a lawyer and former Utah State Supreme Court Justice, has gone so far as to admonish twenty-five hundred seminary and BYU institute teachers at a 1988 BYU conference about any negative information concerning the LDS church with the line, "Satan can even use truth to promote his purposes." He also warned them, "Truth can be used unrighteously."[10] The late Apostle Bruce R. McConkie, in this decade, likewise urged BYU students to "please note that knowledge is gained by obedience."[11]

At the same time, not all Mormon intellectuals and observers are so patently unreflective or docile. Some appreciate the level of threat that any historical "underground" to ecclesiastical power can be, but they accept that parallel scholarly stratum as part of an authoritarian church tradition. "No church can stand a close scrutiny of its origins and history without a good deal of moral and intellectual cringing," Mormon intellectual Sterling McMurrin has stated.[12]

The proud leaders of the LDS Church do not like to cringe from intellectuals' independent pursuit of knowledge. For that reason in 1976 the Church changed its relatively open historical research policies of the past five years, determined to put a lid on its maverick (more objectively oriented) historians as well as on the records of its history. Thus, respected historian Leonard Arrington was demoted from Church Historian to head of the Church's lower status Historical Department, complete with budget and staff cuts, and his works on the history of the Church, under contract to be published by the Church itself, were indefinitely placed on hold while still in press. By the early 1980s Arrington was even removed from the Historical Department, replaced by a Church loyalist who could be counted on not to make waves.

At the same time, the Church became the most enthusiastic of historical document collectors acting in the Underground. It threw itself into the game with more money to bid for documents than any other free-lance agent. And with good reason. The LDS Church was willing to take the chance of buying up false documents, even while suspecting strongly they might be worthless, rather than risk that even one bonafide damaging document might slip past its inspection. With such an attitude, the Church became a prime candidate for victimization.

In this way the LDS Church, with its obsession to control sources about its own history, put a zest into the Underground that the latter otherwise would never have had. Inadvertently, it created a thirst for any and all documents that might challenge the official version of LDS Church history. The situation represented a perfect example of the self-fulfilling prophecy, unintentionally making happen what it feared might happen.

Into this ripe climate of intellectual unease and eagerness to shape (or censor) history strode entrepreneur Mark Hofmann, with the skills to manufacture bogus documents able to survive the tests of suspicious experts and the moxy to try to undermine the church's credibility.

Magic, White Salamanders, and Serial Scams

Mark Hofmann's study of Mormon history told him what controversies still raged among scholars. From history books he learned how to pack his forged documents with enough circumstantial details to give them authenticity in the eyes of experts. Over the years there had been enough rumors about early Mormonism and the life of Joseph Smith to fill an encyclopedia, in part due to lost or nonexistent information from that early era. Hofmann specialized in creating documents that promised to fill in these gaps. The Underground eagerly awaited such morsels.

These were documents that struck at the most sensitive nerve of

Mormonism: the legitimacy of the Church's origins, in particular the truth of Joseph Smith's receiving a revelation that helped him locate fantastic gold plates preserving the Book of Mormon. Hofmann's forgeries also provided a much clearer picture of Joseph Smith's early career. For years there had been speculation about Smith's alleged treasure-hunting in the New York countryside. His past could never be pinned down: was Smith an opportunist-turned-charlatan or a genuine prophet of God? Hofmann tried to lay such questions to rest with his own conjured image of Smith. In doing so he almost altered LDS Church history.

The Anthon Transcription

In April 1980 Mark Hofmann suddenly went from being an unknown university student to an overnight sensation in the Mormon historical Underground. His new career began when he claimed to have bought a 1668 Cambridge edition of the King James Bible once belonging to Joseph Smith's family. In the Bible, stuck between two pages, was the legendary Anthon Transcript. To Mormons this was a stunning find.

The document was named for Professor Charles Anthon, who taught ancient languages at Columbia University in the mid-nineteenth century. Martin Harris, an early Smith follower and New York farmer who put up $5,000 for the first printing of the Book of Mormon, had asked Smith if he could see the original gold plates. Smith, presumably at work transcribing them, refused, but he did show Harris a partial transcript written in what Smith claimed was reformed Egyptian. Harris took the transcript to Anthon in New York City, who analyzed the columns of Greek, Hebrew, and Latin letters randomly inverted, placed sideways, and so forth. Anthon pronounced the transcript nothing but high gibberish and its author a hoaxer. There was, he said, no such thing as Reformed Egyptian.

Returning to Smith, Harris received his reply that Anthon must have been uninformed about this form of Egyptian "shorthand." Harris wanted to believe in the plates and accepted Smith's explanation. Then, despite Anthon's denial that the transcript represented any real decipherable language, Harris began claiming that the document had been authenticated.

Hofmann actually had bought the old but otherwise unremarkable Cambridge Bible from an antiquarian bookshop in Bristol, England, during his mission stay there. However, he now said he had bought it from a Salt Lake City collector after noticing the signature of Samuel Smith, grandfather of the prophet Smith, on the inside. Hofmann deliberately staged the "discovery" of the transcript, stuck within two pages of the Bible by a strange black glue, in the presence of his friend Jeff Simmonds. At the time Simmonds was curator of the Special Collections and Archives at Utah State University.

And to render the possibility that it really *was* the lost Anthon transcript all the more believable, the top of one page was signed "Joseph Smith Jr." and dated 1828—the earliest known autograph of the LDS founder.

Two days after the transcript "surfaced" before Simmonds's and Hofmann's eyes, Hofmann approached several of the General Authorities with the news. Hasty preliminary inspections were made (including one by Dean Jesse, Church expert on Joseph Smith's handwriting) and tentatively but positively confirmed the authenticity of the document. By 1:30 P.M. of that same day, Hofmann was meeting with the three members of the Office of the First Presidency as well as with various Apostles. Hofmann was suddenly moving among a Who's Who of Mormonism at meteoric speed.

The LDS Church, like most large bureaucracies, can act infuriatingly slow when unmotivated to do otherwise. But this time it *was* motivated to do otherwise. The LDS Church was in its sesquicentennial year. The timing of such a find could not have been better. The Brethren were delighted at the thought of such a discovery.

The document's initial reception by Church leaders, in retrospect, was sloppily uncritical. True, later detailed examinations by Dean Jesse affirmed that Joseph Smith's handwriting on the transcript seemed genuine. Later ultraviolet and infrared analyses of the ink by Church archivist Don Schmidt also reinforced the judgment that it was real. Even the paper on which the Anthon Transcript was written passed the aging test. Nothing raised immediate questions. But that was some time after the whole matter was hurridly given the LDS Church's stamp of approval and rushed to the media.

The Brethren had decided to make a show of the Anthon Transcript. In the beginning there was only a *Deseret News* photograph of Hofmann (to one far edge) alongside LDS President Spencer W. Kimball and other Church luminaires gazing fondly down at the alleged document. Included in the crowd were (among others) Apostles N. Eldon Tanner, Boyd K. Packer, and First Presidency counselors Marion G. Romney and Gordon B. Hinckley.

But several months later came a major media event at Palmyra, New York. It was there that Joseph Smith was supposed to have translated the Book of Mormon and thus created the Anthon Transcript. It was a region where for years the LDS Church had been purchasing land with LDS historical significance. As it turns out, the Mormon History Association was also meeting in Palmyra that year, and it was at that event that the First Presidency's Gordon B. Hinckley chose to make the formal announcement that the Church now possessed a document so much a part of its claims to legitimacy. It was a publicity coup for Hinckley. He was to have many more dealings with Hofmann, the finder of Mormon documents, but none would be so useful as this one.

If they had only known how Hofmann must have secretly chortled at the ballyhoo over his forgery. Besides a good laugh and the satisfaction of revenge, however, Hofmann received more from the Church than just its leaders' warm thanks. He asked $20,000 for the Anthon Transcript. The Brethren preferred to pay him in kind with genuine historical items he could easily sell for that much money, including a first edition copy of the *Book of Mormon*, a very old five-dollar gold piece, and Kirtland (Ohio) Safety Society bank notes.

It was, to put it mildly, a promising start. Within the year Hofmann announced that he was abandoning a medical career, dropping out of the university, and going into full-time document collecting/trading.

The Anthon Transcript was the prototype for Hofmann's future frauds against the LDS Church and other collectors. Hofmann knew that to pass the standard authenticity tests he must master four critical dimensions of forgery: (1) handwriting, (2) historical content, (3) sufficiently aged paper, and (4) old ink. His skills came from several sources. He familiarized himself with the nuances and idiosyncrasies of the writing styles of those long-dead persons whose handwriting he forged. He used his knowledge of the "missing gaps" in Mormon written history as well as his imagination to generate a credible "new history." For old paper, he pilfered the end sheets of rare books from a century and a half ago which were stored in the open stacks in the University of Utah library's archives; Hofmann cut the paper out with a razor blade. He also turned to trial and error, ironing and sometimes heating paper sheets in an oven to artificially age them.

Through experimentation based on available formulas in published books, he chemically manufactured styles of ink. His recreation of iron gallotannic ink, the typical ink in use during the nineteenth century, was probably the most difficult of Hofmann's forgeries to detect. Ironically, he had found the recipe in expert Charles Hamilton's *Great Forgers and Famous Fakes*. Hamilton later became Hofmann's professional confidant, friend, and—eventually—another of Hofmann's betrayed victims.

In fact, as prosecutors ultimately learned, Hofmann ran a cottage-industry forgery business out of a single workroom in his basement where his family was routinely forbidden to enter. There he concocted his own ink, sometimes burning old documents for their carbon to mix in the pot and confuse experts using carbon 14 tests. There he practiced his admittedly superb mimicry of historical celebrities' handwriting styles. There, also, he kept the tools for his more sophisticated printing frauds. These included chemicals for etching printing plates, electroplating and photosensitizing equipment, and ultraviolet and infrared lights. When Hofmann worked late into the night, as he did often, the darkness gave the room a natural "black light" effect.

The rudimentary materials which Hofmann used, the primitive working conditions in his basement, and the quality of his craftmanship that fooled experts revealed one other significant fact: having a sociopathic personality was totally independent of being a near-genius.

The Joseph Smith Blessing Letter

That a fledgling document collector stumbled across the lost Anthon Transcript in Salt Lake City was a phenomenal happening. It could, of course, be chalked up to beginner's luck. But that lightning seemingly struck twice, and in such quick succession, should have alerted all concerned to take Hofmann more cautiously.

Less than a year after delivering the Anthon Transcript to the General Authorities, Hofmann was back. Again he had a discovery pertinent to LDS origins, but this time things could not be so faith-promoting. Hofmann said he had possession of an 1844 letter from the prophet Joseph Smith to his adolescent son, Joseph Smith III, bestowing on him leadership of the LDS Church after the father's death. "For he shall be my successor to the Presidency of the High Priesthood: A Seer, and a Revelator and a Prophet, unto the Church, which appointment belongeth to him by blessing . . ." the letter read.

Hofmann asked $5,000 for the letter, counting on its theological significance as bait. For if Joseph Smith, in his own handwriting, had preordained that his son—and not Brigham Young—take over the whole enterprise at his death, then the LDS Church's claim to legitimacy was seriously undermined. Indeed, the Reorganized Church of Jesus Christ of Latter-day Saints, which had split off from the LDS Young-backers at Independence, Missouri, in the 1840s over the succession question, would find considerable satisfaction in the letter. Hofmann hoped the LDS Church would buy the letter just to keep its existence quiet. He played up the rivalry issue, indicating that if the Brethren were not interested, he knew of some folks in Missouri who probably would be.

Don Schmidt, the Church's chief archivist, felt the asking price was too high. Hofmann left and returned another day, bluntly threatening to go to Schmidt's RLDS counterpart if there was no LDS offer. Still Schmidt balked. Hofmann did not bluff; within twenty-four hours Hofmann had the RLDS church historian on a plane heading westward.

During the Anthon transaction with the Brethren, Hofmann had played the role of a deferent, loyal Mormon just trying to help his Church. This time around, however, he was a more aggressive dealer, playing both sides against each other. In the midst of negotiations with the Reorganized Mormons, Hofmann showed a copy of the blessing letter to LDS hand-writing expert Dean Jesse, purportedly to get Jesse's independent opinion of the handwriting but really to circumvent the skeptical Schmidt and stir up some excitement among the Brethren.

Stir them up it did. Jesse thought the piece of paper too important to let it fall into the wrong hands, which by that time was just about anybody outside a very small circle in the Church hierarchy. Soon the First Presidency's Gordon B. Hinckley was putting pressure on Schmidt to obtain the blessing letter, and a chastened Schmidt was swallowing his pride, pleading with Hofmann for the letter.

Hofmann put on a pious show of ethical entrapment: from the begin-ning he had wanted to give the LDS Church—his Church—first option on the letter, but Schmidt had refused, twice. Arrangements were already being worked out with the RLDS church. What could he do? A deal was a deal. He had a reputation to establish and uphold.

LDS leaders' pressure did not let up. Schmidt asked for another confer-ence between himself, Hofmann, and G. Homer Durham (LDS Church historian who had replaced Leonard Arrington and ended the early 1970s era of open scholarship) the morning before Hofmann was to meet with the RLDS historian to conclude the transaction. The message to Hofmann at the meeting was abrupt: forget the ethics of the deal with RLDS and get out of it. The LDS Church *needed* that letter.

Hofmann eventually reneged on the deal by claiming that the RLDS church wanted several more weeks to authenticate the document—which Hofmann had known beforehand—while he now had an immediate buyer without authentication demands. Thus, no sale. The outraged RLDS historian countered with a threat to sue Hofmann for breach of contract and rightly accused him of duplicitous negotiations.

None of this mattered to the LDS side: "Kill the deal at any costs" was the message hammered at Hofmann. Acting the loyal Mormon, Hofmann did.

Meanwhile, the media picked up whiffs of the blessing letter contro-versy and the potential legal fight over who owned it. The usual propriety of the LDS public image, in contrast with such a scandal, would make great news copy. Reporters called from big-city newspapers and national wire services, worrying the normally hypersensitive Brethren about nega-tive publicity. The story proved impossible to keep quiet, and a suit by the RLDS church would be a public relations catastrophe. The whole af-fair became a messy embarrassment. Secretly, it must have been a field day for Hofmann, embarked as he was on his multilayered project to cause major mischief for the LDS Church.

Within a few days Gordon B. Hinckley released an official announcement to the press, acknowledging the existence and the Church's possession of the blessing letter. He discounted its importance with the statement that it was no more than a father's unremarkable sentimental blessing given to his beloved son. The dismissal of the letter's importance seemed lame in view of the clearly controversial contents, but it was the best way Hinckley could manage to control whatever damage had been done.

Two weeks later Hinckley announced that the LDS Church would trade the blessing letter to the Reorganized Mormons for a copy of Joseph Smith's revelations, entitled the *Book of Commandments* (the same price Hofmann had originally asked of the RLDS historian). In this way the LDS Church saved face, avoided a lawsuit with its rival, and obtained a valuable historical document. The RLDS, for its part, received a theological boost (at least until they later learned they had been duped). And Mark Hofmann's credibility with church authorities as a man who could put his finger on rare, important documents was considerably increased. From then on he personally dealt with Elder Gordon B. Hinckley, able even to receive audiences from Hinckley without prior appointments. Within Mormondom that was something in itself worth more than money.

One interesting telltale sign of Hofmann's duplicity passed completely unnoticed by Church officials after the letter deal was settled. When asked for the provenance (conditions of obtaining) of the blessing letter, a normal request among purchasers of historical items, Hofmann pulled a fast one and hid his tracks. He warned Don Schmidt that the person who had sold Hofmann the letter, a descendent of Joseph Smith's early follower Thomas Bullock, also had "dirt" on Brigham Young in the form of embarrassing financial records. When Hofmann handed Schmidt a (forged) notarized statement from the seller Allen Bullock attesting to the provenance, Hofmann warned Schmidt not to make Bullock's identity public or even to contact him, or else Bullock might cause future problems with his documents. Schmidt bought the reasoning, and no one ever checked to see if an Allen Bullock had sold Hofmann a blessing letter. In fact, there had been no such sale.

Document Discovery in High Gear

Over the next few years Mark Hofmann came on strong in the document Underworld. He was a relentless self-promoter, frequently name-dropping his association with Gordon B. Hinckley and other General Authorities. He was also an erratic businessman (but, his clients assumed, a brilliant one) seeming to exist by cellular phone from his flashy Toyota MR2 sports car but rarely accessible except through his message recorder. He lived the life of the high roller on his business trips: in New York, for example, where he attended auctions at Southeby's and became a familiar face at Schiller-Wapner Galleries, he roomed in the finest hotels, wining and dining in the best restaurants.

But wheeler-dealer or not, Hofmann could deliver documents. Not all were as sensational as the blessing letter, but to the Underground many were significant.

Such as old money. The nineteenth century Mormons had organized various cooperatives and utopian communities that often printed their own currency. One example were Valley (or White) Notes, the earliest printed money in Utah. Or Spanish Fork Cooperative Notes. Or Kirtland Safety Society Notes. And minted coins as well. Hofmann consistently found such things that other collectors had given up hope of ever seeing.

Hofmann also began presenting LDS Church officials with a series of seemingly irrefutably authentic documents that raised disturbing questions about Church origins. It had been known since the early 1970s that an 1826 court trial of "Joseph Smith the Glass Looker" took place in Norwich, New York. A farmer had sued a man named Joseph Smith for breach of contract in not producing promised treasure. No one knew for sure if this same Smith was the prophet, but there had been accusations throughout the Church's history that Joseph Smith had chased after buried treasure using special seer stones, divining rods, and other occult devices. Anti-Mormons linked Smith's alleged treasure hunting to their claims that the Book of Mormon was something Smith concocted after he realized that nothing would come of his digging. But the evidence had always been hearsay.

Suddenly Hofmann began discovering harder evidence. In mid-January 1983 he produced an 1825 letter from Joseph Smith to Josiah Stowell, a wealthy farmer in Bainbridge, New York. It was the earliest example of Smith's handwriting, which ordinarily would have pleased Church experts and officials. Instead its contents alarmed them. In the letter Smith advised Stowell in detail on an occult procedure for locating treasure with a bent stick and said he was inclined to accept an offer from Stowell to work for him in locating treasure.

The smoking gun had been found. Joseph Smith the Glass Looker was indeed the prophet himself.

With a total absence of publicity, contrary to the ballyhooed announcement of the Anthon Transcript, Elder Gordon B. Hinckley personally wrote Hofmann a check for $15,000. He reportedly told Hofmann, "This is one document that will never see the light of day."[13]

In the fall of 1984 Hofmann followed up the Stowell letter with an even bigger shocker: the so-called Salamander letter written in 1830 by early Mormon disciple Martin Harris to W. W. Phelps. Harris recounted how Smith had told him of finding the gold plates, and this version was dramatically different from the Church's official story. Instead of an angel Moroni who led Smith to the buried gold plates and visions of God and Christ, there was a mean spirit guarding the plates which violently attacked Smith and transformed itself into a white Salamander (a traditional occult symbol).

After several rounds of cautious negotiations and use of intermediaries—Hofmann did not want to approach the Church directly, and Gordon B. Hinckley likewise did not want to have the Church be the direct buyer—Hofmann himself finally sold the letter to Mormon businessman Steve Christensen for $40,000. Christensen was known to have a personal library of over fifteen thousand history and religion books, making such a sale credible. The arrangement was then for Christensen to donate the letter to the Church when Hinckley personally gave him the go-ahead, that is, when chances of the document leaking out to the public were slim. As with the Stowell letter, none of this was to be made public.

Not long after completing that deal, Hofmann came back to Christensen with still *another* controversial document: an 1825 agreement between Joseph Smith the prophet/glass looker and Josiah Stowell to divide the profits from their treasure-hunt venture (a partnership that fell apart and caused Smith's court trial the next year). Christensen paid Hofmann $15,000 for the contract.

Meanwhile, as the Church was trying to keep word of the emerging crop of damaging documents from leaking out to the press, Hofmann engaged in more troublemaking. He anonymously sent copies of Smith's 1825 letter to Joseph Stowell to various Mormon scholars in the Underground. As an "unnamed expert," he also told religion journalist John Dart of the *Los Angeles Times* about a secret history of the LDS Church which he had seen locked away in a vault. It was purportedly written by early Church historian Oliver Cowdery and told how Joseph Smith's brother, Alvin, originally found the gold plates *sans* any original vision of God, Jesus, or Moroni. The Underground was understandably in a stir.

Eventually the Church was forced to reveal the trio of treasure-digging letters. Too many rumors were afloat (thanks to trickster Hofmann), and the Church could be more damaged by repressing or lying about the letters' existence than by just owning up that it had purchased them. For Church leaders it was essentially a pragmatic decision. Meanwhile, Hofmann had his money *and* the satisfaction of seriously embarrassing LDS leaders, not to mention causing confusion among the faithful.

Ironically, it was the anti-LDS evangelical Christian Utah Lighthouse

Ministry, operated by ex-Mormon Sandra Tanner and her husband Jerald, that first questioned the authenticity of the Salamander letter. To Jerald the Salamander version remarkably paralleled the nineteenth century anti-Mormon book entitled *Mormonism Unveiled* by E. D. Howe. But these suspicions arose a whole year before the truth about the forgeries came out following the bombings. While the documents controversy raged, Hofmann decided to give the Mormon underground a respite and busied himself finding a wider market. His investment partners had raised considerable sums of money for him to buy rare documents, and he was up to his ears in commitments.

Serial Scams in Zion

If anyone had managed to cram all of Mark Hofmann's customers into one room and quizzed them, some disturbing patterns would have become apparent:

Hofmann often queried collectors on the kinds of rare documents they would like to have, then not so long afterwards he amazingly "happened" to have some of the same for sale. Alvin Rust, owner of two coin stores in Salt Lake City, was writing a book on Utah coins and currency and casually mentioned to Hofmann that he wished he had some examples of Valley Notes to describe. Soon after, Hofmann came to Rust with four of them for sale (the *only* four, he swore), then later returned with nine more, selling the latter for even more money. On another occasion, Hofmann conned Rust for several thousand dollars for phony Spanish Fork Cooperative Notes which he produced not long after Rust had remarked that he wanted those, too. This pattern was repeated with other buyers, but none of them seemed to become suspicious at this cause-and-effect regularity.

Hofmann used to claim that he simply beat the bushes for his finds, going door to door in Mormon communities, contacting relatives of famous Mormons, and attending auctions. But as Salt Lake County Sheriff Pete Hayward reminisced about Hofmann's uncanny chain of document finds just after the 1985 bombings, it should have looked fishy to collectors:

> Where does he [Hofmann] get them? All of a sudden there's this one guy who keeps coming up with these things, worth all that money. These kinds of documents don't just lie around for years. I know for a fact that 50 of us couldn't find these papers in 50 years if we were looking for them. But he keeps coming up with them.[14]

Hoffman repeatedly claimed to have a limited set of rare items, then after these were bought up he would suddenly produce additional copies so that earlier buyers were pressured to buy these, too, in order to maintain the value of their initial investments. For example, when Hofmann first approached coin dealer Alvin Rust with eight Valley Notes, Rust said the Church should have first option to buy them. Hofmann sold four to Church archivist Don Schmidt for $20,000, then returned to Rust to sell the other four for $12,000. Several months later Hofmann turned up at Rust's coin shop with *nine* more such notes. To protect his earlier investment now that seventeen notes were on the market Rust paid Hofmann another $27,000 for the nine.

At another time Hofmann went to Don Schmidt with what he claimed was the sole existing ticket to the *Maid of Iowa* riverboat once owned by Joseph Smith, with Joseph Smith's autograph even on it. He sold it to Schmidt for $2,500; then, a few days later, he sold a second "only-one-of-its-kind-in-existence" *Maid of Iowa* ticket to private collector Brent Ashworth. Finally, as he had done with Rust, Hofmann came back to Schmidt with still another "just discovered" ticket. Schmidt followed Hofmann's game and bought the second ticket to preserve the value of the first, or so he thought.

On the suggestion of forgery expert Charles Hamilton in New York City, whom Hofmann had gotten to know in his collection excursions, Hofmann explored the market for signatures by the famous (but illiterate) frontiersman Jim Bridger. He sold one signed Bridger promissory note to private collector Brent Ashworth for $5,000, claiming it was the only known to exist. One week later he came back to Ashworth, saying there were actually four more—and sold Ashworth a second one for *another* $5,000. Later Ashworth found out that Hofmann had sold additional notes to a Salt Lake City bookstore called the *Cosmic Aeroplane.*

Collectors were trading valuable real documents to Hofmann, which he could sell at very good prices, for clever but inexpensive forgeries turned out in his basement. A good example already mentioned was the $20,000 worth of items Hofmann received for the phony Anthon Transcript (much of which he had crafted from sheer imagination) from the LDS Church. In March 1982 Hofmann traded collector Brent Ashworth an alleged one page letter from Martin Harris that recounted for a friend Joseph Smith's version of finding the gold plates in a hillside in upper New York state. In return, Hofmann received from Ashworth $27,500 worth of authentic documents penned by Abraham Lincoln, George Washington, and others.

Later, in July 1982, Hofmann sold Ashworth a purported letter from Joseph Smith's mother, Lucy Mack Smith, to her brother, Solomon Mack, dated January 23, 1829. The contents described some of the lost 116 pages of the Book of Mormon which Martin Harris had misplaced while the LDS scriptures were being transcribed. In his enthusiasm to have the letter (which he later donated to the Church amid much fanfare), Ashworth traded Hofmann an original copy of the Thirteenth Amendment to the Constitution, letters from Andrew Jackson, Ben Franklin, and a copy of a book written by Joseph Smith's grandfather, items worth altogether at least $30,000).

Hofmann turned the business of document-selling and forgery into a unique pyramid hustle. He did this by forming partnerships and investment groups that raised the money to purchase rare items which Hofmann then promised to sell at often double or better the original costs. As in most scams, it seemed too good to be true. Investors could recoup their down-payments and earn ridiculously high returns. But no one could dispute that Hofmann's initial deals had delivered the profits he predicted. He had the golden touch and made believers out of otherwise prudent, skeptical men.

Often he persuaded individual partners to "roll" the profits over to pay for the next rare book or letter he had discovered for even bigger profits. In this way actual profits did not have to be produced, only promised. Money owed to investors was invisibly "tied up" in subsequent investments. Hofmann operated many of his scams on promises, the money being juggled elsewhere while he was supposedly arranging fantastic deals on behalf of his investors.

And secrecy (or, as Hofmann called it, discretion) was always a big part of his strategy. Partners were usually kept in the dark about Hofmann's alleged dealings. They almost never knew who his contacts were or how to check on his stories about the progress of negotiations. He threw out tantalizing tidbits, but he never revealed his entire plan. Thus investors never really knew what Hofmann was up to. Their few attempts to make him accountable, particularly as things began to turn bad, revealed a long trail of lies and inconsistencies. In reality Hofmann was a compulsive liar. Yet to those who trusted him he was an elder in the Church and a brother, with all that means to fellow Mormons, and it seemed wrong to question his methods, particularly if he was making them a lot of money in the end.

But things had to turn bad, for in all pyramid schemes later investors are drawn in by the lure of high profits so that they unknowingly can pay off early investors. Not enough investors can be indefinitely brought in to cover everyone. In Hofmann's case he might have pulled it all off longer than he did, for at least he had real products he was selling, even if they were only phony documents churned out in his basement workshop. What did him in was that too many heavy investors suddenly wanted their documents or their money back all at once. In the crunch, Hofmann could produce neither.

Nevertheless, at his peak Hofmann was hot, raising tens of thousands of dollars almost effortlessly and hundreds of thousands on the bigger deals. He exuded confidence and a "can-do" spirit. Investors bought it.

Mark Hofmann successfully operated a bold but rare type of crime: serial scams. He fleeced the *same* victims repeatedly with a virtually identical ploy. Most con-artists quickly take their leave after fleecing a "mark," particularly if significant amounts of money are involved. Not Hofmann. He was looting people's wallets as well as the LDS Church coffers for tens of thousands of dollars and sometimes more, and he boldly returned to do it again and again.

Hofmann's greatest single victim was the LDS Church, to which he sold forty-eight seemingly authentic but bogus documents for thousands of dollars. Individual collector-investors, such as Brent Ashworth, Alvin Rust, and Steven Christensen also threw money into Hofmann's pseudo-investments as part-owners of documents. As individual investors, they were burned far worse than the LDS Church organization could have been. Coin dealer Alvin Rust, for example, was repeatedly tapped by Hofmann for loans to buy supposedly legitimate documents; for example, Rust loaned Hofmann $10,000 for the Joseph Smith III blessing letter. At one point Rust even took out a second mortgage on his home to raise money for Hofmann.

The nature of Hofmann's forgery made this type of racket possible. (Police estimated that he took in roughly $2 million from just the most important of his bogus documents.) The early profits and the superb nature of his craftmanship disguised his game well. Without the bombings, which brought forensic experts onto the scene, there is no reason to expect that the forgeries could not have continued indefinitely.

A Tightening Vise

By 1984 forger Mark Hofmann operated a thriving documents business. His market ambitiously branched out beyond the Mormon Underground. Throughout North America he forged and sold an incredible number of documents supposedly displaying the signatures and handwritings of such diverse historical persons as George Washington, Paul Revere, John Adams, Betsy Ross, Daniel Boone, Andrew Jackson, John Brown, Francis Scott Key, Billy the Kid, Mark Twain, and Emily Dickinson. He applied his talent for mimicking handwriting across a veritable Who's Who in Americana. He fooled the best experts with his ingenious homemade products and was generating sizable monies to invest in his document "futures."

Then his serial scams began to unravel. Hofmann became a victim of his own aggressiveness and his overconfidence that he could always sell his documents. Within a year he had many more impatient investors than profits to share. Ruthless in conning document collectors, Hofmann reacted equally ruthlessly when cornered by his creditors.

The beginning of the end was Hofmann's "discovery" of the "Oath of a Freeman," a 1639 Puritan testament of democratic values and individual rights, in a New York bookstore. The real Oath was believed to be the earliest printed document in English in the Western hemisphere, with no surviving copies previously known to exist. Actually Hofmann forged the lost document, carried it into the bookstore under his coat with a modest price-tag already stuck on it, bought it, and then had a bona fide sales receipt to prove its provenance. Its appearance was convincing enough that New York's Schiller-Wapner Galleries was willing to offer it for sale to the Library of Congress. Asking price: $1.5 million.

Hofmann fully expected the Oath to sell, either to the Library of Congress or to the American Antiquarian Society which he later contacted. If it had sold, he would have suddenly put his hands on a massive transfusion of cash allowing him to cover his mounting debts. And, as he told prosecutors in his confession, he would not have set the bombs. There would have been no need to stall or distract his creditors. But he needed the enormous sum he was asking for the Oath, for by October 15, the day of the Christensen-Sheets murders, Hofmann owed more than $1.3 million to investors, in amounts ranging from several thousand to almost half a million dollars.

One group of Salt Lake City Mormon investors, led by Thomas Wilding (a former Utah State school chum of Hofmann and his insurance agent) particularly pressured Hofmann to be paid. While the investors had initially raised money for Hofmann's purchases when he told them of the exciting returns of 66 percent or greater, the Wilding group eventually became fed up with Hofmann's "rubber" checks, increasingly unbelievable stalls and excuses, and cancelled appointments and unreturned phone calls. He tried stalling them with his assurances that he would soon sell the "Oath of a Freeman," then tried to convince them to roll future profits from it into purchasing a second copy of the Oath that he had just "discovered."

The Wilding group smelled a rat, but they knew if they turned Hofmann over to the police for fraud—and by now it was apparent that he was double-dealing with many more investors besides just them—there would almost certainly be no chance of recouping any return on their m oney. In many classic pyramid schemes those early enough in on the game often decide not to blow the whistle in the hopes of getting their money out of it. Thus the Wilding investors' group declined to contact police.

Instead, Wilding and his lawyer sat down with Hofmann and made him sign a debtor-creditor agreement that required Hofmann to give Wilding two promissory notes for the amounts of invested money ($188,488) and for the promised profits ($266,667). Hofmann also was to hand over to Wilding the titles to his cars and the deed to the new half million dollar house he was buying in Salt Lake. Moreover, for every day Hofmann was late in paying he would owe an additional $2,000 penalty.

Hofmann was supposed to pay the profits promissory note and deliver the deed to his house to Wilding on October 16, the day after Hofmann was to close on the house, and the day when the bombings took place.

Meanwhile, what Hofmann wasn't telling anyone in Utah was that he had been turned down twice on the Oath of a Freeman. Neither the Library of Congress nor the American Antiquarian Society—the two biggest buyers likely to pay the $1.5 million price tage—wanted it.

Desperate to raise cash, with his checks to large and small investors beginning to bounce, Hofmann tried a new scam. He claimed he had located the McLellin Collection, an alleged treasure trove of early Joseph Smith writings, original Egyptian papyri from which the Book of Abraham (an LDS scripture) was translated, and other early Church memorabilia. The collection was said now to be in the possession of the Texas descendants of William E. McLellin, an early Smith follower-turned-apostate. Hofmann said he needed $185,000 to buy it.

Hofmann told coin-dealer Alvin Rust that the collection was worth $300,000 to $500,000, depending on how fast they wanted to sell the items. They would split the profits evenly within a month's time. More wary now of this young wheeler-dealer who already owed him $100,000 from past deals, Rust was still mesmerized by the promise of high returns. He promptly wrote Hofmann a check for $185,000. Within a week Hofmann called him back to say that the Church had definitely bought it. Yet that same week, on the very day Gordon B. Hinckley reluctantly announced to the press the "official" existence of the controversial Salamander letter, Hofmann went to see the elder in the First Presidency. He said he wanted to sell the McLellin Collection to the church. Hinckley, apparently more wary than Alvin Rust had been about Mark Hoffman and his troubles, said he was not interested.

Hofmann returned again to visit Hinckley in the interim between selling Steve Christensen the Salamander letter and then the Josiah Stowell treasure-digging letter. To manufacture and "find" two such letters in a short a time was dangerous to his credibility, but Hofmann had to risk it. He was a man in a bind. He needed cash, not so much from sale of the Stowell letter but from the larger profits of selling the McLellin Collection to the Church. In hindsight it is obvious that Hofmann was using the Stowell letter to prod Hinckley. The real message to Hinckley was that with the current wave of historical bombshell revelations he could not afford to let a whole collection of more potential ones get away.

On his second visit to Hinckley, Hofmann was more cordially received. The Church was interested, he was told, but it did not want to buy the collection directly. Hofmann would need another "donor" like Steve Christensen who could put up the money to buy the collection.

Hofmann contacted Christensen about a loan. Christensen and the Consolidated Financial Services company were facing bankruptcy, however, so Christensen did not have the funds. But Christensen took Hofmann to see Hugh Pinnock, a member of the board of the First Interstate Bank, a General Authority in the Council of Seventy, and a Mormon reputed to be "going places" in the Church hierarchy. Pinnock realized the value of keeping the McLellin Collection out of non-Church hands. Thus, in a very irregular transaction, with a minimum of paperwork and no word of any collateral being supplied, Pinnock pulled strings and obtained the $185,000 loan for Hofmann. Hofmann agreed to pay it back *with the $1.5 million that he said the Library of Congress had recently agreed to pay him for the Oath of a Freeman.*

The uncritical Pinnock—who had written articles and spoken over several years to wide audiences of Mormons about how their own gullible, trusting natures rendered them easy dupes to con-artists and criminals—even offered to lend Hofmann an LDS Church prop-jet when he went to Texas to pick up the collection.

That was in late April 1985. It was to be a long summer of double dealing. The First Interstate Bank note was due September 3. After weeks of dodging investors such as the Wilding group, Hofmann's check to the bank bounced.

Lies followed lies until it became difficult to know when Hofmann was ever telling the truth, or even if he himself ultimately knew what the truth was amid the weird web of stories he spun. Confronted by Pinnock about the defaulted loan, Hofmann said that he had used the money to buy documents, that he had given the McLellin Collection to Alvin Rust (who kept it in a strongbox) to repay him for a $150,000 loan, and that the American Antiquarian Society had just offered him $250,000 for the Oath of a Freeman.

The Oath again. Hofmann tried to play it like a card in a poker game. Pinnock told Hofmann to repay Rust the $150,000 in cash from the sale, while he personally arranged for his old friend David E. Sorensen, a wealthy retired Mormon businessman serving as mission president in Nova Scotia, to buy the collection and then donate it to the Church.

Private collector Steve Christensen, Pinnock decided, would authenticate the documents in the McLellin Collection when Hofmann delivered them—on October 15.

The Aftermath

Hofmann was arrested soon after he nearly blew himself apart in his own car. There was simply too much circumstantial evidence, including bomb parts and forgery materials in his basement, receipts for printing plates for specific documents, and even witnesses who had seen him dropping off his deadly packages wrapped in plain brown paper. The preliminary court proceedings in early 1986 began with Mark Hofmann's attorneys earnestly proclaiming his innocence, but by the end of the hearings his guilt was transparent. To the chagrin and anger of the families of Steve Christensen and Kathy Sheets, a plea bargain was struck to avoid a lengthy trial. Hofmann agreed to plead guilty to two counts of second degree murder and two counts of felony theft by deception. In turn, prosecutors dropped 26 other felony charges, the U.S. Attorney's office dropped charges of unlawful possession of a machine gun (one of Hofmann's hobbies was firing it in the woods), and New York state authorities agreed not to prosecute him for trying to sell the bogus Oath of a Freeman.

This arrangement translated into a sentence of five years to life for the murder of Christensen, one to fifteen years for the murder of Kathy Sheets, and indeterminate terms of one to fifteen years on each count of theft by deception. In addition, Hofmann was given thirty days to meet with prosecuting attorneys (with his own lawyers present) to answer all questions about the charged offenses. If the interviews were successfully concluded, prosecutors agreed to speak on his behalf to the parole board.

The preliminary hearing captivated an anguished Salt Lake City as well as the families involved. That one of their own could have so skillfully and cynically rewritten LDS history, and murdered two innocent people in the process, made a riveting tale. There was public outrage at the plea bargain, but prosecutors were convinced that the complications of the case would cause it otherwise to drag out for years, possibly even to be lost. And the defense attorneys knew they had a guilty man whose death penalty they were trying to avoid.

Ironically, Hofmann's forgeries might have stood for years as legitimate if the bombings had not taken place. LDS history was already being reexamined, and his documents—accepted as authentic—were part of the modern reinterpretation. In that sense the tragic deaths of Christensen and Sheets were not in vain: the two Church members were inadvertently martyred to reveal Hofmann's greed, compulsive lying, and unscrupulous twisting of history.

The LDS Church turned the Salamander letter and other papers over to the FBI for examination. As presented in testimony at the preliminary hearing, forensic experts George Throckmorton and William J. Flynn discovered a revealing flaw in Hofmann's forgeries: his pseudo-nineteenth-century gallotannic ink was thickened with modern gum arabic. The gum arabic tended to form microscopic but detectable cracks in the ink that would not be the result of natural aging. Hofmann could steal authentically old paper from library archives and mimic the handwriting of famous persons, but there was no way he could convincingly fake old ink.

Meanwhile, documents dealer Kenneth Rendell of Newton, Massachusetts, had originally certified Hofmann's documents as legitimate. But when they were carefully examined under an ultraviolet light they glowed bright blue—an indication that the paper had been artificially aged. It became evident that Hofmann, under pressure to deliver, sometimes cut corners with his materials. And Rendell noticed that the fine edges of the alleged authors' handwriting often appeared shaky, as if copied. "The ink looked good. It looked quite old. The documents were quite well done. But they were obvious fakes," he concluded.[15]

Hofmann's confession to prosecutors revealed much of his methods and motives. He was a sociopathic serial bomber, meaning he put more effort into his construction of instruments of destruction than into the question of who his victims would be. His amoral choice of victims mattered less to him than that the explosions created the necessary diversions to give him breathing space with his creditors. Deputy Salt Lake County prosecutor Robert Stott told one newspaper reporter:

> He's an emotional iceberg. You can't hate or love Mark Hofmann. You can only despise what he did. He seems to have no conscience and very little appreciation of others' suffering.[16]

Notes made by Deputy Salt Lake County attorneys Robert L. Stott and David Biggs from interviews with Hofmann prior to his guilty pleas show that Hofmann cold-heartedly debated in his own mind whom to kill with the bombs, selecting from among past customers like Thomas Wilding and Brent Ashworth. He did not finally decide on his victims until the morning of October 15. Christensen, Hofmann reasoned, would have to die to prevent the exposure of the McLellin fraud. The second bomb was simply to distract from Hofmann's financial mess and give him time to renegotiate his bills. Someone in the Sheets family, such as patriarch Gary who for a time financed the authenticity check of the Salamander letter purchased by Steve Christensen, would further confuse police leads. Prosecutors' notes from interviews with Hofmann recorded:

> He said he only filled the Sheets pipe bomb half full of powder, and he didn't think the rocket ignitor would work because it was three-fourths chipped away. He said it didn't matter to him if the Sheets' bomb went off or not because its purpose was to establish a diversion. For this purpose, the death of someone was not necessary. He realized, of course, that a bomb left at the residence could kill or severely injure someone, but it didn't really matter to him.[17]

Hofmann's dialogue with prosecutors broke down when he objected to his prison conditions and to having a police detective present. Frustrated prosecutors broke off the interviews and reported negatively to the judge who recommended that Hofmann spend the rest of his life behind bars.

Hofmann was never granted parole. Two years and eleven months after the bombings, Hofmann was found comatose, apparently after a suicide attempt or feigned suicide/escape plot using sleeping pills dispensed by the prison pharmacy. His wife had recently won an uncontested divorce. Meanwhile, authorities were trying to have him transferred from the Utah State Prison to a federal pentitentiary after it was discovered that he had plotted to pay two inmates $50,000 to kill members of the Utah State Board of Pardons. Clearly Hofmann's energies at playing games were not exhausted.

Numerous aspects of the police investigation, trial, and aftermath have been examined in books on the Hofmann murders, but two dimensions deserve emphasis here.

1. Immediately after the bombings LDS Church officials hastily interviewed Hofmann, Alvin Rust, and others involved in the serial scams *before* Salt Lake police officials could find them. LDS Church security, which is made up of a disproportionate number of former FBI and CIA employees as well as other retired law-enforcement officials, seemed deliberately to set up a wall of insulation around the General Authorities, hindering the Salt Lake City police investigation. The intent was not full disclosure but damage-control for Church leaders by this time up to their ears in financial dealings with Hofmann. So much for a reverence for historical truth, recent or otherwise.

For example, the Church's official and patently untruthful position was that Elder Gordon B. Hinckley and other officials barely knew Hofmann, Christensen, or any other critical actors in the ongoing scam and had never indicated any interest in the McLellin Collection. In retrospect this subterfuge was an incredible lie. Meanwhile, Hugh Pinnock personally paid back the First Interstate Bank loan to Hofmann as if it were a private family affair. The Church suddenly did not want to be seen as another victim in the obsession for control of LDS history, but by denying its connections to Hofmann it made itself look foolish. LDS leaders were as active in the documents Underground as any individual ever was. Hofmann simply exploited that presence.

Yet every effort was made by Church spokespersons to present the false appearance that LDS leaders had not been involved with the sordid implications of buying forged documents. For example, Apostle Dallin Oaks told the media how Rust had come to him immediately after the bombings, confused and begging to know what he should tell the police. Yet in reality Oaks had summoned Rust to the Church Administration Building before the police could talk to either of them,[18] trying to learn the Church's real role in the document buying.

2. One way or another, after the early 1980s Hofmann managed to influence the study of LDS history for the foreseeable future. He created an intellectual climate in which Mormon historians felt obligated to take a fresh look at Church history. This was not necessarily a bad thing to persons more interested in truth than dogma, but Hofmann inspired criticism sheerly on the basis of phony documents. He undermined Church members' confidence that the official version of historical events was one they could rely on. Many historians had begun working to revise their knowledge with his forged documents, which were assumed to be reliable, truthful sources. Hofmann deliberately mixed uncertainty and torn feelings into the research efforts.

Hofmann also reinforced Church leaders' notions that they had better impose further stifling, authoritarian controls on the study of the LDS Church's history or else such study could prove dangerously threatening. In so doing he also increased the drive of the Underground to subvent the Church's historical bureaucracy. Hofmann's greatest damage may be the mayhem he caused between fearful bureaucrats who were more interested in preserving orthodoxy than in open investigation and those member/scholars who choose truth (wherever it may lead) over cant.

The Hofmann episode also threw into question a basic premise of the LDS Church: that the General Authorities have the inspiration of God with them at all times. During Hofmann's pretrial hearing one employee in the Church's Historical Department said in a conversation that the Hofmann documents could not possibly be forgeries "because God would not allow His Servants [the General Authorities] to be so deceived by one wicked man."[19] The implications of such massive fraud for the authority of inspired LDS leaders are even more faith-threatening to Mormons than the contents of the myriad Hofmannesque forgeries.

After it was all over, prosecutor Robert Stott summed it up best. Addressing an audience at a symposium of historians and the general public at Brigham Young University, he pointed his finger at the whole nexus of Church repression of its own history, the memorabilia-mad collector mentality of the Mormon Underground, and the gullibility of Mormons duped by Mormons. He said:

> Mark Hofmann recognized those areas in which you would be the least objective. He recognized your interest in folk magic, he recognized that you better accept something in that area than something that wasn't. His deception, his creations, then, in part, were fashioned with that in mind, to meet what you wanted.[20]

Mark Hofmann was a businessman, and he knew his market.

5

The Lehi Child-Sexual-Abuse Scare

Mormons like big families with lots of children. They have felt this way since their polygamous days. Birth control is condemned by LDS Church leaders, and married women are discouraged from working outside the home or even preparing potential careers in case they become widowed. The birth of children gives souls in heaven the opportunity to incarnate on earth and begin the spiritual journey toward eventual godhood. Thus Mormon females are divinely destined, so they are told, to become home-makers and mothers. Men are to be their providers and protectors.

The family is the bastion of Mormon virtue. It reproduces, it baptizes, it tithes. Wholesome heterosexual family life, vigorously integrated into the Church's community activities, is a hallmark of Mormonism. Its members and leaders reason that such a tradition ought to help insulate them from the scourge of abuse and sexual perversions now rampant in America.

One day during the summer of 1985 Mrs. Sheila Bowers of Lehi, Utah, went as usual to her job at Utah State Prison, leaving her three small children to be watched by her sister. While babysitting, however, the children's aunt saw and overheard things that disturbed her. When Mrs. Bowers returned home that night her sister bluntly voiced her concern: she had caught the children "playing nasty" with their bodies. For youngsters they definitely seemed to know far too many details about sex, as if they had been tutored by someone older.

A worried Mrs. Bowers remembered a psychologist who worked at the prison and called her for advice. The psychologist recommended that

Mrs. Bowers contact Dr. Barbara Snow, a well-known therapist who dealt with sexually abused children at the Intermountain Sexual Abuse Treatment Center. Mrs. Bowers telephoned Dr. Snow, and not long after this Mormon mother's worst fears were confirmed: her children were apparent victims of sexual abuse. The children had told Dr. Snow that a teenage babysitter was the perpetrator. And it turned out to be not just anyone; the alleged abuser was the daughter of the bishop of the Lehi Eighth Ward of the LDS Church.

Other Mormon parents in the ward who had employed the same babysitter became alarmed. The Treatment Center suggested they bring their children in for similar interviews with Dr. Snow to see if the Bowers children represented just an isolated case. The report came back that unfortunately the problem had affected several other families—the Hadfields, the Walkers, and the Brierlys. All were members of the same Eighth Ward. In one family the alleged victim was only five years old.

The bishop, Keith Burnham, was aghast and disbelieving. His fifteen-year-old daughter resolutely denied ever sexually abusing anyone.

Alan B. Hadfield, father of two of the allegedly abused children, was angry. But he became positively outraged after a small daughter of Bishop Burnham revealed to Dr. Snow that her own mother, Shirley, had "touched" her private parts. Then other children began claiming that both Shirley and Keith Burnham had fondled their genitals. Hadfield later recalled, "I was mad. I was devastated. I thought, 'Here is this man, this moral leader in our neighborhood, doing these things to my children.' "[1] Hadfield became a strident advocate of prosecuting his former friend, the bishop, joining with other parents in retaining an attorney to initiate legal action against Burnham.

The children's claims of sexual abuse split apart this tightly knit Mormon farming community. Lehi had been a place where fathers and mothers alike engaged in all sorts of sports, scouting, and recreational activities with one another's kids. People in the Eighth Ward trusted other people as part of a church family and shared tradition.

The controversy spilled over into hostile feelings and factions at ward meetings. Some people would not speak to others and certainly not sit near them. One group of neighbors rallied to support Bishop Keith Burnham and his wife as falsely accused; others joined in sympathy with the seething parents of the young victims. Hadfield remembered, "There was a spirit in church, and it was not a good spirit, that was so thick you could cut it with a knife."[2]

While the parents of the young victims were meeting in parent-therapy group sessions with Dr. Snow, officials from the State Division of Family Services came and took away the Burnham children. They were placed in foster homes where they underwent physiological and psychological tests. Contrary to what Dr. Snow's interviews suggested, however, no evidence of harm was discovered, and the Burnhams regained their children after several weeks. But things were never again the same in the ward.

The Utah County Sheriff's Office and the Utah Attorney General's Office began an extensive, often exasperating, investigation. Rumors abounded, but hard evidence that would stand up in court for prosecutions seemed elusive. As the months went on victims' families grew impatient that arrests were not being made and criminal charges weren't yet filed. In the uncertainty, neighbor began to suspect neighbor. The dense LDS ward networks of committees, associations, and "telephone trees" were abuzz with gossip. Accusations flew about wildly, needing only the slightest provocation. One resident had his home searched on suspicion of being a child pornographer simply because he was the only person in the neighborhood who owned a video camera.

Meanwhile, Dr. Snow continued to interview and counsel the children. And accusations continued to be made.

The next shocker came some months later in February 1986. Rex Bowers, a prominent figure in the parent-therapy group and as outspoken as Alan Hadfield in demanding Bishop Burnham's hide, had his own son accuse him of sexual molestation. In interviews with Dr. Snow, other children suddenly recalled Bowers' molesting them as well. His wife left him immediately.

Soon after, children named both Earl and Cindy Walker as abusers, and then they accused Paula Brierly as well.

Then, in May, Dr. Snow interviewed Alan Hadfield's ten-year-old daughter, who said her father had forced her to have oral intercourse with him and fondled her vagina and anus. One day later Dr. Snow interviewed Hadfield's twelve-year-old son, who told her he had been sodomized by his father. That same night Hadfield's wife of twelve years walked out permanently.

Someone from each of the original parent-therapy families had now been named as an abuser. To investigators, the allegations were spreading like a contagion. To LDS Lehi residents once horrified by the thought that their bishop's teenage daughter might have abused kids in her care, the allegations suddenly indicated a huge rent in the moral fabric of their community.

The fear grew with the children's increasingly bizarre testimonies. For example, during the Hadfields' divorce proceedings and bitter custody battle, their children widened the list of former abusers beyond their father to the entire Hadfield clan, naming cousins, uncles, and aunts. Hadfield's adolescent son claimed to have engaged in sex acts over the years with as many as fifteen other children and fifteen adults, including Keith and Shirley Burnham. Children began to tell Dr. Snow stories of orgies where participants wore costumes and the adults took photographs. Worship of Satan was demanded. On some occasions as many as four adults and six children from the neighborhood allegedly played sex games involving oral and anal intercourse. Even the grandparents in one family became suspects.

Dr. Paul L. Whitehead, public-affairs representative for the Utah Psychiatric Association, also interviewed some of the children and claimed that mental health professionals had already identified sex abuse rings in communities across the state.[3] Two and a half years after an anxious Sheila Bowers first called her for an appointment, Dr. Snow testified in court that she believed forty adults were involved in Lehi's child sexual-abuse scandal.[4] Under oath Dr. Whitehead concurred.

Satanic child-sexual-abuse rings at large among the Saints in Zion? *Made up of Saints?* It all seemed such a gross inversion of Mormon values. No one wanted to believe that it could be true. Yet out of the mouths of innocent children came the shocking indictments that inspired lurid headlines and sensational copy to the news media.

In the two and a half years of the official investigation, the public and experts alike were to disagree about how reliable the children were as informants. Who could be believed? Children with wild imaginations, possibly coached by entrepreneurial therapists who subtly fed them cues as to what to say? Some experts claimed such youths were incapable of constructing such explicit tales. Parents who tearfully professed complete innocence but who might conceivably be part of a sinister conspiracy of perversion? Experts like psychiatrist Whitehead said they were capable of such deception. They would act distraught and innocent to dummy up and protect each other—as perpetrators of organized sexual abuse of children could be expected to do.

Letters to the editors of newspapers across family-oriented Utah took sides as if the controversy were a political debate. Indeed, politics soon entered the fracas. Citizens, particularly in Lehi, contacted their state legislators and officials. Some demanded severe punishment for the heinous abusers. Some others called for a halt to the "witch hunt" harassment by officials, which ruined reputations and turned victims into suspects overnight. In response, some state legislators began to question future funding for the Intermountain Sexual Abuse Treatment Center. Friends and supporters of the suspects wrote letters to the General Authorities of the LDS Church, and some Church officials tried to pressure county investigators either to make their arrests or drop the scandal. "It has been a political nightmare," admitted Utah's Deputy Attorney General Paul Warner to one reporter in the midst of the investigation.[5]

The Lehi episode dramatically showed how the flip side of virtue can be dark indeed. As the tragedy unfolded, the same network of LDS ward contacts that promoted strong family values and high rates of religiosity also facilitated the spreading of rumors, fears, suspicions, and false accusations that ruined reputations and broke up families. Yet at the same time the scare caused by the alarming possibility that Lehi was harboring child-sexual-abuse rings distracted attention from the real problem of child abuse in Mormon communities—a problem they shared with the entire nation.

The Lehi case was entangled in many of the same controversies, emotional and legal, that characterize the child-abuse problem generally. Only in the past several decades has the American public become sensitized to child sexual abuse as a serious problem more widespread than most people previously believed. Many holes in our knowledge of how to detect and prosecute it still remain. And there are some who feel that our newly acquired national concern has reached a point where the fear of such abuse often displaces our good sense not to rush to immediate judgment of those merely accused.

Child Abuse in Utah: The Family Secret

Child abuse in Utah in 1985 was something that presumably didn't happen in "strong"—i.e., Mormon—families. At least that was the prevailing wisdom of many people, including LDS Church members themselves. This stereotype of Mormon families as somehow uniquely protected from sordid things like incest owed its existence in part to aggressive public relations efforts by the Church's Public Communications Department, established in 1972 to promote a positive image of Mormonism throughout the Gentile world, and in part to the Church's production of the "Homefront" public service spots widely seen on television and heard on radio. (The brief "Homefront" vignettes emphasize traditional family values and make a low-key connection between them and the LDS Church.)

Child abuse and, worse, sexual molestation, were thought to be the preserve of disreputable, lower-class characters and sleazy, leering perverts. That belief made it very difficult for many of the Lehi neighbors—and the local investigators—to accept the possibility that some of their respectable fellow citizens might be sexual abusers.

"We're more comfortable dragging a guy up on stage with a four-day growth of beard wearing a trench coat with nothing under it," James J. Mead, a former police officer who founded a private corporation working to educate the public about child abuse, told an audience of professionals in Salt Lake City.

But when you're handed the bank president, a lawyer or a psychiatrist, you don't believe it. In 20 years I've had one who fit the category of dirty old man. Most are gentle, kind, caring, and charismatic.[6]

Professionals working with abusers, of course, know that fact, but the public image of sexual moleters in Utah even in 1985 was some years behind the times. The truth was and is that Mormon households as a group are no more immune to the many sources of child-sexual-abuse than any other homes, however much the LDS Church would like to minimize the reality or Mormons themselves would prefer to disbelieve it. At present Utah and its residents are caught up in a national wave of concern about the problem, and the stereotypes are beginning to fall.

At the same time, most experts agree that our nation as a whole is not undergoing any serious upsurge in the proportions of child-abuse and sexual-abuse cases; instead, we as a population are becoming more attuned to recognizing such abuse. Douglas J. Besharov, former director of the National Center on Child Abuse and Neglect, observed that "years of public-awareness campaigns and professional education have had their intended effect. Americans are much more sensitive to the plight of maltreated children, and are more willing than ever to report suspected cases."[7]

The same is true for Utah. Statewide, investigations of child abuse and neglect rose in Utah from 8,423 in 1983 to 11,390 in 1986, and both those numbers were considerably higher than the 4,209 investigations in 1978–79. In just four years (1983–1986) the number of recorded sex-abuse victims quadrupled—from 264 to 1,022.[8] In 1985, the year that Lehi's citizens were appalled by an apparent outbreak of child sexual abuse in their community, Utah ranked thirty-fourth of the fifty states in population but thirteenth in reported cases of child abuse.[9]

Even in the Utah prison population, which represents only a fraction of the number of criminals apprehended in the general population, the number of convicted molesters has been going up. One expert in the Utah Department of Corrections found that just in the short interval between 1986 and 1988 the number of convicts sentenced for child-sexual-abuse crimes (including lewdness, incest, sodomy, rape, rape with an object, and aggravated sexual assault) rose 30 percent.[10]

Utah's recent figures on child abuse are right in step with trends in the nation. A 1988 national study sponsored by the U.S. Department of Health and Human Services, the National Center on Child Abuse and Neglect, and other federal agencies found that since the last major national survey in 1986 there had been significant increases in reporting different kinds of child abuse. Reports of sexual abuse had tripled in just two years.[11] Two social scientists compared Utah's rates of family violence with national trends for the 1980s and discovered that "substantiated [investigated] cases of child sexual and physical abuse in Utah increased during the past decade." Yet they also confirmed what Douglas J. Besharov and others have claimed: such an increase is undoubtedly the result of a greater willingness to report and investigate acts of child abuse rather than of any growing epidemic of new violence. Most important, they concluded that there "is no evidence that the situation in Utah is much different from the U.S."[12]

State and federal statistics do not break down the forms of abuse by religious affiliation. Therefore they cannot be of use to detect how much of child and sexual abuse violence is LDS as opposed to Gentile. But Utah is approximately 70 percent Mormon. Is the one-third of the population that is Gentile disproportionately engaging in child abuse? Counselors and coordinators of social services for abused victims and abusers doubt it.

For example, Gary Jensen, a Child Protective Services specialist in Utah's Division of Family Services, estimated that 50 to 60 percent of the child-abuse cases he regularly has seen have been LDS. The abusers were generally in all outward respects proper, churchgoing, and solid citizens.[13] Leslie Lewis, deputy Salt Lake County prosecuting attorney, has worked on the legal end of such abuse for over a decade and concurred with Jensen: two-thirds of all the child abusers she has prosecuted were active Mormons.[14]

In fact, the same proportion has been estimated by various professionals working directly with the child-abuse problem in Utah. Thomas Harrison, a clinical social worker and for seven years coordinator of a child-sexual-abuse unit in Salt Lake City's Primary Children's Medical Center, reported that 55 percent or more of the child-abuse cases he had seen were Mormon. The percentage generally went up in areas more heavily populated by LDS members.[15] Dr. C. Y. Roby, whose credentials include serving as director of the Intermountain Sexual Abuse Treatment Center, having been chief consultant during the late 1980s for the Church's own LDS Social Services, and having co-authored a training manual on dealing with child abuse for LDS Social Services counselors, likewise estimated that 70 percent of those he counseled came from strong LDS backgrounds.[16]

In short, professionals in Utah who handle reported child abuse and counsel the perpetrators as well as the victims believe they see about the same proportion of Mormons among their clients as are in the general population. This observation does not mean Mormons are any more prone to child abuse, pedophilia, or incest than Gentiles, only that as a religious group they account for their "fair share" of the state's problem.

But why is this so, given the LDS Church's penchant for encouraging strong Judeo-Christian family values? After all, Church leaders abhor such abuse and speak out about it. At one 1982 semiannual Church General Conference at Salt Lake City's Temple Square, Elder Gordon B. Hinckley told the faithful: "It is a terrible thing that we hear occasionally of child abuse. This is a growing evil across the world. . . ." And LDS spokesperson Bill Bosh, acknowledging the problem among Church members, said, "We"re doing everything we can think of to teach fathers and mothers not only the sacredness of rearing children but how to effectively parent."[17]

Indeed, that is one major mission of LDS Social Services. The Church has its own psychologists and counselors to help members cope with violence problems. In the early 1980s Mormon men who applied for a "temple recommends" from their local bishop in order to participate in temple rituals began being queried about any possible abusive incidents involving their wives or children. In 1986, at a session of the 156th General Conference, Elder Gordon B. Hinckley bluntly admonished Mormons that family violence and child abuse were unequivocal grounds for excommunication if abusers did not confess and pray for forgiveness.[18]

However, not all aspects of LDS Church concerns about child abuse work to disclose and treat it. The all-male priesthood is a good example.

Most LDS bishops (nonpaid, lay clerics who serve for several-year stints) are inadequately trained to deal with the problem of child sexual abuse, much less to detect it. Often when they try to counsel sexually abusive men they err in the direction of minimizing the seriousness of the problem or agreeing with the abuser's patriarchal rationalization that engaging in abuse really functions to educate or discipline the children. Or, out of embarrassment, bishops simply allowed the problem to fester past a point where it could have been treated by professionals before emotional/physical damage was done to children. Observed Barbara Thomas, a clinical social worker and director of the Salt Lake County Child Abuse Coordinating Committee:

> We've found a lot of [LDS] bishops still trying to handle this problem themselves. It is a lay clergy problem—there is a big turnover of LDS clergy. Not enough are trained to recognize the seriousness and scope of the problem.[19]

There is also a tendency of some bishops and even some LDS health professionals to "cover up" for their fellows in the priesthood in a misguided attempt to protect the sancitity of the office. It is one thing to pay lip service to the notion that priesthood-holders, bishops, and other leaders are fallible human beings; it is another to find that someone "called" to Church service has such a problem. There is an implicit threat to the Church's legitimacy. Child-abuse counselor Gary Jensen in Utah's Division of Family Services recalled: "We've had enough cases come to this department where a physician never reported abuse of the child due to the important religious standing of the man in the community."[20]

One former LDS woman who had experienced child abuse and seen this "cover-up" pattern angrily termed it a "circle-the-wagons" damage-control ploy. "Such abuse is neither uplifting nor faith-promoting when discovered among such leaders," she told me in a conversation. For that reason many cases may not be reported. In fact, a frequent question asked by appointment secretaries in the Utah offices of psychologists and psychiatrists is whether the visitor is LDS or non-LDS; the question thus screens the problem by religious denomination.

Many Utah abuse counselors do not think the LDS Church is concerned enough about the child-abuse problem. It is, to borrow the title of a book on family violence published in the early 1980s, a nasty "family secret."[21] Counselor Gary Jensen acknowledged the value of the LDS Church's positive "Homefront" television messages but added: "The irony of all of this is when you get down to the nitty gritty the [LDS] church is not very cooperative and prefers to keep the child abuse matter closed when it involves their own members."[22] Likewise, deputy Salt Lake County attorney Leslie Lewis criticized the Church's handling of such cases:

> They do a very poor job of reporting child abuse cases to us as they should. They don't give either the police or other agencies the necessary information needed. They try to resolve these problems internally. It's almost like pulling teeth sometimes to get them to cooperate and give us the data we need on victims as well as perpetrators.[23]

Modern Mormon families are subjected to the same problems and strains that social scientists believe contribute to domestic violence and child abuse generally. But they also face special factors that can add to the risk of abuse in the home. Mormon households encounter economic pressures from the Church's well-known emphasis on large families and condemnation of birth control while simultaneously discouraging women from working outside the home. For example, President Ezra Taft Benson (when he was still an Apostle) once told the 152 General Conference that women who feel the allure of careers or outside employment to supplement their husbands' incomes contribute to the breakdown of the American family as well as to drug abuse, vandalism, alcoholism, pornography, and homosexuality.[24] As a result, wage-earning responsibility is frequently shifted solely onto the husband's shoulders. Mormon families also encounter marital tensions that result when their patriarchal subculture (with its emphasis on the obedience of women to men) runs up against the expanding opportunities and rising expectations of women for equality in the larger American society.

In fact, despite idealized portraits of Mormonism's values, which might suggest a lower-than-average rate of child abuse, it would be surprising, given the stresses and frustrations inherent in some aspects of church-promoted family life, if LDS members *didn't* show an average amount of abuse problems.

In any event, it was the idealized model of Mormon families the general public believed in that underlay the shock many felt when the Lehi child-sexual-abuse scandal became public.

Alan B. Hadfield—Enemy of the People?

The trial of Alan B. Hadfield in 1987 was a microcosm of the destructive conflict set loose in the community of Lehi. After two years of extensive police investigations, Hadfield was the only Lehi adult charged with child sexual abuse, and he became—depending on one's point of view—either an archetypal symbol of the scandal's drama or a scapegoat to satisfy those who felt *somebody* ought to hang for whatever it was that had gone wrong in the community.

Most important, Hadfield's case offered a clear test of the power of the Lehi children's awful testimonies. Previously considered a model Mormon father, he had been initially outraged when the children's stories of child abuse were first aired in Lehi. Having taken the reports at face value, Hadfield led the attack on his own bishop, pressing for criminal prosecution. Then, shortly before he himself became labeled a molester, he came to question (however indirectly) the whole process of adults in the neighborhood being denounced one after the other as pedophiles. Like others who sensed something amiss in the "discovery" process, Hadfield began to cultivate the suspicion that more was going on in Dr. Snow's counseling sessions than just the rehabilitation of alleged sex-abuse victims. But it took the adversarial context of a criminal trial in Utah's Fourth District court to expose those dynamics.

Hadfield was formally charged with four counts of sodomy on a child and three counts of sexual abuse of a child, all serious felonies carrying sentences ranging from ten years to life in prison. Ironically, he had once made a joke prophesying a predicament somewhat like this. While he and his wife were still attending Dr. Snow's parent-therapy meetings and the abuser suspect list began to grow, he remarked that he was about the only man left in the neighborhood who had not been accused. "Am I going to be next?" he asked her in a lighthearted way.[25]

Two weeks later his ten-year-old daughter had an hour-long session with Dr. Snow and accused her father of incest. The next day his twelve-year-old son told Dr. Snow that Hadfield had sodomized him.

His children's testimonies were the strongest evidence confronting Hadfield and were thus the logical focus of the defense attorneys' attacks. It was true that a pediatrician at Primary Children's Medical Center in Salt Lake City had examined the two children and concluded that they both showed some signs of abuse, particularly the boy. But child-abuse experts know that such "evidence" is often subjective and frequently not as clear-cut as, say, a bullet wound would be. Often such exams are rudimentary, as doctors guess if a girl's hymen or a child's sphincter has been suspiciously stretched or enlarged. Through it all, Hadfield staunchly denied that he had ever molested his chidren.

Thus the future of the entire Lehi scandal, and Alan Hadfield's guilt or innocence, hinged on the credibility of these children. And their initial testimonies against their father did seem damning. They spoke to the court in detail about how he had sexually abused them and what he had said during the acts. Dr. Paul Whitehead said that Hadfield's son and daughter had told the psychiatrist that Hadfield claimed he would kill their mother and drown them both if they ever revealed what he had done. During the son's testimony the trial had to be recessed after the boy became so emotionally upset that he vomited on the witness stand.

Surprisingly the first questions about the prima facie validity of any of the children's testimonies had been raised before the trial began. Wayne Watson, chief deputy Utah County attorney at the time the first accusations came out, was overseeing the investigation and witnessed through a two-way mirror one of Dr. Snow's therapy sessions with a Lehi child. According to him she would sit on the floor with the child, both of them surrounded by dolls and cuddly stuffed animals. If the child reacted negatively to her questions about abuse, she maintained a stiff, formal posture. If the child confirmed abuse and provided details, she then embraced the child warmly, holding him on her lap and praising the youngster for good behavior.

To Watson the scenario was transparent: Dr. Snow, by subtle and not-so-subtle cues, was coaching the children, encouraging them to bring forth stories of abuse and withholding approval if they did not.

"I was appalled," Watson recalled. "I had deep reservations about whether the ideas expressed by the child related to what had actually happened to them or whether they were the product of ideas placed in their minds by Barbara Snow. . . . She had so conditioned those children that I had serious concern about using them as witnesses in cases."[26]

Dr. Snow repeatedly countered the "coaching" charge during the trial.

Her defense was that she was a therapist, not a law-enforcement investigator. And, as she observed, child-abuse victims, particularly younger ones, cannot easily or readily tell the complete stories of sexual abuse that involve nurturing/authority parent figures. Many times abused children have been warned about what horrible things could happen to them, other family members, or even beloved pets, if they dared tell anyone. Young children's ambivalence and confusion over the right and wrong of what happened can mean that the stories must sometimes emerge a bit at a time, in a loving, accepting atmosphere that is the opposite of the formal setting of a courtroom or police interrogation.

But the credibility of the "coaching" charges picked up momentum as the trial proceeded. Dr. Snow gradually began to look like a person who had implanted ideas of abuse in the children's minds when she was ostensibly only eliciting them. Judy Pugh, a therapist who had worked with Dr. Snow at the Intermountain Sexual Abuse Treatment Center, told the court that during the months of counseling she experienced a growing concern about initial inconsistencies in the stories of the children. Yet after the children continued to meet with Dr. Snow, the stories became homogenous, and whenever one child accused an adult of abuse, fairly soon after another child would tell essentially the same story, making themselves new victims of new abusers.

One ten-year-old girl, who had earlier claimed to be a victim, testified that in the beginning she told Dr. Snow several times that no one had abused her but that the therapist refused to accept that answer. "She kept asking and asking" about Alan Hadfield, the girl told the court, perhaps as many as fifty times in one session. The girl said she finally relented and said she had been "touched" by someone, afraid that the therapist would "yell" at her if she did not confess to something.[27]

Dr. Stephen Golding, director of clinical psychology at the University of Utah in Salt Lake City was brought in as an expert witness by the defense lawyers. Dr. Golding had evaluated a videotape of Dr. Snow conducting a therapy session with Hadfield's son. His conclusion: Dr. Snow used leading, suggestive, and directed questions, putting words in the mouth of the boy. He testified that her techniques were "subtly coercive and highly questionable."[28]

There were also inconsistencies in testimonies about the events that incriminated Hadfield. The children claimed that on the night of April 6, 1986, while their mother was away in Salt Lake City visiting the estranged wife of another Lehi man accused of sexual abuse, Alan Hadfield had fondled and sodomized them on his bed as they watched a television program before being sent to their rooms for the night. However, at that time, during the same television show, Hadfield was in reality talking on the telephone with Dr. Snow. Ironically *she* had called *him*, concerned about statements she had heard made by other social workers critical of her treatment techniques. Defense attorneys even produced a copy of her telephone bill to prove it.

The children told the court that their father had promised to buy them a "four-wheeler" riding toy if they would not tell about the sex abuse. Yet attorneys showed the court a sales receipt demonstrating that Hadfield had purchased the "four-wheeler" two weeks *before* the sexual abuse was supposed to have occurred.

Furthermore, Hadfield had an unusual birthmark in his groin area that anyone engaging in oral sex with him could not have missed—yet neither child had seen it nor could describe it.

In the high emotion of the trial, Hadfield and many of his sympathizers in the courtroom broke down and wept during the proceedings. Everyone agreed that an upset Hadfield did his case no good when, during questioning by a prosecuting attorney, he blurted out, "If I did those things, I don't remember."[29]

On December 19, 1987, after ten hours of deliberation, an eight-member jury convicted Alan B. Hadfield of all four first-degree counts of sodomy on a child and all three second-degree felony counts of sexual abuse of a child. Under Utah's mandatory minimum sentencing law, Hadfield would have to serve at the very least ten years with no probation.

But Hadfield still had one narrow window of hope. Under a special incest exception, intended by predominantly Mormon legislators to preserve the family unit if at all possible, a judge could place the convicted abuser on probation after six months in the Utah County Jail (with work release allowed) if he paid restitution to his children for their therapy and successfully completed a sex-abuser-therapy treatment program. The judge had to decide that Hadfield met each of the twelve guideline requirements in the incest exception law.

The difficulty faced by Hadfield was twofold: first, he and his wife were now irreconcilably divorced and there was no longer any family to preserve. Second, most therapy programs demanded that clients confess on admission that they have an abuse problem. Alan Hadfield never wavered in affirming his complete innocence of all abuse charges.

The judge took Hadfield's attorneys' request for the incest exception under advisement while they scrambled to find a therapy program that would accept an unrepentent client convicted of child sexual abuse.

Meanwhile, Lehi remained a community divided in opinion. Those who believed Hadfield an unconscionable liar wrote letters to newspapers clamoring for a hefty prison sentence. But Hadfield's supporters, who now numbered among them Bishop Keith Burnham (with whom Hadfield had tear-

fully reconciled) and whose numbers had been growing as the trial pro-
gressed, went to work to convince the judge to grant Hadfield probation.
They organized a rally that attracted eight hundred persons, including several state legislators, and staged a ten-dollar-a-plate benefit banquet at the
Lehi Junior High School, which drew nearly a thousand. A Hadfield defense fund was created to help with his legal expenses, among other things;
townsfolk raised almost $20,000, although because of the trial's notoriety
they had trouble finding a bank that would accept the account. Friends
of Alan Hadfield collected hundreds of signatures on a petition for probation and started a letter-writing campaign to the Fourth District judge.

Dr. Paul Whitehead, the psychiatrist from Salt Lake City who supported Dr. Snow's analyses throughout the trial, clung to the belief that
Lehi was in the grips of a child-sexual-exploitaiton ring and pointed to
the support for Hadfield as evidence of it. He reasoned:

> If one accepts the fact, as I do, that there are a lot of people involved,
> then some of them have a major vested interest. To protect one is to
> protect all. . . . If many were not involved, it's very unusual that people
> would come to the response to this degree of one individual who has
> been convicted by eight impartial people.[30]

Despite Dr. Whitehead's beliefs about child-sexual-abuse rings, the trial
of Alan Hadfield ended the sexual-abuse scare in Lehi. The Hadfield court
drama had exhausted the community, and evidence to support the other
children's accusations was dubious. No other persons were ever charged.
The deputy Utah County attorney's office stopped the investigation.

Meanwhile, Hadfield's lawyers found a therapy program that would
accept him despite his refusal to admit he was an abuser. The judge sym-
pathized with Hadfield's backers and granted the incest exception despite
Hadfield's divorced status. A howl arose from angry prosecuting attorneys that this exception would send a clear message to child abusers everywhere that Utah would be a haven for their actions, but at least for the
time reports of child sexual abuse ceased altogether in Lehi.

The families that had divorced or split up over the children's accusations remained severed, and many of the children would undoubtedly
continue to receive therapy for an indefinite time, if not for being sexually abused then for the trauma of the trial. But much of the community
spirit of Lehi returned—in large part, ironically, because of the rally of
support behind Alan Hadfield during his trial. His detractors simply lost
out to majority public opinion. Some measure of neighborhood solidarity
returned to the Eighth Ward.

Amid the controversy over her interviewing methods before Hadfield's trial even began, Dr. Barbara Snow had resigned her position at the Inter-mountain Sexual Abuse Treatment Center and moved on. She reopened her therapeutic practice in Salt Lake County, and in early 1987 allegations of child-sexual-abuse rings started anew in another community. Children initially brought to her for counseling started accusing adults in their neighborhood of sexual abuse, then often implicated their parents, and particularly their fathers.

During the spring of 1988 a female private investigator originally hired by the Lehi friends of Alan Hadfield publicly announced the results of her own investigation into similarities between Dr. Snow's involvement in the Lehi scandal and the later Salt Lake County sexual-abuse probe. The private eye also told media reporters that Dr. Snow had been entangled during 1986 in yet a third, similar rash of sexual-abuse accusations by children in Bountiful, Utah. The pattern of events there, including counter-accusations that Dr. Snow "coached" her clients, had been identical with Lehi's.

In April 1988, after fourteen months of investigation, Salt Lake County officials abruptly decided, with minimal fanfare, to drop their probe.[31] In November 1989, when I visited Utah, I attempted to learn the post-Lehi fate of Alan Hadfield, but he had disappeared into the population.

Lehi, Urban Legends, and the Collapse of Scares

One immediate consequence of the Hadfield trial and the Lehi sexual-abuse scare was a new law passed by the Utah legislature, creating a criminal penalty for persons who raise false accusations of child abuse or who induce children to make false accusations thereof. Another bill, requiring therapists and police to record on video or audio tapes their interviews used in determining criminal charges for sexual abuse, cleared a House of Representatives committee but failed in a floor vote. Critics said it would have been prohibitively expensive. Other legislation was proposed that would temporarily halt any divorce-related proceedings, including custody hearings, when child abuse or molestation was alleged. The Hadfield case was often referred to in deliberations. Reading between the lines of such bills, it was apparent that elected officials sensed that the authorities' handling of the Lehi children's accusations had gotten terribly out of hand.

Lehi had experienced a social scare of epidemic proportions, which finally crystallized into the prosecution of one man, and it was never even certain he was a sexual abuser. A number of observers, including Hadfield's attorneys, made more than one comparison of the prosecution to the alleged outbreak of witchcraft at Salem, Massachusetts, in 1692. In that colonial settlement a handful of young girls made a series of accusations of demonic possession against persons who then had to assume the burden of establishing their innocence. As in Lehi, those who voiced opinions that things might be going to extremes (as Alan Hadfield had suggested to Dr. Snow) soon found themselves accused or, in the vein that Dr. Whitehead suggested, were discredited as part of an alleged self-protecting conspiracy. Salem undeniably produced more gruesome results: twenty-two persons either went to the gallows or died in prison. But the dynamics seemed similar.[32]

In other terms, Lehi experienced what David Hechler has termed "sex accuse" and what David L. Kirp, in an article entitled "Hug Your Kid, Go to Jail," called the "Child Sexual Abuse Accommodation Syndrome."[33] Both authors refer to an exaggerated fear of child sexual abuse coupled with a willingness to suspend normal assumptions of innocence until proven guilty; they also comment that when children, particularly younger ones, report on the world around them, their stories are generally unrealistic and incomplete. Kids' versions of reality, in other words, become automatically accepted as fact with no allowance made for the latitude of fantasy.

In writing about investigations of child sexual abuse Mary Pride refers to this phenomenon as the doctrine of "immaculate confession":

> Social workers are taught that any time a child accuses his parents (even if his confession occurs under pressure from the worker), this confession must be taken as gospel. However, if he denies everything from the start, or later denies his accusation, his denials mean nothing.[34]

In this mind-set considerably less emphasis is placed on how the very process of eliciting information from a traumatized (or perhaps nontraumatized) child shapes and guides what the child says.

At the same time, this genuine concern about child abuse occurs in a modern urban society where authentic communities are being replaced by residential islands of superficial pleasantries, where stores and commercial enterprises with distinct identities are being bought out by chains and/or relocated in shopping malls, and where much of the nation's population doesn't stay in one place for very long.

Cultural analysts tell us that accompanying such change is a drop in civility and community spirit, even a breakdown in civic and personal morality. Values and loyalties are relativized. The "glue" among neighbors is weak to nonexistent. One result of these social changes is the fear of strangers and of the terrible things they are presumably capable of doing. Such fears translate into a belief that these faceless strangers *are* doing these things and *will* do them if given half a chance. The mass media, which focus on the unusual, the sensational, and the exceptional in the world around us, only reinforce such concerns.

Stories of child-sexual-abuse rings in particular have become what folklore specialists and social scientists refer to as "urban legends" and "subversion myths."[35] It is not that such things never occur; obviously, they do. But people pass on hearsay, rumors laced with personal concerns, and speculations that come to be taken as established facts. Somewhere there are child-sexual-abuse rings, just as there are real Satanic cult groups and other monstrosities, and people imagine that perhaps the problem has finally come to their neighborhood as well.

In this way, children's faces began appearing on milk cartons during the 1980s with pleas to report their whereabouts, as if they had been snatched by white slavers, pimps, or Satanic cults. In reality, most were runaways or the victims of parental custody battles. At Halloween, parents now worry that their children may become victims of poisoned candy or the razor-blade-in-the-apple trap, despite the fact that only a very few isolated cases of this danger have ever materialized.[36] Urban legends touch at our basic concerns and worries; as terrible as the deeds often done in such stories, the telling and retelling reflects more about us than about what is actually going on "out there."

This argument is not intended to detract from the seriousness of the child-abuse problem or demean professionals who work to mitigate it. However, child abuse has become the major family problem of the late twentieth century, surpassing even concern over women-battering. The relative helplessnsss and innocence of the victims, the invasion of the privacy and sanctity of the home, and the staggering implications of widespread sexual abuse for the American family lend the problem a drama, a horror, and an urgency it has never before possessed.

But if real fears and "urban legends" in the popular culture fuel social scares like the one at Lehi, why do they end? If prosecutors at Lehi obtained a conviction in the Hadfield case, why didn't they press charges against other adults accused by the children?

There are several immediate answers, and perhaps one not so obvious possibility.

First, the Hadfield trial was an emotionally charged, embarrassing moment for this largely Mormon community. Since the evidence against Hadfield was certainly contestable, prosecutors no doubt questioned the value of putting more adults and children through a similar murky ritual.

Second, the public and experts alike had grown uncomfortable with the inconsistencies in the children's testimonies and were dogged by the suspicion that the kids had been coached by Dr. Snow. And other than that claimed in the Hadfield case, no one discovered even a trace of physical evidence to support the abuse stories; in an alleged abuse ring of the magnitude the stories suggested, there should have been a great deal.

Third, there really was no evidence of a child-sexual-abuse ring. That possibility was largely the psychotherapists' conjecture, which they apparently never relinquished. In the aftermath of the Hadfield trial, horrific possibilities gradually receded to become grotesque improbabilities. LDS Church leaders were undoubtedly relieved to see the controversy die (and there is *no* evidence they played any role in discouraging further prosecution). The "scandal" collapsed of its own weight, not on account of outside pressure.

But there was a final reason Lehi saw no more trials or convictions. The children's accusations initially divided the community, but then, paradoxically, the ritual-trial of Alan Hadfield pulled much of it back together. The testimonial evidence of the trial seemed to lay the truth of the sex-abuse urban legend out on the table for dissection, and most people saw with relief that it wasn't happening in their community after all.

Most important, the dense LDS ward network of households, men's/women's/children's groups, and communication "paths" via telephone could be used efficiently either for spreading gossip and fear *or* for mobilizing support for Alan Hadfield. Hadfield had become a symbol of injustice done to one of their own, just as the entire sexual-abuse scare had hurt the reputation and self-esteem of Lehi in general. Vindication of Hadfield was vindication for the community. In the end a lack of community, which some scholars believe underlies the conditions ripe for the spread of urban legends, was reversed.

The effort to persuade the judge to grant Hadfield the probation/therapy option, even though Hadfield technically did not qualify for it, was a communal reassertion that the urban legends were not true in Lehi. The unfortunate truth for Hadfield was that he was no more likely to be an abuser than were his neighbors.

Perhaps, after the Hadfield trial, the Lehi prosecutors also sensed this when they declined to press charges against anyone else accused. Certainly the investigators in Salt Lake County, where Dr. Barbara Snow took her counseling practice when she left Lehi, had some inkling of what they might be getting into when they decided to drop their sex-abuse probe.

6

LDS in the FBI:
The Case of the Mormon Mafia

Mormons are famously conservative and patriotic. Like the late Las Vegas recluse-millionnaire Howard Hughes, President Richard Nixon surrounded himself with such Mormon assistants because of their loyalty and integrity. They could be trusted.

President Ronald Reagan followed Nixon's lead, Indeed, the years of the Reagan administrations witnessed an unprecedented influx of Latter-day Saints into key positions in the federal government, including the White House staff.

Mormons support the Constitution. Themselves once the victims of religious persecution, they are keenly sensitive about civil rights, church-state boundaries, and religious freedom.

The flip side of this patriotism and loyalty is the "Mormon Mafia," a good-ol'-boy system of LDS favoritism in the FBI that surfaced during the 1980s. Charges of its influence eventually provoked a legal scandal in 1988 that rocked the FBI and irrevocably changed the way in which that agency handles its internal affairs. But to understand the issues involved, one first has to recognize how important Mormons have become to the U.S. intelligence community.

Both the Federal Bureau of Investigation and the Central Intelligence Agency eagerly recruit Latter-day Saints. Overseas missions have provided many male missionaries with valuable foreign-language experience and contacts. FBI Special Agent Lou Bertram, who coordinated recruiting efforts in Utah during the 1980s, claimed that "Utah, because of all the returned missionaries, leads the nation in the number of new recruits" for his agency.[1] One LDS recruiter suggested well-known Mormon virtues that make LDS members especially desirable in "The Company" (the CIA nickname): their reputation for "a sense of conformity and respect for authority," their sobriety, and their patriotism.[2] Mormon applicants rarely have backgrounds that would even hint at their being security risks.

Thus Brigham Young University, which many returning LDS missionaries attend, has become a hotbed of activity for CIA and FBI recruiters. In fact, Jeffrey Willis, personnel director for the CIA during the early 1980s and himself a former Mormon bishop, confirmed that former LDS missionaries are preferred over any other kind of applicant to the CIA. Having "returned missionary of the Church of Jesus Christ of Latter-day Saints" on either a CIA job application or a personnel dossier, he said, was a "definite plus" for one's career. Likewise, the FBI's Special Agent Lou Bertram, who coordinated FBI recruitment in Utah during the mid-1980s, claimed that "Utah, because of all the returned missionaries, leads the nation in the number of new recruits under the language program."[3]

Just how much of a "plus" it is, at least within the FBI, was only recently made clear.

On January 14, 1987, a Hispanic FBI agent, Bernardo Matias "Mat" Perez, filed a $5 million suit in a U.S. District Court against the Bureau on behalf of all Hispanics working for it. Perez charged the FBI with systematic discrimination—*largely religious discrimination*—against its Hispanic agents and employees, most of whom are Roman Catholics.[4]

The immediate discriminators, he claimed, were Mormon superiors in the field, supported by FBI officials in the Washington headquarters. Latter-day Saint superiors had come to constitute what he and others called a "Mormon Mafia" in the FBI. Perez accused them of selecting out the better (and sometimes less dangerous) field assignments for their fellow religionists as well as giving them promotions at the expense of non-Mormon agents, particularly Hispanic Roman Catholics.

The charge was not made, or taken, lightly. It was particularly serious in view of the fact that the FBI is responsible for enforcing federal civil rights statutes. Moreover, Mat Perez was the highest ranking Hispanic in the FBI, a tough twenty-seven-year veteran with a distinguished record of field investigations, who served under the legendary J. Edgar Hoover. He was the agent who in 1983 collared Richard W. Miller, the first FBI agent in history to be charged and convicted of espionage.

Indeed, it was the arrest and sensational trial of Miller—a lapsed Mormon who had sold classified secrets to the Soviets for sex and money—

that eventually brought to light the emerging network of discrimination in America's most prestigious law-enforcement agency. For Perez it was the beginning of a personal ordeal that became a crusade, pitting more than three hundred Hispanic FBI agents against many of their Mormon superiors.

Richard W. Miller—Double Agent

Mat Perez fits the profile of a modern FBI agent; well-educated and sophisticated, he is a man of many talents who had various promising career options available in his youth. His paternal grandparents had crossed the border into this country fleeing the Mexican Revolution. He is a sixth generation American on his mother's side, and of Spanish-American, Yaqui Indian, and French Basque heritage. The oldest of ten children, Mat Perez started out adulthood in a seminary, then dropped out to join the FBI as a messenger. He returned to his education, graduating from Georgetown University in Washington, D.C., with a major in Spanish literature and a minor in classical languages.[5]

Fluent in several languages, he originally had plans to join the Department of State but sought a temporary job with the Bureau again, this time as a translator. His specialty was Spanish. Ironically, Perez was never a native Spanish speaker. He learned the language at Georgetown University, afterwards speaking it with an American accent.

Ultimately, he became a Special Agent in 1963, one of only five Latino FBI agents out of approximately six thousand.[6] In time Perez began to establish a reputation as a resourceful field investigator. He performed well undercover in dangerous situations, perhaps creating an impression in some superiors' minds that his unconventional demeanor made him a maverick. Perez sometimes wondered if his successes, accomplished as they were by a Hispanic, presented some form of threat to his Anglo colleagues and superiors.[7]

Perez supervised important infiltration work while stationed in Puerto Rico and became the Special Agent in Charge of its San Juan office. Earlier, in 1976, as a Supervisor of the Los Angeles Division, he had been responsible for breaking up a violent Weatherman terrorist cell.[8] It was Perez, again working out of the L.A. Division in 1982 as Assistant Special Agent in Charge, who attempted unsuccessfully to fire Miller. (They had met as young agents in San Antonio in 1964 where Miller was already becoming the butt of jokes.) And it was Perez who in 1984 arrested Richard W. Miller.

Miller was a twenty-year veteran with a history of family problems, debts, and poor job performance. He was the complete opposite of the public image which the FBI wished to promote. Overweight and often slovenly dressed, Miller had received two disciplinary reprimands, including one for selling Amway products out of the trunk of his FBI vehicle. Moreover, he was incompetent.[9]

Some fellow agents ignored the black marks on Miller's record; others avoided him. Perez, as the number two official in the L.A. Division, tried twice to have Miller removed, but the Special Agent in Charge, Richard W. Bretzing, and P. Bryce Christensen, Miller's immediate supervisor on his foreign counterintelligence assignment, kept Miller on the payroll despite his failings. Some agents grumbled that religious favoritism played a role. "He just did not fit the FBI image," one agent later recalled, "and it sure looked like somebody was protecting him just because he was a Mormon."[10] Bretzing and Christensen, the agents knew, were also LDS. Bretzing in fact was an LDS bishop, and some members of the L.A. Division were in his ward.

Finally, Miller crossed over the line from merely incompetent to treasonous. As his financial problems mounted (he was part-owner in a failing avocado farm, among other things), the forty-seven-year-old Brigham Young University graduate fell in with two scheming Russian emigrants: Svetlana Ogorodnikov and her husband, Nikolay, a sometime meatpacker. Both claimed exaggerated ties to higher-ups in the Kremlin and hinted they might have some mysterious KGB mission in this country.

Whatever his attraction to this eccentric couple, Miller completed a triangle that soon turned sordid. Eventually he began a romantic affair with Svetlana as the Ogorodnikovs became legally separated yet continued to live together. The couple promised money for secrets that they knew Miller could deliver. Prosecutors later believed the Ogorodnikovs thought they could use Miller to build their own credibility with the Soviet government. Miller may or may not have believed them, but he needed relief from his debts. Miller struck a deal to provide them classified documents for $50,000 in gold and $15,000 in cash.[11]

During the trial it emerged that sometime before his arrest Miller had been excommunicated by the LDS Church, though he had previously been an active ward member. During the investigation Special Agent in Charge Bretzing met with Miller and appealed to his past faith, urging him "to repent of his mistakes."[12]

Rumors of preferential treatment circulated freely in the L.A. FBI office and came out during the trial. As a result, Miller's defense attorney later asked a U.S. district judge to dismiss the charges on the never-substantiated grounds that Miller was being used as a scapegoat by Bretzing to prove that he did not discriminate in favor of Mormon agents. For the first time the term "Mormon Mafia" made it into the news as a few Hispanic agents used it in interviews with reporters outside the courtroom.

Meanwhile, Bretzing issued a news release irately denying that any special treatment for LDS agents existed in the FBI and claiming that the defense was simply clutching at straws to save a transparently guilty man. He also lashed out against the discrimination claim, saying it unfairly cast aspersions on hundreds of loyal FBI employees who happened to be Mormon.[13]

Richard W. Miller was convicted of espionage, bribery, and conspiracy to copy and pass classified documents to the Soviet Union knowing these would "be used to the disadvantage of the United States." His sentence was harsh: two life-terms in addition to fifty years in prison and a $60,000 fine.

Significantly, Perez and Bretzing gave conflicting testimonies at the trial and a long-existing tension between them became evident. Perez made no secret of the "Mormon Mafia" accusation. Soon it was no longer just an internal suspicion or rumor. Even the LDS Church-owned *Deseret News* printed the damaging quote of one anonymous Hispanic FBI agent who supported Perez, saying, "The Mormon Mafia was running the [Los Angeles] office and giving choice assignments to their own people."[14]

In one sense, the Miller espionage was unrelated to the later class-action suit filed by Mat Perez and other Hispanic FBI agents against their federal employer. After all, Miller's spying had nothing to do with ethnic or religious discrimination. But it has been briefly discussed here for another reason. This case provided the first public forum for a rather unpleasant internal FBI matter to receive serious inspection: the perception by Hispanic agents that there was a definite pattern of discrimination against them in terms of assignments and promotions, conducted in part by fellow Mormon agents. Miller was a lapsed Mormon, and the same Hispanic agent who had repeatedly protested Miller's continued incompetent presence in the FBI had been the one to arrest him. Complaints of favoritism to Miller because of his former religious affiliation, which came out during the trial, became the beginnings of a scandal within this nation's premier law-enforcement agency.

For Mat Perez, who over the next four years was to file fourteen complaints against the FBI claiming discrimination toward himself and other Hispanic agents, the "Mormon Mafia" was to become more than an issue of office politics.

Favoritism in the Los Angeles Division

In 1982 Matt Perez had left Puerto Rico under a cloud. The official reason for his transfer to the Los Angeles Division and demotion to Assistant

Special Agent in Charge alleged "administrative shortcomings." Perez had been an outgoing, energetic boss in the Puerto Rican division who often went out on field assignments with his agents and personally made arrests on the street. However, superiors in Washington claimed he needed "retooling" before being put in charge again of any of the FBI's 58 field offices. His interpersonal and investigative skills might be superb, but he was a bit sloppy on administrating an office full of Special Agents.

So they said. Perez suspected otherwise.

Puerto Rico had been a tough assignment. This U.S. territory is the crossroads for much cocaine and narcotics traffic from Central and South America. Beyond the drug trade, however, there is a volatile political situation on the island. FBI agents in Puerto Rico confront terrorism spawned by some extremist groups in a movement to declare independence from the United States. For these reasons seasoned investigators consider Puerto Rico one of the most dangerous posts in the FBI.

Perez had thrown himself into investigative missions there with gusto and worked closely with other police groups. He appreciated the undervalued role that Spanish-speaking agents play in surveillance and undercover assignments.

But in the process of getting personally involved, it is likely he uncovered information implicating some local police in criminal activity. Certainly in the world of competitive law-enforcement agencies Perez's successes posed a threat. One U.S. Marshal later testified in a federal court that in his opinion in one particular case Perez had been set up by Puerto Rican police to be embarrassed—even putting him under surveillance and bugging his residence.[15] But, in any event, Mat Perez was transferred out of the San Juan Division after just two and a half years. (The FBI's normal period of assignment in that city is a minimum of four years.)

The new position for Perez in Los Angeles might genuinely have been intended by his superiors to improve whatever flaws he had as an administrator, but the situation was set for disaster. The Special Agent in Charge of the L.A. office, Richard W. Bretzing, possessed a personality completely opposite to Perez's. Where the Mexican-American-Indian Special Agent was gregarious and upbeat, Bretzing was cool and detached. Perez enjoyed hands-on investigative work and thrived on the involvement. Bretzing was first and foremost the administrator. One prized outcomes and effects over style; the other went by the book.[16]

For example, Perez helped solve a kidnapping in Alhambra, California, in 1983 and even received a commendation from local law-enforcement officials. However, Bretzing ignored the praise and merely sent Perez a memorandum reprimanding him for having worn jeans and cowboy boots in the field instead of a three-piece suit.[17]

It was clear from the beginning that the chemistry between the head of the L.A. Division and his new number two man was going to be bad. Apparently, word of Perez's advocacy of Hispanic FBI agents' concerns had preceded him. Skipping the usual courtesy of arranging a meeting for the new Assistant Agent in Charge to be introduced to other agents and staff members in the office, Bretzing bluntly told Perez, "I understand you are coming here as a special representative of Hispanics."

Perez icily replied: "You are insulting me. I am here as an FBI agent."[18]

Their working relationship started off sour and stayed that way. Bretzing was in constant contact through conferences and telephone calls with other agents in the L.A. Division, but Perez was kept "out of the loop" despite the fact that his office was next to Bretzing's. Special Agent John Hoos, whose office was across the hall from both Bretzing and Perez, watched the Bureau chief create a "cold-shoulder" atmosphere that others in the office could almost tangibly feel. Hoos was in charge of handling all media inquiries and was kept busy when the L.A. Division was involved in providing security for the 1984 Olympics held in the city. Yet during this time Perez was completely left out of things. Hoos recalled:

> Numerous times . . . I would go to see Mr. Perez and he had no idea what was going on in the division. He said he had "never been told anything about that." Mr. Perez was kept totally in the dark about numerous investigations.[19]

When Perez did initiate activities they were given a negative spin by his boss. Once Hoos set up an interview on Spanish-language station KMEX-TV in Los Angeles with Perez and another Hispanic agent, Auellio Flores, to discuss FBI recruitment of minorities. The live program was sent out by satellite dish across the country to more than two hundred stations. Soon after, switchboards at FBI divisions in Los Angeles, Chicago, San Antonio, and even Washington headquarters lit up with requests for applications. Calls came in from as far away as New York City. The program was unquestionably a public relations success for the FBI.

Yet Bretzing was not pleased. He summoned Perez and curtly told him: "Your job is not recruiting. Your job is sitting behind a desk, being administrative ASAC of this office."[20]

During the 1982-83 year the religious factor began to rear its ugly head in an office where 50 of the 450 employees were LDS members. And Perez found he was not the only one feeling discriminated against.

Special Agent Paul Magallanes, for instance, had filed a complaint against the FBI with the Equal Opportunity Employment Commission and soon after found himself transferred from the more desirable Ventura office (near where he lived) to the L.A. Division, an hour and a half away. When he and five other senior Hispanic agents submitted applications for a program providing polygraph training, they learned that the slot was given to a junior Anglo colleague—a Mormon whose wife gave Bretzing's children piano lessons.[21]

Cliques of agents that already existed began to solidify, not just around the office watercooler but in other ways. Perez came to work one day to find his office moved from the seventeenth floor, where the Division's administrative officers were located, to the fifteenth floor, the working area for new junior street agents. Moreover, Perez was told by Bretzing that he had been demoted in rank to Assistant Special Agent in Charge of Investigations, perhaps a task more suited to Perez's streetwise talents as an investigator but a humiliation nonetheless. To complete the slap in the face, Perez's former office next to Bretzing was now occupied by P. Bryce Christensen, whom Bretzing had just promoted to Assistant Special Agent in Charge of Administration.[22]

Secretarial, clerical, and other employees with Hispanic backgrounds who felt a heavy-handed LDS presence began meeting with Perez in his office to air their complaints of discrimination, and Perez began advising them how to file grievances. One female Hispanic agent told how in training at Quantico a Supervisor had pulled her aside and recommended she read a fashion magazine because she "looked too ethnic."[23]

Meanwhile, Richard Bretzing was actually working two jobs: as Special Agent in Charge of the L.A. Division and as bishop of his ward, including supervising distributions from his local Church welfare warehouse. His secretary complained often to Special Agent John Hoos about the time he spent out of the office doing Church business and the time he spent *in* his office on government time taking care of those same Church matters. Hoos knew firsthand that Bretzing had his secretary prepare notes for speeches to LDS groups. Bretzing had given his secretary a list of a dozen LDS General Authorities with firm instructions to pull him out of any conference, including one with the director of the FBI, if anyone on the list telephoned him. In her absence he gave the same instructions to Perez's secretary.[24]

Hispanic agents and staff began to see a conflict of interest between Bretzing's LDS Church responsibilities and his treatment of Roman Catholics. It is true that Mormons, like most Protestants, reject the ecclesiastical authority of Rome and have been hostile toward Catholicism in the past. But these agents detected distinct sectarian partisanship issuing out of the office of the Agent in Charge. Such was the feeling when a minor scandal broke out in the Division over Bretzing "lending" several off-duty

LDS agents to a Church official as bodyguards. One of the agents turned out to be a homosexual (a sexual preference anathema to church doctrine), and in the end Bretzing saved face by "strongly suggesting" that they all resign. FBI headquarters for its part turned a deaf ear.

During this time spy-to-be-revealed Richard Miller was still being tolerated by Bretzing despite the former's record of inept conduct as a Special Agent. Yet to come would be charges of passing classified documents to the Russian couple. Perez and others who felt the FBI was being embarrassed by Miller could neither ignore him nor get Bretzing to act on removing him.

In sum, the L.A. Division atmosphere was poisoned with tension and a belief that discrimination was rampant. Finally, in 1983 Mat Perez had had enough. He filed a discrimination grievance with the Equal Employment Opportunity Commission. As a Hispanic and a Roman Catholic, Perez claimed, he was not being treated equitably. He convinced several other agents and employees, including his secretary and Special Agent Paul Magallanes, to provide supporting testimony for his case.

Then the retaliations began.

The Mormon Mafia Moves

Five years later Special Agent Aaron Sanchez was asked in a U.S. District Court why he had waited so long to join Mat Perez in a class-action suit against the FBI if discrimination was so blatant. Sanchez replied, "The first commandment in this outfit is that you do not embarrass the Bureau."[25]

And charges of ethnic and religious discrimination within the very federal agency sworn to uphold minority rights *were* embarrassing. In FBI jargon, "the thumb" would have to be "put on someone" to prevent these sorts of disclosures.[26]

Special Agent in Charge Bretzing initiated a string of actions that Hispanic employees and agents recognized as retaliation and harassment. Mat Perez's secretary, Aileen Ikegami, was suddenly removed and demoted in rank from secretary to a significant Assistant Agent in Charge to a lowly supervisor of xeroxing and telecopying.[27] Special Agent Arnold Gerardo, who helped Mat Perez prepare for his EEOC hearing, had several top superiors at Washington headquarters approach him and threaten him with "long-term consequences" for his involvement. Subsequently he was denied promotion to a supervisory position (despite being qualified), then demoted, transferred, and finally forced out of the FBI. (Today Gerardo is a successful supervisor with the U.S. Customs office in San Diego.)[28]

Special Agent John Hoos, the non-Hispanic media liaison who witnessed first-hand Perez's shabby treatment by Bretzing, found that he had suddenly become unwelcome in the L.A. division chief's office. Before he had routinely checked Bretzing's calendar with the latter's secretary to see when the chief would be available for interviews. The day after he testified at the hearing for Perez, Hoos learned that he no longer had access to Bretzing's calender. Both Hoos and Hoos's assistant suddenly found Bretzing aloof, noncommunicative, and difficult to locate—this was a distinct change from the previously (and recently) cordial working relationship between Hoos and his boss. (Hoos had been approached by lawyers representing Bretzing to convince Hoos to testify for Bretzing, but Hoos leaned toward Perez, who had also asked him to testify. "This is a catch-22 situation," he told them. "I am damned if I do, and I am going to be damned if I don't.")[29]

In fact, immediately after Hoos had testified in Perez's EEOC hearing, government attorneys who had asked numerous questions about LDS Church business that Bretzing allegedly worked at on FBI time went immediately to Bretzing and briefed him on Hoos's testimony. Exactly one year later to the day Bretzing announced to Hoos that he was reassigning him from the media position, no reason provided.

"I am seriously considering that you are removing me from this position because of my testimony on behalf of Mr. Perez with the EEOC complaint," Hoos said, confronting his boss.[30]

According to Hoos, Bretzing smiled back but said nothing in response.

Later Hoos spoke by telephone with a former Assistant Director of the FBI and a personal friend. "John," the friend cautioned, "Bretzing got you for your testimony and you will never be able to prove it."[31]

The thumb was ultimately put on Special Agent John Hoos. He was reassigned to the narcotics squad, the most dangerous duty in any FBI division.

But Hoos was more fortunate than special Agent Paul Magallanes, who had already been punished for his own EEOC complaint by being transferred from an office near his home to the distant Los Angeles Division. Magallanes, too, was transferred to dangerous narcotics-squad duty —but first Bretzing made Magallanes turn in his gun and then refused to allow the Hispanic agent use of an agency car with a radio. Throwing Magallanes onto the streets to investigate drug dealers with no weapon— not even a two-way radio to call for back-up help—was tantamount to declawing a cat and abandoning it in the jungle.[32]

Perez's 1983 hearing did not find compelling evidence for discrimination. But the Richard Miller espionage debacle in 1984, compounded with Perez's embarrassing complaints of discrimination, set the stage for more systematic and systemic reprisals. One came that same year. Perez was transferred to El Paso, Texas, as Assistant Special Agent in Charge of that division.

Vindication

Mat Perez filed another grievance with the EEOC, claiming that as a Roman Catholic he had been discriminated against by Mormon superiors in the FBI, that his transfer to El Paso was really an act of retaliation. But this grievance, like the others, was dismissed.

By now Perez had few illusions. Internal correction of the discrimination problem seemed impossible without some intervention from outside. Yet for a lone agent to try to take on the Federal Bureau of Investigation in court was a David-and-Goliath proposition. Moreover, as Perez well knew, the costs could jeopardize his career and ruin him financially.

On the other hand, Perez and fellow Hispanic agents felt this entire discrimination problem was a moral issue, bigger than just individual complaints and promotions. Hispanic agents genuinely loved the FBI—*their* FBI—and to allow these mounting instances of favoritism and religious prejudice to pass unchallenged threatened the very premises on which the agency was founded.

Thus on January 14, 1987, Bernardo M. Perez filed a $5 million lawsuit in El Paso's U.S. District Court. Perez maintained he had been deliberately kept from promotion and career mobility through no fault of his own but as the result of ethnic discrimination heavily laced with religious bias. Moreover, he asserted that this was not just his problem but one for many Hispanics working in the FBI. People who had supported him in previous grievances, he added, had been demoted, harassed, reassigned to less desirable locations, or forced to resign from the FBI, all because they dared speak aloud about the unmentionable problem.

Later that year Perez went before Judge Lucius Bunton in the U.S. District Court with a motion to allow him to be certified as a class representative for all Hispanic FBI agents. He got the certification, and suddenly Perez was the center of a massive class action suit.

Of the approximately nine thousand FBI agents during the late 1980s, four hundred were Hispanics. Until this time only one, Perez, had ever headed any of the fifty-eight FBI field offices. Word of the suit spread quickly among minority agents; the response was phenomenal. By the time the suit went to Judge Bunton for a non-jury trial, 311 of the 400 Hispanic FBI agents had signed on with Perez. For many, joining the suit came only after much soul searching and first-hand experience with inequities in the system. Special Agent Rudolph Valadez recalled: "It was a long time coming for us to admit we were discriminated against, because we did not want to face the fact that we could not rise to the top. We don't have any shortcomings; we are up against institutional bigotry."[33]

That was Perez's undisguised public posture as well. After *fourteen* failed grievances, he pulled off the gloves and said publicly: "There are administrators at the top levels of the FBI, at headquarters, and in the field, and they are bigots!"[34]

One could conceivably dismiss Perez's words as those of an embittered employee who more than once received less than satisfactory performance ratings, who as a consequence failed to win promotions, and who was projecting the causes of his failings onto everyone but himself, were it not for the avalanche of support he received from fellow agents, both Hispanic and Anglo. When three-fourths of the FBI's entire Hispanic force stepped forward to join his suit, many offering to testify against their employer, the horror stories of religious and ethnic discrimination came out.

Those in the L.A. Division revealed Bretzing's LDS preferences and retaliations. Agents testified to the cliquishness of Mormon agents and superiors that seemed to make "blue flamers" (fast-track promotable agents) out of their LDS colleagues.[35] Special Agent Valadez, passed over for promotion twenty times in six years, had clashed with Richard Bretzing and been told to his face by that Special Agent in Charge that he would never be promoted to a supervisory position, regardless of how qualified he was, until Valadez "changed his attitude about management." Valadez understood the clear implication: Bretzing meant *Mormon* management.[36]

Others accused the "Mormon Mafia" and FBI headquarters in Washington of "tracking" Latino agents into translation assignments that removed them from the frequent special training opportunities occurring in the FBI and earned them career ruts. Such tedious translation work added long hours which more often than not meant time spent beyond their regular duties. Agents referred to such dead-end assignments as the "Taco" or "Tortilla" circuit." An informal FBI tradition of assigning such agents to areas with large Hispanic populations (such as Miami, Los Angeles, New York, and San Juan) also functioned to reduce their chances for promotion. Some Hispanic agents even told of having to do basic janitorial jobs.

In the case of Special Agent Samuel Martinez, a Mormon superior wrongly accused him of illegally selling weapons in Mexico City where Martinez was stationed. (Agents sometimes find themselves involved in what might at first glance seem "shady dealings," in this case helping a valued informant raise cash by [legally] selling a gun.) Martinez intended to request an extension as assistant legal attaché to the U.S. embassy in Mexico City. Such extensions are commonly granted. The other three attachés were LDS members, however, and Martinez concluded that his Legal Attaché in Charge had "wired" or reserved the fourth position for still another LDS colleague and thus had "flagged" Martinez's record with a major black mark to insure that he would not get it. With the false accusation, the Legal Attaché had Martinez demoted in rank and salary and ruined his chances for the attaché post.[37]

Martinez filed an EEOC complaint on grounds of discrimination which fell on deaf ears. Through the FBI's Merit System Protection Board he was eventually exonerated with full payment of attorney's fees and restoration of rank and pay. In fact, had he not been a veteran, his demotion would have stood. But he paid a price for complaining. The false charge stayed on his record despite his demands for expungement. In turn, he was ostracized by fellow agents when assigned to FBI headquarters in Washington. It was not uncommon for Anglo agents to discuss lunch options openly in front of him and then deliberately exclude him when they left the office. Not a killing blow, to be sure, but professionally insulting and personally aggravating on a daily basis.[38]

Another agent, seventeen-year veteran Ernesto Patino, was turned down five times for a position as legal attaché to either Bogotá, Columbia, or Mexico City. He, too, ran up against the "Mormon Mafia" which seemed to screen out non-Mormons from those offices.[39]

It was not always easy to separate testimonies of religious discrimination from ethnic discrimination. Frequently they were interwoven. Professor Gary LaFree, a sociologist at the University of New Mexico, testified that Hispanic FBI agents were more likely to be sent to dangerous or less desirable locations and significantly less likely to serve in supervisory positions—even though Hispanics scored the same or higher on the barrage of tests the FBI gives.[40] Hispanics were also more likely to experience disciplinary action. Indeed, run-ins between Roman Catholic agents and LDS supervisors as reported during the trial accounted for many such "actions."

At the end of each testimony attorneys asked the agent if he or she feared retaliation for appearing in court. All replied in the affirmative.

At the end of the ten-day trial, the U.S. government had spent more than one million dollars to defend the FBI against the suit by its own agents. The trial cost the suing agents over $800,000. Perez obtained donations from Hispanic civic groups and even used his expected retirement funds as collateral for loans to pay his lawyers. When the trial concluded he was $140,000 in debt. Perez et al.'s attorneys announced they would be paid only if they won, though one of the lawyers, Antonio Silva, told reporters he had spent so much time on the case that if they lost his own firm would be bankrupt.

Over ninety agents testified in the El Paso courtroom. When all plaintiffs in the suit tallied up the income lost in denied promotions, the extra time they had put in over the years doing Spanish-language work from which Anglo agents were spared, the seniority equity lost, and their legal fees, the figures were astronomical. The Perez team of lawyers raised the amount requested in their suit to $9.2 million.

There were controversies within controversies over the course of the trial. The plaintiffs' lawyers accused the government attorneys of manipulating and withholding evidence and not cooperating with the court. Hispanic agents were photographed as they left the courtroom by someone suspected of being an FBI agent. It even turned out that during the El Paso trial Mat Perez became the subject of an internal, probably punitive three-year FBI investigation that sought evidence that he had perjured himself as a witness in the trial of the agent convicted of espionage for the Soviets, Richard Miller.[41] However, nothing ultimately came of this transparent attempt to harass him.

The only LDS agent of any real consequence called to testify by government lawyers was Richard Bretzing himself. Bretzing denied any motives of religious prejudice and claimed his only intentions toward Mat Perez had been to help the Hispanic agent with his "leadership shortcomings." "I did everything I could to keep my faith, my religion, out of the administration of the office," he testified.[42]

To Hispanic agents who had witnessed Special Agent in Charge Bretzing occupy so much of his daily office routine with Church-ward matters and so completely erode any reasonable chance of Mat Perez exercising real leadership responsibilities in the L.A. Division, his protestations of neutrality seemed ludicrous.

Mat Perez and the Hispanic agents won their suit. Still, the victory was not complete. Judge Bunton found them the victims of a class-wide "pattern and practice of discrimination in employment and promotional opportunities." However, he ruled that only Perez—not the other agents—had been the unfair victim of FBI retaliations. And the judge rejected a separate claim of religious discrimination, though at the same time he noted that much of the trial testimony did, in fact, support "the proposition that Mormon supervisors made personnel decisions which favored members of their church at the expense of Hispanic class members."[43]

A separate trial was to be held several months later to determine the amount of compensation to be awarded to the Hispanic agents, and the haggling commenced. The government tried to settle for one payment of $175,000 total, to be divided among the agents and their attorneys, but the individual agents' claims ranged from $11,000 to $300,000 *apiece*. Trial and appeal continued on the compensation issue and was still not settled a year later.

Meanwhile, shortly after the initial verdict, Perez's lawyers found themselves swamped with a new kind of clientele. Minority agents in the U.S. Secret Service, the Alcohol, Tobacco and Firearms Bureau, the U.S. Marshal's Office, and the Drug Enforcement Administration—one-third of those querying were women—quickly made contact to discuss their own possible suits.[44]

The most important long-range outcome of the trial was the attitude of change it fostered in the front office of the FBI. William Webster, former director of the FBI and recently appointed head of the CIA, publicly admitted that there were occurrences of individual discrimination against some Hispanic agents but did not concede a widespread or systematic problem in what was formerly his FBI. But new FBI director William S. Sessions pledged to stamp out racism and ethnic discrimination. He approved a new five-year Affirmative Action program to hire and promote more minority employees.[45]

As a result, a little more than one year after Perez's suit was filed, four Hispanic agents—*not* members of the class suit—had been promoted to visible upper-management positions in the FBI. Perez et al.'s attorneys dismissed the reforms as window dressing, asserting that the problem was not simply due to Anglo insensitivity but was fundamentally grounded in religious bigotry.[46] Still, the trial had drawn attention to precisely the career problems in the FBI about which Perez and his colleagues had first complained, and a public relations-sensitive FBI responded.

The entire problem of religio-ethnic discrimination in the FBI, which also happened to involve some Mormon agents, revealed a seldom discussed aspect of LDS members' highly visible conservatism and patriotism. It is the tendency for Saints in public positions of trust and authority to err in the direction of favoring their fellow religionists, even to the point of violating those trusts. To want to help a fellow member of one's religion in career advancement is normal for anyone, regardless of creed. To do so at the expense of a colleague of a different faith, in a government agency responsible for enforcing such neutrality, exceeds the bounds of legal and moral propriety.

Does this mean that those FBI agents who were also LDS members, even if they unconsciously or inadvertently discriminated against Roman Catholic and other non-Mormon agents, were not loyal Americans and patriotic? I do not mean to suggest it.

Rather, all the factors creating a separate Mormon subculture and worldview, which Mormons themselves readily admit exists, can create something beyond a simple patriotism/pseudo-patriotism split. Mormons have a profound, deeply held allegiance to this nation as the home of their founder and Church as well as of their faith's trials and triumphs. No one has a better claim to its citizenship.

But many Latter-day Saints also put their governmental duties in the same relative perspective as that of Mormons in other regimes and cultures (which was suggested in the earlier chapter on missionizing). Their attitude can often become one of "parapatriotism," combining a natural love of one's country with a more abstract sense that its rules of law and government are transient things. Parapatriotism is a spinoff of the once more frequently found Mormon sense of millennialism: that the current order of things in society will soon be displaced by Jesus Christ's return. With such a view, ultimate allegiance in a conflict of interest involving like-minded religionists should go to one's Church and fellow believers, for they alone will persist.[47]

Parapatriotism, thus, is not a conspiracy. It is an attitude and a tendency, however unreflected upon by its promoters.

Epilogue

By the end of the first trial Mat Perez had two and a half weeks to serve before he became eligible for retirement. Still, like other agents who had testified, including non-Hispanic ones like John Hoos, Perez was leary of further retaliation. "I have already been told by my superiors that harsh things have been said, and this matter is not going to end," he said in his court testimony.[48] His El Paso Special Agent in Charge, Richard Schwein, retorted that any talk of future retaliation was ridiculous.

Nevertheless, enough testimonies by worried agents convinced Judge Bunton to issue a caution in his ninety-seven-page decision: there were to be no future FBI retaliations of any kind, not only against Hispanic agents who had participated in the suit but also against groups that had supported Perez, such as the Texas chapter of the League of United Latin American Citizens.

Mat Perez did not immediately retire. In 1989 he was at FBI headquarters in Washington, D.C., now Deputy Assistant Director of the Bureau's main laboratory. Judge Bunton had awarded him restoration pay and promotion (the first such instance in FBI history), but Perez had to remain in the agency another year in order to be eligible for retirement benefits.

And what of Richard T. Bretzing? Shortly before the trial in El Paso had even begun, he retired from the FBI. He became a counselor in the Newbury Park (California) state presidency and took a new job as Managing Director of the LDS Church Security Department in Salt Lake City where many former FBI and CIA Mormon agents work after retiring from the intelligence community. A Bretzing weary of the "Mormon

Mafia" criticisms told reporters: "The position where I am going will not be visible at all. I welcome that."[49]

7

The Challenger Shuttle Disaster: Elite Crime and the LDS Church in America's Space Program

Once proponents of theocracy in the United States, LDS Church leaders now accept the principle of a division between church and state. The Brethren in Salt Lake City are solely guardians of the spiritual and material welfare of their fellow believers. While members of the LDS ecclesiocracy of course encourage the prosperity of Utah and regions where Church members predominate, they seek to minimize Church presence in public policy debates. Now integrated into all major American institutions, LDS members can, without Church pressure, separate their public roles from their religious loyalties.

The "can-do" optimism of America's space program was dramatically ruptured on the morning of January 28, 1986. At precisely 11:38 A.M., barely seventy-three seconds into its liftoff from the Kennedy Space Center at Florida's Cape Canaveral, the space shuttle Challenger exploded horrifically on live television. Hot pressurized gases escaped from the field joint between the sections of one booster rocket and, once ignited, acted like a huge blow torch that cut its way into the fuel tank. The two booster rockets each contained over five hundred thousand tons of rocket fuel. Within seconds fire transformed the Challenger into a giant incendiary bomb rising in the sky. The wings flew off, the booster rockets careened wildly upwards, and the main aluminum cabin, along with the seven crew members inside, fell almost five thousand feet before crashing into the ocean with a force of over two hundred G's. It was March before divers could recover the cabin section with Challenger's flight and mid-decks; inside the cabin they found the bodies of the astronauts still strapped in their seats.

"It was a catastrophe and tragedy of such great proportion that it stopped the nation—not unlike President Kennedy's assassination or the Japanese attack on Pearl Harbor," wrote one journalist.[1] Indeed, it was the world's most spectacular and fatal space disaster, broadcast on prime-time television. The only parallel in our nation's space program was the Apollo 1 launch-pad fire in 1967 that killed Virgil "Gus" Grissom and two other astronauts, halting the progress of the moon landing project for twenty-two months. The shuttle program after Challenger was to be stalled even longer.

The Challenger tragedy was the NASA shuttle program's twenty-fifth flight. After so many successful missions, both NASA officials and the public had come to accept shuttle flights as commonplace, so safe in fact that a New England public school teacher and mother of small children, Christa McAuliffe, was given rudimentary training and dubbed a "payload specialist" as part of the crew. The preflight publicity helped set up the country and the world even more for the post–disaster shock and disillusionment.

President Ronald Reagan soon ordered an investigation. Former Secretary of State William Rogers headed the special commission with a thirteen-member panel that included three astronauts and several engineers. After weeks of hearings and scores of witnesses as well as the review of thousands of documents, the Rogers Commission's five-volume report was issued. The main conclusion of its investigation focused on a technical point of failure in the Challenger's booster rocket design: the thin rubber "O-rings," or sophisticated gaskets, which, along with a special chemically treated putty, were supposed to form pressurized seals to keep flammable gases from escaping at the booster rocket segments' connecting joints. The unusually frigid temperature on that January morning in Florida rendered the O-rings more rigid than expected. At blast-off they failed to form tight seals.

But the O-rings were only the immediate cause of the disaster and the endpoint of a much longer story that science writer Malcolm McConnell in *Challenger: A Major Malfunction* termed "a low point in squalid political intrigue."[2] It is a story of white-collar crime that includes many actors, among them the LDS Church, the head administrator of NASA, several U.S. Senators from Utah, and a Utah-based company that built the shuttle booster rockets. It is the story of political favoritism and a conflict of interests. It is a story that explains why NASA adopted a flawed and inferior rocket design and how the vested interests involved in the procurement decision have remained generally unpublicized. Indeed, as Malcolm McConnell writes, "as Challenger's crew smiled down from the launch pad catwalk at the massive white columns of the solid rocket boosters, they were looking at the fiscal product of flawed policy and political corruption."[3]

This is the chronicle of the involvement of the LDS Church itself in our nation's worst space disaster. Incredible as it may at first seem, the disaster need never have happened were it not for a confluence of factors closely related to that Utah-based religion.

Warning Signs Ignored

The Challenger's massive 149-foot booster rockets resembled roman candles the height of fifteen-story buildings, powered by solid rocket fuel that, once ignited, could not be shut off. These rockets provided 80 percent of the 7.7 million pounds of thrust needed to lift the 4.5-million-pound shuttle into space. They would finally burn out their fuel approximately twenty-five miles up as the shuttle left Earth's atmosphere at four-and-a-half times the speed of sound.

The booster rockets' force was awesome, combining "the brute power of a bomb and the delicate precision of a fine watch."[4] Each booster rocket was constructed of four reusable cylindrical segments twenty-five feet long and twelve feet in diameter, harnessing a thrust of hundreds of pounds per square inch. Writes Malcolm McConnell of the force propelling Challenger: "On launch day, when the external tank was loaded with the liquid hydrogen and oxygen, the combined load of liquid and solid propellants would equal the explosive power of a small tactical nuclear weapon."[5]

The Solid Fuel Factor

Years later the use of solid fuel in booster rockets (or Solid Rocket Boosters —SRBs) would become a major criticism of the shuttle program. Cost, however, had been the original criterion in 1973 when NASA chose solid over liquid fuel. The former was, simply, much cheaper. The shuttle program, which had started off as only one part of the space agenda mapped out by President Richard Nixon's Space Task Group, had witnessed the scrapping of construction of an orbiting space station and a manned exploration of Mars as the Vietnam War gradually drained America's economy. Suddenly the shuttle *was* NASA's space program. And cost-cutting in the face of niggardly congressional funding became a way of daily operations at NASA.

The biggest problem with SRBs was their lack of a fundamental safety factor. The main engines of the orbiter vehicle itself were powered by liquid fuel that could be throttled back or even turned off. However, after ignition, the SRBs could not shut down even if ground controllers suddenly learned that the mission had to be aborted. Nothing could cancel the explosive power of the SRBs once released. Joseph Sutter, a respected aeronautical engineer who was a member of the Rogers Commission investigating the Challenger disaster, warned that "solid rockets are so dangerous that only seasoned crews who have no families and who realize the risks should be sent on Shuttle missions." According to Sutter, "Practically all of the experts of rocketry say that one of the biggest mistakes in the Shuttle program was the decision to go with solid rocket boosters."[6]

The O-Rings Glitch

It is an old truism that a chain is only as strong as its weakest link. In the case of the Challenger, the failure of the weakest link had fatal consequences.

More immediately threatening to shuttle flights than the nature of solid fuel was the defective design of the "O-rings" intended to prevent the escape of dangerous gases, released on ignition, between the segments (or at the field joints) of the booster rockets. O-rings were flexible, pencil-thick rubber gaskets held in place by gas pressure and backed up by a thick sealing putty. The O-rings would adjust to the extremely rapid "rotation," or flexing, of the boosters' metallic joints under the tremendous lurch of blast-off. Though the O-rings were locked in place by 177 thick steel pins, the key to their functioning was their flexibility under stress. The O-rings were meant to be the answer to the millisecond of shifting alignment between booster rocket joints.

They turned out to be an unreliable answer. If the O-rings did not set properly after joint rotation at blast-off, particularly because they and the metallically treated putty packed in around them might be stiffened by cold temperatures, the superhot pressurized gases from ignition—at 5,600 degrees Fahrenheit—could burn through or erode them. On more occasions than the public realized, past shuttle flights had courted disaster on account of the O-ring problem. Almost half of the first twenty-three shuttle flights had experienced partial failure of O-rings in the field joints between booster rocket segments. In fact, the previous five shuttle missions before Challenger had partial field-joint failure during launches.[7] Moreover, in nine of the ten shuttle flights before Challenger's January 28 disaster, heat had damaged the primary O-ring in at least one of the shuttle's two boosters. In an April 1985 launch the primary O-ring was completely lost.[8]

The Rogers Commission pinpointed the source of the Challenger explosion: the failure of the O-rings to seal in flammable gases at a field joint of one rocket. The temperatures at Cape Canaveral had been uncommonly cold on January 28. At the time of the Challenger's launch the air temperature was only thirty-six degrees Fahrenheit—fifteen degrees colder than on any previous launch. (Ice literally covered the walkways and girders of the Fixed Service Structure beside the shuttle earlier that morning.)

Later studies of recovered pieces of the booster rockets, films, and NASA computer tapes revealed that an O-ring at the right booster rocket's aft-field joint had burned through. (Cameras recorded small black puffs of escaping gases.) Glassy aluminum oxide residues from the burning propellant temporarily sealed the field joint, but when the Challenger hit a severe windshear at 11:38 A.M. the booster's flames burned through.

The Rogers Commission also discovered a shocking record of coverups surrounding the O-ring design problem. As Malcolm McConnell details, both the Utah-based Thiokol Corporation that built the shuttle's booster rockets and NASA's Marshall Space Flight Center in Alabama covered up engineers' reports that the O-rings were dangerous. The frantic pace of preparing shuttle flights and the attitude that NASA could accept growing risk "because they got away with it the last time" led a variety of Thiokol and NASA officials to cavalierly dismiss O-ring problems as "within an acceptable limit."[9]

Meanwhile, whistle-blowing engineers within Thiokol, performing their jobs conscientiously,, were either ignored or stifled. Roger Boisjoly, for example, was a senior engineer at Thiokol who later testified about the coverups to the Rogers Commission. In July 1985 he had warned Thiokol officials of a "possibly catastrophic failure of seals on the Shuttle booster rockets." But his report was withheld from launch directors at NASA. It was labeled by Thiokol as "company private." At the same time that company officials suppressed such information, Boisjoly charged, Thiokol was receiving funds from NASA to recruit eighteen quality-control and safety inspectors who were never actually hired.[10]

Boisjoly and two other Thiokol engineers, Allan McDonald and Arnold Thompson, along with Joe Kilminster, Thiokol's Solid Rocket Motor Project Manager, arranged an "eleventh hour" meeting with Thiokol executives and NASA officials the night before the Challenger's final launch to plead their case about the O-ring danger. But the engineers' warnings were overruled as "inconclusive" by Thiokol's own executives and therefore failed to impress NASA. After the Challenger disaster Boisjoly filed a one billion dollar personal injury and damages suit against Thiokol (formally known as Morton Thiokol, Inc. after being bought by Morton Norwich Products, Inc. in 1982), accusing the company of branding him a malcontent and demoting him for his role in testifying before the Rogers Commission. He accused the corporation of, among other things, fraud, negligence, manslaughter, racketeering, defamatory statements against him, and untruthful testimony to congressional and presidential commissions.[11]

The Challenger incident opened up the administration and operating procedures of NASA for an intense scrutiny long overdue. Much of America's space program had become mythologized since the 1960s by public-relations agents and the public's wishful thinking. The true state of lax safety precautions and shoe-string budgeting had been virtually whitewashed. Unfortunately, it took a tragedy that cost seven lives to stimulate the investigations to follow.

Challenger also brought to light the circumstances surrounding how a contract was ever awarded for booster rockets with serious design flaws. Indeed, there was controversy back in 1973 when the selection of Thiokol to build the rockets was made by NASA officials, and it resurfaced after Challenger.

Influence Peddling at NASA

That favoritism and special interests played a role in NASA's awarding the booster rocket contract to Thiokol is no longer speculation. It is undeniable fact, the product of illegal behavior conducted in corporate board rooms and high government offices. To understand how a problematic rocket design passed muster in the competitive world of space-industry bidding, we need to return to the years immediately preceding the shuttle program. We need to turn to Utah and a union of economic and religious interests that biased NASA's booster-rocket decision.

The Pro-Utah Connection

Cities, towns, states, and even regions have long formed business associations to encourage industry, tourism, and trade. There is nothing unusual in such commercial boosterism. Thus a group organized in 1965, calling itself Pro-Utah and promoting local economic growth, fit this national trend.

But in Utah all aspects of culture and society, including business, have to take into account one inescapable presence: the Church of Jesus Christ of Latter-day Saints. The LDS Church is the state's single largest employer. Its historical primacy in what used to be barren mountains and desert has left a distinctive mark on modern Utah mores, media, and economics. The chairman of General Motors once quipped, "What is good for General Motors is good for America." And the same is often thought for the LDS Church in Utah. Mormon leaders treat Utah as their special economic trust as well as their Church's spiritual heart. Journalists Gottlieb and Wiley, writing in *America's Saints* about the Church's vast fiscal clout in Utah, summed it up: "Unlike any other American church . . . the [LDS] church's economic decisions, and the sheer weight of its massive holdings, including its participation in the campaign to bring corporations to the Wasatch Front and its plans for downtown Salt Lake City, have a major impact on large numbers of people, both Mormon and non-Mormon."[12]

Pro-Utah uniquely reflected both the state business community's and the LDS Church's interests in attracting lucrative outside industries. It was a lobbying group simultaneously made up of Utah businessmen and Mormon Church officials. Prominent among the latter in the late 1960s were Loren C. Dunn (Pro-Utah's Vice-President and a member of the LDS Church's First Council of the Seventies, a high ecclesiastical administrative rank), C. Taylor Haight (a former Director of Industrial Development at Brigham Young University), and N. Eldon Tanner (a councilor in the LDS Church's highest executive office, the First Presidency).

Tanner in particular was a tireless booster for Utah's economy. He equated such growth in the state "as being in the best interest of the Church."[13] A successful businessman before being called to full-time duties in the upper Church hierarchy, Tanner had been active throughout the 1960s and into the 1970s in efforts to expand Utah's economy. He was a strong supporter of Utah Governor Calvin L. Rampton's campaign to diversify Utah's industrial base. While in the Church's First Presidency, he also served four years on the State Coordinating Council of Development Services and met frequently with Calvin L. Rampton to promote industrial development in the state.[14] Said Milton Weilemann, who served as Executive Director of the Department of Development Services throughout most of the Rampton administration years:

> There was probably no one who ever did more in the state of Utah for industrial development than President Tanner. He was without question the most actively involved person I ever knew, who made great efforts and spent considerable time in trying to bring industry into this state. Quite often, I remember, he would accompany the Governor and members of his staff to other states to meet with heads of large corporations and persuade them to expand or relocate in Utah. Because of his efforts and as a gesture of appreciation to him, we offered one important chair in the Department of Industrial Promotion to him. He politely declined, however, saying he wished to remain in the background, but [he] recommended Elder Loren C. Dunn instead to fill that position. It was Elder Dunn's responsibility to report directly to President Tanner on a weekly or frequent monthly basis concerning what the Department of Industrial Promotion was engaged in or had just accomplished. President Tanner then reported these matters to the Quorum of the Twelve Apostles.[15]

Pro-Utah and the indefatigable LDS Elder N. Eldon Tanner aggressively courted corporations and contracts for Utah industries.[16] When the space industry became an important presence in the American economy, it was only natural that Utah, a state with a lot of defense-contract business, would be interested. But one as-yet-unmentioned actor helped finally to connect Utah's economic development concerns with the shuttle booster rocket: Dr. James C. Fletcher, NASA head and member of the board of directors of Pro-Utah.

James C. Fletcher—Head of NASA

When Dr. James C. Fletcher was recruited in 1971 by President Richard M. Nixon to become the head administrator of the National Aeronautics and Space Administration, he had already established impressive careers in both higher education and industry. Fletcher received his bachelor's degree from Columbia University and his doctorate from the California Institute of Technology. He had also done research at Harvard University and taught at Princeton as a graduate student. He later worked as a scientist for over a decade, developing components for sonar devices and guided missle systems. In 1958 Fletcher cofounded and became president of the Space Electronics Corporation (later the Space General Corporation) which developed and manufactured the upper-stage parts of rockets. Six years later he stepped into the office of President of the University of Utah.[17]

During these years Fletcher came to know and work with LDS leader N. Eldon Tanner in two ways that were to become important while Fletcher was head of NASA.

First, as the LDS Church's premier advocate of industrial development in Utah, Tanner came to be deeply involved with the University of Utah as a grant-drawing institution. Tanner arranged frequent meetings that included himself, Fletcher, and various representatives from large out-of-state corporations. The purpose of the meetings was to persuade industries to relocate in Utah. Such meetings took place with increasing frequency toward the end of 1969 and throughout much of 1970. Meanwhile, either Governor Calvin L. Rampton or Milton Weilemann, his Executive Director of the Department of Development Services, met with Tanner on a weekly basis to provide updates on the progress of industrial development statewide and to discuss various ideas for attracting new industries to Utah. LDS Church official Loren C. Dunn, an officer in Pro-Utah and later in the state's Department of Industrial Promotion, also reported directly to Tanner on a regular basis.[18]

A second area of mutual interest for Fletcher and Tanner during this same time was their LDS Church involvement. Fletcher rose into the upper echelons of LDS Church leadership. While living on the West Coast he became a member of the high council of the Los Angeles Stake and then a Regional Representative (above the rank of Stake President) to the LDS Church's First Presidency. These Church activities brought him into contact with Tanner.

Finally, Fletcher had at least some indirect connections with Thiokol before he ever faced the decision to award the company a lucrative contract. Fletcher's wife was from Brigham City, Utah, where Thiokol had its aerospace plant. He was to make oblique reference to this connection, as will be shown, in his eventual complaint that he was being squeezed to give preference to Utah in awarding the booster-rocket contract. Because of his own science background Fletcher was, of course, familiar with Thiokol's prominence in the space industry. And during the time that Fletcher was meeting with Tanner and others regarding plans to bring more business to Utah, Tanner and Milton Weilemann held meetings with executives from Thiokol about planned expansion of its facilities.

The Pro-Thiokol Lobby

Insofar as his Utah connections could help, James C. Fletcher received strong support when he was nominated by President Richard Nixon to be NASA's head administrator. Before hearings of the Senate Space Committee in April 1971, Utah Senators Frank E. Moss and Wallace F. Bennett (both Mormons) led the witnesses buttressing Fletcher's case. (One of Fletcher's brothers was also Bennett's son-in-law.) Senator Bennett referred to Fletcher as "one of our state's outstanding citizens," while Senator Moss declared Fletcher to be one of the "most able administrators in the state."[19] With such endorsements the former space scientist and entrepreneur now presiding over the University of Utah could hardly lose. Fletcher took over NASA.

Two years later NASA announced that it intended to employ solid fuel rocket boosters on the shuttle. By that time Utah's Senator Moss had been named Chairman of the Senate's Committee on Aeronautical and Space Sciences which oversaw NASA's policies and budget. All of Utah appreciated the economic and employment windfall that such a rocket contract would bring, not least of all Moss. He announced to the press that such a contract would be worth one billion dollars to his state.

The Thiokol Chemical Corporation's Wasatch Division, outside of Brigham City, Utah, also recognized the value of such a contract. Thiokol had come to this area of Utah near the Wasatch Mountains in the 1950s. By the 1960s it had government contracts to make tactical and strategic missiles such as the Minuteman ICBM and the Poseidon and Trident submarine-launched ballistic missiles. The sixty-five hundred workers at the Wasatch plant marked it as the largest industrial employer in Utah and the second largest overall employer in the state (next to the LDS Church).

Cynics would say that the stage was set for reciprocity on Fletcher's part because of his key position and the help Mormon politicians had given him. Soon after the solid-rocket-booster announcement was made, NASA administrator Fletcher provided his home state's Senator Moss with a special briefing on the forthcoming Request for Proposals (RFP).[20]

And the lobbying began.

Thirteen years later, as the nation reeled in a sense of disillusionment following the Challenger disaster, the General Accounting Office (GAO) conducted an investigation into how Utah-based Thiokol obtained the booster-rocket contract in the first place. But many had forgotten that this was the *second* GAO investigation into the contract issue.

The first inquiry occurred in 1973. That year, when James C. Fletcher (as NASA's Source Selection Official) had announced his decision to award Thiokol the rocket contract based on advice from NASA's Source Evaluation Board, there were protests from other competing bidders—principally the Lockheed Propulsion Company, the United Technology Center, and the Aerojet Solid Propulsion Company—as well as from congressmen and at least one governor from states that would have welcomed the contract. Later it would become known that two members of NASA's Source Evaluation Board had been former Thiokol employees. Aside from the potential bias issue, the secretive deliberations of the Source Evaluation Board were protested. The Lockheed Corporation, which lodged the formal complaint and sparked the first GAO investigation in 1973, contended that NASA had overestimated Lockheed's projected costs and underestimated Thiokol's figures.[21]

Moreover, the Thiokol production plan was to ship rocket segments twenty-five hundred miles overland by railroad, laying the segments horizontally on flatbed cars which could (and often did) damage their outer edges. (Lockheed would have shipped rocket segments vertically by river barges.) The 1973 GAO investigation found in its ninety-eight-page report that cost estimates from Thiokol's rocket design versus Lockheed's were miscalculated. Actually the two corporations' projected costs fell within a fairly close range. Nor was technological excellence an issue. In fact, the Aerojet Solid Propulsion Company had presented a booster-rocket model with no joints in its steel casing, eliminating the risk of any "joint rotation" on lift-off.

The 1973 GAO review recommended a "reconsideration" of the contract decision, in which Fletcher had the final say. Comptroller General Elmer

B. Staats, head of the GAO, wrote Fletcher. "Your attention is invited to the conclusions reached in our decision. Please advise of the actions taken with respect thereto."[22]

NASA administrator Fletcher stuck by his original decision. Much of his reasoning was buried in techno-bureaucratic jargon. However, Fletcher strongly defended the Thiokol booster-rocket design, in particular the O-rings and field joints. Praising the design as "innovative" Fletcher said: "The Thiokol motor case joints utilized dual O-rings and test parts between seals, enabling a simple leak check without pressuring the entire motor."[23]

But later in 1986 the entire matter of the Thiokol-NASA relationship was reopened and thrown back to the GAO. On December 18 of that year, almost twelve months after the Challenger explosion, Senator Albert Gore of Tennessee ordered a congressional probe into possible conflict-of-interest violations in NASA's awarding the booster-rocket contract to Thiokol. Gore cited as a prime reason several articles written by science journalist William Broad and published December 7 and 8 in the *New York Times*. These articles discussed a connection between Fletcher, Pro-Utah, and LDS Church lobbying. Gore said the disclosures in the articles "give rise to serious questions about the propriety and legality of the contract" and may have violated Executive Order 11222, a bill signed by President Lyndon B. Johnson in 1965 prohibiting federal officials from actions that might result in, or create the appearance of, "giving preferential treatment to any organization or person."[24]

Some of the most critical proof of LDS lobbying that journalist Broad presented in his articles was provided by research done for this chapter, not simply on the LDS Church offices and connections held by James Fletcher but also on the extent of LDS Church-related contacts with Fletcher on behalf of Thiokol during the early 1970s. Up until the late 1980s the public had complete access to the collection of Frank E. Moss's personal papers at the library of the University of Utah in Salt Lake City. That is where evidence of a pattern of such lobbying by the LDS Church was discovered. The Moss papers showed the following sequence of events:

On January 12, 1973, James C. Fletcher wrote Senator Moss, Chairman of the Committee on Aeronautical and Space Science, in response to Moss's efforts to convince Fletcher to give Thiokol preferential treatment. Fletcher acknowledged previous conversations with Moss about Moss's past inquiries into the booster-rocket contract. Though Fletcher was to later say (after the contract was awarded) that Thiokol's rail-delivery plan for rocket segments was superior to Lockheed's river-barge plan, in his January letter to Moss he questioned Thiokol's plan, writing "Would it be cost-effective enough for us in the long run?" In the remainder of the letter he referred explicitly to the Utah pressure groups that had lobbied him. He also expressed his hope that such forces could be kept at bay:

> I know that President Tanner and various of your state officials have manifested an unusual zeal in hopes that NASA would send some of our business your way. As you probably already know several firms have recently approached me in person, which I suspect was through your persuasions no doubt.
>
> Undoubtedly whatever decisions in regard to such matters that are made will ultimately come through your Committee. But it would be comforting to know that amicable solutions can be reached without any undue pressure on our part or the intervention of politics as such.[25]

But lobbying pressures on Fletcher intensified. A little over one month later Fletcher had become resentful of LDS-related "hard-sell" tactics to award Thiokol the booster-rocket contract. He seemed frustrated that those lobbying him did not appreciate, or care about, his ethical dilemma in this situation. He was appealed to on the basis of his LDS Church loyalty, his previous high Church responsibilities, and his relationship with Elder N. Eldon Tanner. He was keenly aware of the ethical bind that confronted him. It arose, on the one hand, from the direct pressure from a Mormon Utah Senator's office as well as from indirect leverage from the LDS Church's premier economic booster, N. Eldon Tanner, and, on the other hand, from Fletcher's obligation of professional neutrality as a federal official evaluating contract bids.

A crucial letter from Fletcher to Frank E. Moss, dated February 23, 1973, is presented below in its entirety. This letter provides a window into the intense lobbying climate which Fletcher faced from Thiokol and LDS-related contacts. He wrote:

Dear Mr. Chairman:

> I feel an obligation to respond to the numerous efforts made by your office of late to have this Agency, and, in particular myself, look with considerable favor at the placing of some of our business in your State. Not only would it be highly irregular to say the least, but might provoke the kinds of inquiries we are not prepared at this time to handle.
>
> However, I am in sympathies with you regarding the future potential that your State holds. Bear in mind that I also have roots there too, which may not run as deeply as yours do, but are, nevertheless, there and obviously form some kind of positive attachments during the period I was at the University. And while I may not have a particular constiuency [sic] to serve as you might, yet there are particular individuals whom I hold in high regard and have tried to help from time to time when

it was within my power to do so.

One of these as you may well know, is President Tanner. He has exhibited considerable energy and determination in revitalizing some of your downtown areas in Salt Lake City. And on more than one occasion, he has expressed pretty much the same sentiments that you have in regard to giving your State's economy a bigger boost. We've explored together various options at great length as to how this might be achieved with a minimal amount of attention being drawn to either of us.

But the fact remains, Mr. Chairman, that my hands are tied for the time being. In my present position here at this particular Agency, it would be extremely difficult if not somewhat unethical for me to channel any more of our contracts towards your State without arousing further suspicion. As I explained to President Tanner before, I didn't mind helping out once, but I feel that anything else in the forseeable [sic] future would simply be improper.

I would also like to call your attention to another matter along these same lines. One of your staff—I think you probably know who I am referring to—went so far as to insinuate sometime ago that I had a moral, if not a spiritual obligation to acquiese [sic] on some of business issues previously raised by President Tanner. This person voiced an unthinkable opinion to the effect that my Church membership took precedent [sic] over my Government responsibilities.

Knowing that you share similar sentiments with me in the clear separation of Church and State, I would like to request that you take this unpleasant matter under advisement with the individual in question and explain just how serious and unconscionable [sic] those inferences were. In the meantime, I will see what else can be done for you.

But for right now I must pursue a course that, at least, seems to be equitable to all parties concerned. Sometimes substantive actions don't count as much as how others perceive them to be. Who would know better about this, Mr. Chairman, than someone in your position. I'll be in touch.

The letter was signed "Jim F."[26]

Fletcher did not identify the specific person connected to Moss who had appealed to his Church membership. Malcolm McConnell, in *Challenger: A Major Malfunction*, relates how Pulitzer Prize–winning journalist Mark Thompson tracked down Ken C. Gardner, Senator Moss's former top aide, and interviewed him on this subject. McConnell quotes Gardner (as reported by Thompson): "There is no question that one of the main reasons Thiokol got the award was because Senator Moss was Chairman of the Aeronautical and Space Sciences Committee and Jim Fletcher was the administrator of NASA."[27]

According to journalist Thompson, Gardner remembered a "furious battle" among the various bidders and at the same time a frustrating "aloofness" of Fletcher to the lobbying, as Fletcher's earlier January 12 letter (quoted above) reveals. Fletcher was struggling to maintain his integrity amid the various pressures to show favoritism to Utah's Thiokol. Later, reported Gardner, Moss's status on the Senate's Committee on Aeronautical and Space Sciences "gave us major clout in lobbying for it. . . . That's where I think our lobbying paid off; that's how these decisions are made."[28] Perhaps the Moss staff person referred to by Fletcher was Gardner; at the very least it was someone like him from Senator Moss's office.

At one point in the 1986 hearings into the booster-rocket-contract controversy, South Carolina's Senator Ernest Hollings, outraged by the evident trail of influence-peddling, accused Fletcher of being part of a "Utah conspiracy."[29] That judgment may seem harsh (Hollings later softened it with a public apology so as not to seem anti-Mormon), but it was echoed by others.

"The only reason we selected that terrible (Thiokol 0-ring) design to begin with was that Fletcher was a Mormon and from Utah," recalled William C. Bush, an engineer now retired from the Marshall Space Flight Center in Huntsville, Alabama. John E. Pike, director of space policy for the Washington-based Federation of American Scientists, concurred: "It's difficult to avoid the conclusion that this is bias and favoritism. Certainly the record suggests that Thiokol should not have gotten the contract."[30] William Wright, an investigator from the GAO representing Senator Gore's Senate committee of inquiry, commented that Pro-Utah and its lobbying efforts had "the imprint of the LDS Church all over it."[31]

Fletcher later gave conflicting accounts of his relationship with Pro-Utah. At his 1971 confirmation as NASA administrator he had never mentioned Pro-Utah *even though he had joined its board of directors in 1965 and as of 1971 served on the lobbying group's executive committee.* Amazingly, in 1986 Fletcher told reporters that he "did not recall" ever having been a part of Pro-Utah. Yet he also admitted:

> I worked with those folks very closely. We were trying to promote Utah
> as a high-tech state successfully. But I don't remember being a member
> of the group."[32]

At the same time, Raymond L. Hixon, Pro–Utah president in 1973, claimed he had visited Fletcher as NASA administrator to lobby for Utah as a site for future shuttle investments and contracts. But Fletcher said he remembered no such Pro–Utah visits while at NASA.[33]

In the Wake of the Challenger: Business as Usual?

The Pro-Utah/Pro-Thiokol/LDS/Moss lobby won. Thiokol received the lucrative contract for a basically flawed booster-rocket design, and as Senator Moss had predicted, it did bring a billion dollars worth of business to Utah. But the odds eventually caught up with the risks, and seven astronauts died as a result. The U.S. space program ground to a halt for over two years. Public confidence in NASA was shaken. Ironically, James C. Fletcher, the man who more than any other was responsible for awarding the booster-rocket contract to Thiokol, was asked to return to NASA in the spring of 1986 to help restore its image. (He had resigned in 1977 to become a faculty member at the University of Pittsburgh, simultaneously starting a successful consulting firm and serving on various corporations' boards of directors.)

In 1986 the GAO probed for any conflict of interest on James C. Fletcher's part and found the former NASA administrator with an unblemished record. They did not uncover any evidence that as NASA's Source Selection Official he had profited personally from the Thiokol contract and had thus (in the GAO's eyes) not violated Executive Order 11222. Fletcher's executive membership in Pro-Utah, from which he later claimed he had "orally resigned" in 1971, was not considered significant grounds for a conflict of interest. The GAO report concluded: "In general, in the absence of some continuing financial interest in an organization, a prior affiliation with that entity is not viewed as raising an 'appearance' problem that would warrant disqualification from official actions affecting that organization."[34] The GAO focused solely on the possibility that Fletcher benefited financially from the Thiokol contract. Failing to find evidence that any member of the Fletcher family enriched himself or herself, the issue was dropped.

But Executive Order 11222 covers more than simply financial enrichment. It also addresses favoritism more generally. Its most critical section reads:

> It is the intent of this section that employees avoid any action, whether or not specifically prohibited . . . which might result in, or create the appearance of—
>
> (1) using public office for private gain;
> (2) giving preferential treatment to any organization or person;
> (3) impeding government efficiency or economy;
> (4) losing complete independence or impartiality of action;

(5) making a government decision outside official channels; or
(6) affecting adversely the confidence of the public in the integrity of the Government.[35]

The GAO actually cleared Fletcher only of the first possible violation. The evidence reviewed here definitely points to a violation of (2) and strongly suggests that violations (3) through (6) occurred as well. However, at this time the U.S. government apparently considers the entire affair closed, however much the public trust appears to have been violated.

Fletcher's return to NASA did not herald the return of the "can-do" optimism that characterized the U.S. space program twenty years earlier. Much of the controversy continued and centered around Morton Thiokol, Inc. Engineers who had unsuccessfully tried to warn Thiokol (as most people still refer to Morton Thiokol) and NASA about the O-ring hazards were hounded or removed to other duties. Not all went quietly, such as Roger Boisjoly. Meanwhile, Morton Thiokol began an extensive fifty-million-dollar effort to redesign the booster rocket in a way that would reduce the O-ring dangers; heaters were added near the rocket's field joints, for example.

But the company was plagued by internal leaks about lax safety procedures, poor morale, hectic schedules that pressed employees into periods of intense fatigue and carelessness, and attempts by the company to suppress criticisms of the rocket design. For example, Morton Thiokol engineer George Schick wrote a four-hundred-page report outlining problems in the company's operating procedures six months after the Challenger explosion, but the report was allegedly destroyed by company executives who were worried that it would encourage more "Thiokol-bashing."[36] Poor observance of safety precautions and a lack of bonafide quality checks had been a major criticism of Morton Thiokol by the Rogers Commission. After Challenger things did not improve.

A June 1986 audit found that Morton Thiokol was not following proper procedures to ground its missile motors to lessen electrical hazards.[37] In December 1987, five Morton Thiokol workers were killed in the explosion of an MX missile motor caused by the discharge of static electricity and friction heat. Air Force investigators blamed the tragedy on poor discipline and faulty observation of safety rules. In its 634-page report, it told how workers had entered a building to remove an internal mold from an MX missile motor filled with one hundred thousand pounds of volatile solid rocket fuel when they should have done the task by remote control. The ensuing fire and explosion were caused by a static electrical spark. Within two months Senator Jack Brooks of Texas requested a congressional investigation of Morton Thiokol.[38]

In November 1986 an engineer named Steven Agee was hired by Morton Thiokol as a safety trouble-shooter. Quickly, however, his identification of obvious safety violations and hazards earned him the label of "troublemaker." In a period of only a few weeks Agee wrote a total of 221 hazard reports on the booster-rocket design, which he referred to as "221 Ways the Space Shuttle Could Blow Up." By January 1987 he found the reports all shelved and his efforts resented by the Morton Thiokol leaders. Agee went to the Federal Bureau of Investigation. The FBI encouraged Agee to stay on at Morton Thiokol as an undercover agent and to continue to observe and report safety/design problems. Agee eventually received court authorization to smuggle out documents and clandestinely record conversations. By June 1988 the FBI had learned enough to begin its formal investigation; it served a number of subpoenas at Morton Thiokol. NASA's inspector general's office also began its investigation of the company.[39]

Unpleasant suspicions were spreading about Morton Thiokol's post–Challenger handling of the booster-rocket controversy. Voices from the aerospace industry, such as Aerojet-General, United Technologies, and Hercules, Inc. began pressuring Congress to end Morton Thiokol's monopoly on booster-rocket production. Competition, some companies contended to budget-minded legislators, could lower rocket costs by as much as one-third. NASA administrator Fletcher came under Senate criticism for not involving other companies in the redesign of the booster rocket. Memories of the suspicions that Fletcher had been too cozy with the Utah connection when the first booster-rocket contract was awarded resurfaced. In late 1986 Fletcher hinted that he would seriously consider removing himself from all future shuttle-contract determinations. Abruptly in early 1987 he did an about-face in defiance of his critics.[40]

But the pressures did not let up. Post-Challenger NASA officials began to speak of a government-owned plant considerably nearer Cape Canaveral where parts for the next generation of booster rockets could be produced and assembled. Morton Thiokol had a virtual monopoly on such production as long as competitors had to bear the tremendous costs of setting up factories without the assurance of a contract. If the government had its own plant, it could lease the facilities and simply contract for the technology. In the twilight of his second administrative era at NASA, a suddenly more independent administrator Fletcher defended the idea, arguing that space-agency officials believed this development would be in the best cost-efficient interests of the future space program.

Yet in spite of this overwhelming evidence of corruption, incompetence, and the economic logic of moving the booster-rocket plant closer to the shuttle's launch site, Utah's two Mormon Senators stubbornly opposed the relocation idea. Their appeal to keep Morton Thiokol's contract in Utah was transparently in the self-interest of keeping government money in their state at any cost. Senator Jake Garn, ranking Republican on the Senate Appropriations Committee that oversaw the NASA budget (and an alumnus of a shuttle flight himself), said the proposal was "stupidity on NASA's part" and said he expected President Reagan (with Garn's urging) to kill it. Meanwhile, Senator Orrin Hatch denounced calls for further investigations of Morton Thiokol as "hitting below the belt."[41]

But their protests sounded like feeble, last-ditch politics. With Morton Thiokol facing criminal prosecution from the FBI's investigation and repeated postponements of the next shuttle launch, Fletcher found his old job would never be like it once was. Early in 1988 Fletcher announced that he would step down at the end of Ronald Reagan's second term.[42]

Conflicts of Interest, Favoritism, and Elite Crime

This chapter has attempted to untangle the complex mesh of religious contacts, favoritism, and conflicts of interest underlying a genuine American tragedy. The cause of the Challenger shuttle's explosion did not begin with the frigid weather conditions on a Cape Canaveral launch pad in January 1986. Those were merely precipitating circumstances. Instead, the causes can be traced back to a faulty rocket design that most likely would never have been adopted were it not for what appears to be, on the basis of strong circumstantial evidence, the religious loyalty of a federal administrator and his bowing to the pressures of a unique religious/business/geographic alliance which coveted the booster rocket for the sake of local development.

It has not been my purpose to single out James C. Fletcher as the prime villain in the Challenger drama. In fairness to Fletcher, he accomplished many remarkable projects during his first six–year term at NASA while working under tightening financial constraints. He supervised three successful moon flights, the entire Skylab space station endeavor, the Apollo-Soyuz project, and unmanned Viking landings on Mars. The Voyagers 1 and 2 solar-system probes were funded and built while he was at NASA and launched shortly after he left to become a businessman and professor at the University of Pittsburgh.[43]

The LDS Church has been previously involved in such patterns of inside influence and use of positions of public trust occupied by its loyal members to benefit its own goals. In *The Mormon Corporate Empire* anthropologist John Heinerman and I analyzed in detail how members of the Church of Jesus Christ of Latter-day Saints who have assumed the Chairmanship of the Federal Communications Commission, ambassadorships in the Foreign Service, seats in Congress, responsible offices in the CIA-FBI intelligence community, and even sensitive positions in the Pentagon have shown little compunction about giving the interests of the LDS Church and/or its members preferential treatment over the interests of non-members.[44] James C. Fletcher, in this sense, deserves credit for having wrestled so long with such pressures for favoritism.

But whether it be an FCC official awarding radio and television-station licenses to Mormons rather than to Gentiles as a matter of policy or a NASA administrator yielding to LDS Church-based pressures to deliver lucrative space-program business to the state where the Church is headquartered, the indications are the same. Elite crime may be more difficult to detect and, in many cases, less sensational. But it is almost always the most expensive and damaging kind of crime.

In this case the space-exploration and national-defense policies of the United States were seriously compromised by Morton Thiokol's mishandling of its booster-rocket responsibilities. Billions of dollars were squandered and seven lives on the Challenger, as well as five lives in the missile-motor explosion at Brigham City, were lost. This was a heavy price to pay for Mormon influence-peddling at NASA, which began in the early seventies.

Epilogue

There is one curious postscript to the LDS/Challenger story. It illustrates the kind of obstacles investigators encounter when they try to uncover information about sensitive scenarios about which the public has a legitimate right to know but which influential interests do not deem "open for inspection."

During research related to *The Mormon Corporate Empire* John Heinerman was the first to discover important correspondence from NASA's James Fletcher to Senator Frank Moss complaining of LDS pressures to give Utah's Thiokol preferential treatment in the booster rocket contract procedure. He inadvertently made this discovery in the University of Utah's collection of Frank E. Moss papers. These letters were shown to several journalists doing post-Challenger stories on Fletcher, NASA, and Morton Thiokol and were shared with William Wright, GAO investigator. One journalist, William Broad, a *New York Times* science journalist, briefly quoted from them in articles he wrote, publicly identifying them for the first time.

Shortly after, during May 1988, Heinerman temporarily misplaced his own copies of the letters and returned to the University of Utah library to make additional ones. He discovered that the originals were missing. Reporting this fact to the librarian, he was surprised at her apparent lack of concern.

Possessing my own photocopies but concerned that the originals might be jeopardized, I soon after contacted the library by telephone in June and requested confirmation that the letters in question were or were not there. After a search a manuscripts staff member replied in writing that the letters could not be found. Later that month, as a check on what I was told, I asked Heinerman once again to return to the library. He found not only that the letters were missing in the Moss collection but that *their very entries in the collection's registry, where he had first discovered them, had been removed.* A pair of smoking guns pointing to the booster-rocket scandal seemed to have been purged from the public record by persons unknown. Later, in November 1989, as a follow-up encouraged by a skeptical colleague who did not believe such a scenario was possible, I made a third attempt to ascertain the existence of the letters. Gregory C. Thompson, Assistant Director for Special Collections, replied to me by letter that the January 12, 1973 letter of James Fletcher to Senator Frank E. Moss was in the collection but that there was no record of the more important February 23, 1973 letter in the files. "It is my understanding that you are indicating you have a copy of the February 23 letter in your possession," Thompson wrote me on November 22, 1989. "If this is so, I would appreciate your sending us a copy of both the letter and the university stamp."[45] I obliged.

Personal copies of the Fletcher letters, bearing the official stamp of the University of Utah libraries, still exist. But someone apparently sought to cover up basic facts of the shuttle booster-rocket controversy once the location of these letters was revealed. The most incriminating one has been removed and either hidden or destroyed.

8

The Shadow of Mormonism

The televangelist scandals of the late 1980s placed conservative Christianity in a fish bowl for millions of Americans to examine, and cynics were not alone in having a good chortle at the antics of Oral Roberts, Jim and Tammy Faye Bakker, and Jimmy Swaggart. First there was Roberts' grotesque "Donate-$8-million-or-God-will-call-me-home" plea (a sort of Divine hostage hustle). Then came the Bakkers' unrepentent greed unappeased even after fleecing PTL Club donors on a scale worthy of the Philippine's Marcos family. And then there was Swaggart's hypocritical refusal to seek help after being defrocked by the Assemblies of God denomination when a third-rate prostitute revealed the Louisiana reverend's voyeuristic fetish. All these controversies provided a virtual carnival for the news media. By June 1987, for example, ABC's "Nightline" had devoted eleven full programs to the PTL affair, the Bakkers delivering to host Ted Koppel his highest ratings ever.[1] It was the most publicized scandal since Watergate.

In comparion, the darker side of Mormon virtue has received much less light. Relatively little has been written on what seems to be a considerable subject, and such revelations have generally been ignored or disbelieved. Partly this is due to the fact that the LDS Church jealously guards its good image. Indeed, through its vast media holdings, broadcast facilities, and public-relations offices, the Church vigorously promotes the ongoing wholesome stereotype of itself that for many persons passes as the complete story. Utahn journalists and other writers also feel considerable pressure to avoid subjects unpleasant or unflattering to Church leadership in a state where so much of the legal, governmental, and law-enforcement establishment is closely aligned with Church loyalties.[2] There is also some reluctance by Mormons and non-Mormons alike to let go of the nostalgic notion that somewhere in this post-Watergate nation there is a fully functioning body of religionists who exemplify the best mythic qualities of indepen- dence, patriotism, sobriety, thrift, and honesty. It is almost as if our Ameri- can romance with the frontier would have made it necessary to idealize and lionize some other sect if the Mormons had not conveniently existed to personify such traditional virtues.

To treat a religion as any other institution, subjecting the consequences of its operations to investigation minus any attempt to promote its faith, is rarely appreciated by either its believers or its leaders. The outside observer invites a defensive response from the religionists. In the case of a religion like the Mormons', with its history of violent persecution and in recent times a complete reversal of its public image from immoral menace to quintessential moral Americana, criticism also ensures that someone will invariably hurl charges of prejudice and bigotry against the critics. There remains not much middle ground for the open discussion of a religion's less-than-ennobling qualities without raising hackles and prompting accusations of hate-mongering.

Yet as this volume and *The Mormon Corporate Empire* have docu- mented, there is undeniably a "shadow" behind the public reputation and unique, complex subculture of the LDS Church. The term "shadow" is used by psychologists to refer to the "dark, feared, unwanted side" of human personality. The "shadow" represents those qualities that are kept hidden, out of sight, and out of conscious thought so as to preserve a more acceptable, flattering self-image.[3]

Mormondom has an analogous "shadow." It is discussed from time to time by relatively small groups of Mormons at formal meetings, such as the annual Sunstone Symposia, but only in fragments. The Hofmann bombings, for example, are usually understood as the desperate acts of a lone sociopathic con-artist and are seldom linked to the LDS hierarchy's Orwellian determination to put a lock on the Church's history and stifle authentic scholarship. Discrimination against Hispanic FBI agents by Mormon superiors is never connected to other patterns of apparent favoritism in the U.S. government, such as the circumstances surrounding NASA's awarding a rocket contract to Utah's Morton Thiokol company. The pattern emerges in pieces but is not acknowledged as a whole.

The courage and tenacity with which LDS Church members weathered their first half-century of persecution have been rewarded with regional power and national acceptance. But there is a profound price paid when any religion makes its peace with the world and accommodates comfortably to society's institutions. A successful movement transforms itself into a church bureaucracy which comes to prize its own sociological imperatives of protecting growth and authority above all else. Diversity becomes heresy, dissent turns into danger, and human needs become sacrificed to organizational requisites. Preserving the official party line of its own history by secretly purchasing and then hiding away documents that the leadership believes to be authentic is merely one such telling example.

So is quashing the spirit of criticism and dissent. In 1985 Dallin Oaks, a former Utah judge and member of the Quorum of the Twelve Apostles, warned LDS followers that group-think is the order of the day. "Criticism is particularly objectionable when it is directed toward church authorities," he said. "Evil speaking of the Lord's annointed is in a class by itself. . . . It does not matter that the criticism is true."[4]

A generation before, this authoritarian mind-set had already been established for the Mormon rank and file. Wrote one leader in 1945:

> *When our leaders speak, the thinking has been done.* When they propose a plan—it is God's plan. When they point the way, there is no other which is safe. When they give direction it should mark the end of controversy. God works in no other way.[5] [Italics in the original.]

Contrast that lockstep marching mentality with a 1852 editorial in the *Millennial Star* (an English Mormon periodical) and its freer, more fallible image of hierarchical authority as the original converts understood it:

> The question is sometimes asked to what extent is obedience to those who hold the Priesthood required. This is a very important question, and one which should be understood by all Saints. In attempting to answer this question, we would repeat, in short, what we have already written, that willing obedience to the laws of God, administered by the Priesthood, is indispensable to salvation. *But we would further add, that a proper conservative to this power exists for the benefit of all, and none are required to tamely and blindly submit to a man because he has a portion of the Priesthood.*[6] [Italics added.]

The slide down the slippery slope of accommodation to the world involves compromise, temptations to employ coercion rather than reason or inspiration to enforce ideals, and the enjoyment of worldly integration into secular corridors of influence. In the Mormon case this progression has been accelerated by the LDS Church's original postmillennial theology. This expectation that Christ will return to rule among the Saints has, at least indirectly, come to justify and even glorify worldly success apart from its meaning as a sign of spiritual blessing. As modern Mormon critics themselves have noted, greed has moved in with only the slimmest veneer of theological rationalization.

To be sure, Mormons are not special in being susceptible to fraud and come-ons laced with religious overtones. In 1989 the National Council of Better Business Bureaus and the North American Securities Administrations Association issued a report that surveyed religion-based business scams over the previous five years. It found that fifteen thousand American citizens lost a minimum total of $415 million in such crimes. Many of the victims were fundamentalist Christians, many of the schemes were familiar Ponzi pyramids, and most involved networks of church-going believers manipulated by charismatic and, surprisingly, sincerely self-believing leaders. One Utah investment expert, noting the lack of comparative data available either on a state-by-state basis or by religious group, nevertheless cited the report as relevant to the fraud problem in Utah if only because this particular economic problem contrasts so sharply with the popular image of Mormons. He said:

> I think we set ourselves up for this. We portray ourselves as being awfully, awfully good. And when we aren't awfully good, it makes news and that makes grist for the rumor mill.[7]

What the economist did not say was that even if the economic fraud problem is no worse among Mormons in Utah than among, say, United Methodists or Southern Baptists, then why are many Utahn Latter-day Saints increasingly preoccupied with talking about it? And at that meeting it was announced that the U.S. Attorney General's office in Utah had established a Fair Business Unit, staffed by six full-time attorneys, to prosecute fraud.

Meanwhile, the LDS Church strenuously pursues its mandate to spread the Reformed Gospel revealed by Joseph Smith across the globe, its determination unchecked by reflection on its shadow aspects. The sudden receptivity of the Soviet Union and other Eastern bloc countries to religious missions has encouraged the Church, and prospective LDS missionaries are now studying Russian along with Japanese, Finnish, Polish, and dozens of other languages. The Church mission machinery has never been more mobilized to take advantage of this new political situation.

And amid such developments in 1990, LDS Church headquarters in Salt Lake City unexpectedly issued a low-key announcement that in some ways rocked Mormondom and even briefly caught the attention of the rest of North America. In April of that year Church spokespersons issued a proclamation that, among other things, secret Temple rituals for married couples would no longer require wives to swear absolute allegiance to their husbands (just as the men swear allegiance to God and the LDS Church) and that an unflattering caricature of a non-Mormon preacher in one of the sacred dramas would be dropped. Given the little publicized but widely shared repugnance of many Mormon women to the allegiance-swearing part of the temple ceremony, this first change was heralded by the more feminist oriented Saints as a positive move into the late twentieth century. Much less was made of ending the practice of portraying non-Mormon clergy as Satan's agents on earth, but it, too, was a positive step toward the LDS Church accepting its place in American religious pluralism.

Small changes to outsiders, perhaps. In the long history of religious and human liberties the LDS Church's modification of its temple ceremony, a catechism as far removed for most Americans as a Siberian shaman's dance, will probably set no memorials or holidays. But such charges demonstrate the truism that no religious faith or church is immutable, and that includes the shadow side of virtue as well.

Notes

Chapter 1: The Darker Side of Virtue

1. "Pres. Reagan Writes to Elder," *Church News,* August 22, 1981, p. 11.
2. "Elder Decries Criticism of LDS Leaders," *Salt Lake Tribune,* August 18, 1985.
3. "What's Wrong," *Time Magazine,* June 27, 1987, p. 22.
4. Mark E. Peterson, "When Shall It Be?" *Church News,* December 2, 1981, p. 16.
5. Thomas G. Alexander, *Mormonism in Transition* (Urbana, Ill: University of Illinois Press, 1985), p. 139.
6. Leonard J. Arrington and Davis Bitton, *The Mormon Experience* (New York: Alfred A. Knopf, 1979), p. 292.
7. Linda Cicero, "How the Mormons Helped Scuttle ERA," *Miami Herald,* June 20, 1980.
8. John Heinerman and Anson Shupe, *The Mormon Corporate Empire* (Boston: Beacon Press, 1985).

Chapter 2: The Myth of Mormon Missionizing

1. Neal A. Maxwell, "The Church Can Now Be Universal with Priesthood Revelation of 1978," *Church News,* January 5, 1980, p. 20.
2. See Arrington and Bitton, *The Mormon Experience,* Chapter 7, for a comprehensive picture of the roles that immigration and conversion played in building the early LDS Church.
3. Rodney Stark and William Sims Bainbridge, "Networks of Faith: Interpersonal Bonds and Recruitment to Cults and Sects," *American Journal of Sociology* 85 (May 1980): pp. 1386–1387.
4. For a description of similar tactics, see David G. Bromley and Anson D. Shupe, Jr., *Strange Gods: The Great American Cult Scare* (Boston: Beacon Press, 1981), pp. 92–127.

5. "Three Missionary Milestones," *Church News,* April 21, 1985, p. 10.

6. John Heinerman and Anson Shupe, *The Mormon Corporate Empire* (Boston: Beacon Press, 1985), pp. 46–56.

7. Ibid, p. 57.

8. *Deseret News 1985 Church Almanac* (Salt Lake City: Deseret News Press, 1984), pp. 227–234.

9. Author's interview with Walter Cannells, vice-president of international public relations, Bonneville Media Productions, Salt Lake City, May 20, 1985.

10. Ibid.

11. Ibid.

12. Arch Madsen, quoted in Richard Barnum-Reece, "Arch Madsen," *This People* 2, no. 6 (1981): p. 46.

13. "Orthodox Jews Hold Mass Pray-in Against Construction of LDS Center," *Salt Lake Tribune,* July 17, 1985.

14. Heinerman and Shupe, *The Mormon Corporate Empire* (see note 6), pp. 229–233.

15. Bob Gottlieb and Peter Wiley, "Triad Utah: Angels or Flying Carpetbaggers?" *Utah Holiday* (March 1983), p. 45.

16. Robert Gottlieb and Peter Wiley, *America's Saints: The Rise of Mormon Power* (New York: Putnam, 1984), pp. 115–117.

17. Author's interview with an anonymous informant, LDS Church International Mission Office, Salt Lake City, January 19, 1984; also personal correspondence with Jan Krancher, July 29, 1983, from Madinat Al-Jubail Al-Sinaiyah, Saudi Arabia.

18. Author's interviews with two ARAMCO employees at Star Valley, Wyoming, May 7, 1986, and with an anonymous LDS bishop in Ridyadh, Saudi Arabia, by telephone, May 7, 1986.

19. Ibid.

20. Author's interview with Paul Grimshaw, Salt Lake North Mission, Salt Lake City, May 15, 1986.

21. R. Clayton Brough, *His Servants Speak* (Bountiful, Utah: Horizon Publishers, 1975), p. 77.

22. LDS Church, *My Kingdom Shall Roll Forth* (Salt Lake City: The Church of Jesus Christ of Latter-day Saints, 1980), p. 108.

23. Alexv Adjoubey, *The Silver Cat, Or Travels in America* (Moscow, 1956). A portion of the English translation was discovered in the Frank Moss Papers, Box 215, Folder 22, Western Americana Section, Marriott Library, University of Utah Library, Salt Lake City.

24. Author's interview with Dr. Phyllis Jacobson, chairperson of the Dance Department, Brigham Young University, Provo, Utah, January 16, 1982; also interview with the director, Office of Performance Scheduling, Brigham Young University, Provo, January 16, 1982.

25. "Y Dancers Honored," *Church News,* October 6, 1979, p. 13.

26. "Touring Groups Touch Hearts," *Church News,* June 20, 1981, p. 4.

27. Mark Jackson, "Communist Lands Have Future," *Daily Universe,* Provo, Utah, November 9, 1978.

28. Letter of O. Kendall White, Jr. to LDS President Hugh B. Brown, Salt

Lake City, October 30, 1967. Copy provided to the author by O. Kendall White, Jr., Department of Sociology and Anthropology, Washington and Lee University, Lexington, Va.

29. "Are Russians Ready for the Mormons?" *Latter-day Sentinel,* October 15, 1988; "Has the First Missionary to Russia Already Been Called?" *Latter-day Sentinel,* October 15, 1988.

30. "DDR Will Allow Exchange of Missionaries," *Deseret News,* November 5, 1988.

31. Cited in Philip Yancey, "Czechoslovakia's Theater of the Absurd," *Christianity Today,* April 23, 1990, p. 64.

32. Arthur D. Moore, "After the Thaw," *Christianity Today,* April 23, 1990, p. 24.

33. A chronology of the modern LDS "China mission" can be found in Heinerman and Shupe, *The Mormon Corporate Empire* (see note 6), pp. 219–222.

34. News broadcasts on KSL-TV, Channel 5, Salt Lake City, July 17-18, 1989.

35. Kenneth L. Woodward, "Onward, Mormon Soldiers," *Newsweek,* April 27, 1981, pp. 87–88.

36. Howard M. Bahr and Stan L. Albrecht, "Strangers Once More: Patterns of Disaffiliation from Mormonism," *Journal for the Scientific Study of Religion* (June 1989), pp. 180–200.

37. John Heinerman and Anson Shupe, "Book of Mormons and Baseballs," paper presented at the annual Sunstone Symposium, Salt Lake City, August 1989.

Chapter 3: Wolves Among the Fold: Scams and Schemes in Zion

1. Author's interview with Brent Hunsaker, KSL-TV reporter and bureau chief for Utah County, Salt Lake City, December 29, 1982.

2. Muriel Dobin, "Mormons Put Faith, Money in Fellow Man: Men Cash In," *The Oregonian,* March 12, 1982; "Con Man's Paradise," *Austin American Statesman,* July 8, 1983; and *NBC Nightly News* broadcast, December 29, 1983.

3. Dobin "Mormons Put Faith" (see note 2).

4. Author's interview with Tony Mulbury, investigator for the U.S. Postal Service, San Francisco, January 15, 1983.

5. "Educator Says Utahns Financially Gullible," *Salt Lake Tribune,* August 1, 1983; Dobin, "Mormons Put Faith" (see note 2).

6. "LDS Aide Attacks Rise in White Collar Crime," *Salt Lake Tribune,* June 25, 1982.

7. *General Handbook of Instruction* (Salt Lake City: Church of Jesus Christ of Latter-day Saints, 1983).

8. "Utahns Are Natural Targets for Fraud, Dialogue Guests Say," *Deseret News,* June 26, 1983.

9. See, e.g., Stephen D. Nadauld, "Welcome to the Church of Hakeem: Recognizing Frauds and Scams," *Exchange* (Fall 1982): pp. 3–6; and (same issue) Paul R. Timm,"Editor's Corner," p. 1.

10. Hugh Nibley, "Leaders to Managers: The Fatal Shift." *Dialogue: A Journal of Mormon Thought* 16 (Winter 1983): p. 15.

11. Marden Clark, "Whose Yoke Is Easy?" *Sunstone Review,* November-December 1982, p. 43.

12. David W. Maurer, *The American Confidence Man* (Springfield, Ill.: Charles C. Thomas, 1974), p. 4.

13. Brett DelPorto, "3,800 Victims of Scam May Never Recover Funds," *Deseret News,* June 18, 1983.

14. Charles Seldin, "Complex Dealings Surround Fraud Charges," *Salt Lake Tribune,* June 30, 1983.

15. Author's interview with William Fowler, attorney for the Bankruptcy Court trustee, Salt Lake City, June 30, 1983.

16. Author's interview with Linda Campbell, assistant to attorney Robert Merrill, court-appointed trustee for International Clearing House, Salt Lake City, June 31, 1983.

17. Ibid.

18. Author's interview with Ronald W. Goss, attorney for the Bankruptcy Court trustee, Salt Lake City, June 30, 1983.

19. Hugh W. Pinnock, "Ethical Consistency: Tuning Out Misguidance," *Exchange* (Fall 1982): p. 20.

20. "Authorities Arrest Suspect in Fraud," *Salt Lake Tribune,* September 4, 1983.

21. *United States of America vs. Grant C. Affleck,* United States District Court for the District of Utah, Central Division, Salt Lake City, September 26, 1984, *Reporter's Transcript,* vol. 17, p. 3180.

22. Victor F. Zanana, "Leaders of Mormonism Double as Overseers of a Financial Empire," *Wall Street Journal,* November 9, 1983.

23. *United States of America vs. Grant C. Affleck* (see note 21), vol. 1, p. 17.

24. "Affleck Begins 10-year Term in California Prison Camp," *Salt Lake Tribune,* January 3, 1985.

25. *United States of America vs. Grant C. Affleck* (see note 21), final volume, pp. 16, 18.

26. From a prospectus issued by Memorial Estates Security Corporation, August 20, 1960. It is attachment III of evidence in Civil No. C-98-67 field by James F. and Caroline B. Cottam in United States District Court for Utah, Central Division, in Salt Lake City, but currently stored at the Federal Records Center in Denver, Colorado. Hereafter we refer to this file as Civil No. C-98-67. All quotations of plaintiffs originate in this document. Because of the controversial nature of this case and the fact that one of the participants became an LDS Apostle, we have placed our more detailed research notes in the archives of Dr. J. Gordon Melton, Director, The Institute for the Study of American Religion, University of California, Santa Barbara, Calif.

27. Letter of Royal K. Hunt to Joseph C. Rich, November 1960, Civil No. C-98-67, item no. D-26.

28. "Minutes of a Board of Directors Meeting of Mountain View Memorial Estates, Inc.," Civil No. C-98-67. Item no. D-25.

29. "Stockholders Report," Civil No. C-98-67.

30. See note 26.

31. "Deposition of Scott B. Passey," Civil No. C-98-67, p. 35.

32. See note 26.

33. A copy of the letter from Morris A. Shirts to Bruce R. McConkie is attached to Shirts's copy of "Written Instructions and Answers Thereto," filed January 7, 1969, in Civil No. C-98-67.

34. "Order Approving Settlement and Respecting Settlement and Distribution Procedures," p. 2, filed June 13, 1969, in Civil No. C-98-67.

35. Stan Jones, "Anatomy of an International Adoption Network," *Fort Worth Star-Telegram,* June 27, 1984.

36. Carolyn Poirot and Stan Jones, "Mormons Revising Policy in Adoptions," *Fort Worth Star-Telegram,* February 14, 1984.

37. Stan Jones, "U.S. to Contend Adoption Ring Built on Fraud," *Fort Worth Star-Telegram,* February 14, 1985.

38. Stan Jones, "International Adoption Network" (see note 35).

39. Stan Jones, "U.S. to Contend Adoption Ring" (see note 36).

40. Stan Jones, "International Adoption Network" (see note 35).

41. Ibid.

42. Stan Jones, "El Paso Bar Owner Enters Guilty Plea in Adoption Fraud," *Fort Worth Star-Telegram,* June 10, 1985.

43. In order for Mormons to enter and participate in temple functions they must obtain "temple recommends." These are endorsements or certifications by their bishops and stake presidents confirming that they faithfully tithe, attend LDS Church functions, and contribute to Church projects as well as lead generally righteous lives. The tithe is, of course, a biblical injunction to give one-tenth of one's (gross) income to the Church. Fast offerings are collected periodically when members eat nothing or relatively little at certain meals and contribute the money otherwise spent to Church-sponsored charities.

44. Author's interview with Kathryn Lynne Bird Johnson, Heber City, Utah, January 1983.

45. Ibid.

46. Ibid.

47. "Utahn Sentenced to 5 Prison Terms for Bilking Mormons," *Deseret News,* February 2, 1983; KUTV-TV news broadcast, Salt Lake City, December 22, 1982.

48. Paul Swenson, "Nostrums in the Newsroom," *Dialogue: A Journal of Mormon Thought* 10 (Spring 1977): p. 50.

49. Ibid, p. 52; John Heinerman and Anson Shupe, *The Mormon Corporate Empire* (Boston: Beacon Press, 1985), pp. 40–41.

50. Letter of Sterling W. Sill to James W. McConkie, Attorney at Law, Salt Lake City, June 2, 1981.

51. "Affidavit in Support of Motion for Reduction of Sentence," Docket No. CR79-00062, *United States of America vs. Snellen M. Johnson,* United States Court for the District of Utah, Central Division.

52. Sill letter (see note 50).

53. Letter of Victor L. Brown to James W. McConkie, Attorney at Law, Salt Lake City, June 30, 1981.

54. "Amended Judgment and Probation/Commitment Order," Docket No. CR-79-62 A, *United States of America vs. Snellen M. Johnson,* United States Court for the District of Utah, Central Division.

55. Author's interview with Kathryn Johnson (see note 44).

56. Author's interview with Delane Findley, trial attorney for the Security and Exchange Commission in Salt Lake City, January 6, 1983.

57. Author's interview with Kathryn Johnson (see note 44).

58. "Utahn Sentenced," *Deseret News* (see note 47).

59. "Eight-Year Prison Term Given in Fraud Trial," *Deseret News,* June 11, 1983.

60. Author's interview with Kathryn Johnson (see note 44).

61. Author's interview with Delane Findley (see note 56).

62. Letter of Victor L. Brown to James W. McConkie, Attorney at Law, Salt Lake City, January 9, 1981.

63. "Utahn Sentenced," *Deseret News* (see note 47).

64. "Judge Denies Bid to Close Hearing in Granada Case," *Salt Lake Tribune,* May 2, 1989; "Businessman Going to Prison for Fraud," *Salt Lake Tribune,* August 7, 1990.

65. Jerry Spangler, "Telemarketing Frauds Find Utah," *Deseret News,* March 18, 1989.

66. "S.L. Stock Promoter Is Target of Federal Fraud Probe" and "Suspect in Massive Fraud Flaunts His Wealth," *Salt Lake Tribune,* January 8, 1989.

67. Author's interview with Delane Findley (see note 56).

68. Ibid.

69. Ibid.

Chapter 4: The Tales of Hofmann: Forgery, Deceit, and Murder

1. "These Are Our Suspects," *Salt Lake Tribune,* October 16, 1985.

2. Robert Lindsey, *A Gathering of Saints* (New York: Simon & Schuster, 1988), p. 21.

3. Ibid; Steven Naifeh and Gregory White Smith, *The Mormon Murders* (New York: Weidenfeld & Nicholson, 1988); Linda Sillitoe and Allen D. Roberts, *Salamander* (Salt Lake City: Signature Books, 1988).

4. Naifeh and Smith (see note 3), p. 75.

5. Sillitoe and Roberts (see note 3), pp. 216-17.

6. Naifeh and Smith (see note 3), p. 374.

7. Lindsey (see note 2), p. 373.

8. Naifeh and Smith (see note 3), p. 374.

9. Sillitoe and Roberts (see note 3), pp. 304-305

10. "Teachers Given Formula for Reading LDS History," *Church News,* August 25, 1988. John Heinerman and Anson Shupe, *The Mormon Corporate Empire* (Boston: Beacon Press, 1985), pp. 202-15, discusses the LDS church's meager toleration for internal criticism and its penchant for censorship of its own, not only of church-salaried historians and member scholars but also even of university students.

11. Bob Gottlieb and Peter Wiley, "Mormon Infighting Intensifies as Theologians Vie for Power," *Daily Californian* (Berkeley), April 16, 1982, p. 20.

12. Blake Ostler, "7EP Interview: Sterling M. McMurrin," *Seventh East Press,* January 11, 1983, p. 3.

13. Naifch and Smith (see note 3), p. 112.

14. "Police Find Fat Checks in Blown-up Car," *Salt Lake Tribune,* October 18, 1985.

15. "Eastern Dealer Calls Documents 'Obvious' Fakes," *Deseret News,* February 7, 1987.

16. Jan Thompson, "Prosecutor Says Confession by Hofmann Was Chilly," *Deseret News,* January 25, 1987.

17. From transcript titled "Supplementary Notes to Transcripts of the Confession of Mark Hofmann, prepared by Deputy Salt Lake County Attorney's Robert L. Stott and David Biggs, titled *Hofmann's Confession,* vol. I (reprinted by the Utah Lighthouse Ministry, Salt Lake City, 1987), p. SS-8.

18. Author's interview with Alvin Rust, Salt Lake City, June 26, 1986.

19. Anonymous informant, LDS Church Historical Department, Salt Lake City, Utah.

20. Sillitoe and Roberts (see note 3), p. 504.

Chapter 5: The Lehi Child-Sexual-Abuse Scare

1. Paul Rolly, "Did Hadfield Case Leave Nothing But Losers?" *Salt Lake Tribune,* December 27, 1987.

2. Paul Rolly, "Hadfield Challenges Children's Testimony." *Salt Lake Tribune,* December 18, 1987.

3. JoAnn Jacobsen-Wells and Ken Perkins, "Utah Shows Caution, Concern About Sex Abuse," *Deseret News,* January 13, 1988.

4. Paul Rolly, "Therapist Testified Children Named 40 as Sex Abusers," *Salt Lake Tribune,* December 16, 1987.

5. Paul Rolly, "Lehi Sex Case Yields First Set of Charges," *Salt Lake Tribune,* May 20, 1987.

6. James J. Mead, quoted in Carol Sisco, "Child Abusers Rarely Fit Stereotypes, Expert Says," *Salt Lake Tribune,* March 25, 1988.

7. Douglas J. Besharov, "The Child Abuse Numbers Game," *Wall Street Journal,* August 4, 1988.

8. *Annual Report: 1986. Central Register for Child Abuse and Neglect.* State of Utah, Department of Social Services, Division of Family Services: 3-8.

9. "Utah 13th in Child Abuse," *Sunstone Review,* October 1985, p. 5.

10. Author's interview with Christine Mitchell, Director of Planning and Research, Utah Department of Corrections. February 9, 1988.

11. *Study of National Incidence and Prevalence of Child Abuse and Neglect: 1988* (Washington, D.C.: U.S. Department of Health and Human Services et al.), pp. xiii-7.5.

12. Boyd C. Rollins and Craig K. Manscill, "Family Violence in Utah," in

Thomas Martin, Tom B. Heaton, and Stephen J. Bahr, eds., *Utah in Demographic Perspective* (Salt Lake City: Signature Books, 1986), pp. 163–164.

13. Author's interview with Gary Jensen, Child Protective Services specialist, Utah Division of Family Services, December 18, 1987.

14. Author's interview with Leslie Lewis, Salt Lake County deputy prosecutor, January 22, 1988.

15. Author's interview with Thomas Harrison, clinical social worker, December 29, 1987.

16. Author's interview with Dr. C. Y. Roby, Intermountain Sexual Abuse Treatment Center, Salt Lake City, January 8, 1988.

17. "Utah 13th in Child Abuse," *Sunstone Review* (see note 9).

18. Opening remarks by Elder Gordon B. Hinckley, 156th General Conference of the LDS Church, April 1986, Salt Lake City. Personal observations by the authors.

19. Author's interview with Barbara Thomas, clinical social worker and director, Salt Lake County Child Abuse Coordinating Committee, December 22, 1987.

20. Author's interview with Gary Jensen (see note 13).

21. William Stacey and Anson Shupe, *The Family Secret: Domestic Violence in America* (Boston: Beacon Press, 1983).

22. Author's interview with Gary Jensen (see note 13).

23. Author's interview with Leslie Lewis (see note 14).

24. "Social Ills Created At Home," *Salt Lake Tribune,* October 13, 1982.

25. Rolly, "Hadfield Challenges Children's Testimony" (see note 2).

26. Rolly, "Did Hadfield Case Leave Nothing But Losers?" (see note 1).

27. Paul Rolly, "Psychologist Says He Was Forced to Investigate Abuse Stories," *Salt Lake Tribune,* December 17, 1987.

28. Ken Perkins, "Hadfield Testifies He Didn't Abuse His Children," *Deseret News,* December 18, 1987.

29. Paul Rolly, "Did Hadfield Case Leave Nothing But Losers?" (see note 1).

30. JoAnn Jacobsen-Wells and Ken Perkins, "Utah Shows Caution" (see note 3).

31. Paul Rolly, "Is Therapist Child Sex-Abuse Link? Investigator Places Ad for Lawyers," *Salt Lake Tribune,* May 8, 1988; Paul Rolly, "Sexual Probe Dropped, Sources Say," *Salt Lake Tribune,* April 26, 1988.

32. See Marion L. Starkey, *The Devil in Massachusetts* (Garden City, N.Y.: Doubleday, 1969); Chadwick Hansen, *Witchcraft At Salem* (New York: New American Library, 1969).

33. David Hechler, *The Battle and the Backlash: The Child Abuse War* (Lexington, Mass.: D.C. Heath–Lexington Books, 1988), p. 3; David L. Kirp, "Hug Your Kid, Go to Jail," *American Spectator,* June 1985, p. 33.

34. Mary Pride, *The Child Abuse Industry* (Westchester, Ill.: Crossway Books, 1986), pp. 43–44.

35. David G. Bromley, "Folk Narratives and Deviance Construction: Cautionary Tales As a Response to Structural Tensions in the Social Order," unpublished paper presented at the annual meeting of the American Sociological Association, Washington, D.C., August 1989.

36. John Crewdson, *By Silence Betrayed* (Boston: Little, Brown, 1988), pp. 95–113; Joel Best and Gerald Horiuchi, "Rhetoric in Claims-Making: Constructing the Missing Children Problem," *Social Problems* 34 (1987): pp. 101–121; Joel Best and Gerald Horiuchi, "The Razor Blade in the Apple: The Social Construction of Urban Legends," *Social Problems* 32 (1985): pp. 488–499.

Chapter 6: LDS in the FBI: The Case of the Mormon Mafia

1. Jerry Spangler, "FBI Slips into a More Comfortable Image," *Deseret News,* December 23, 1984.

2. CIA recruiter cited in "Missionaries and the CIA," *Sunstone Review,* November-December 1981, p. 9.

3. Author's interview with Jeffrey Willis, personnel director, Central Intelligence Agency, Sterling, Va., April 1, 1982; see a longer description of CIA recruiting of LDS missionaries in John Heinerman and Anson Shupe, *The Mormon Corporate Empire* (Boston: Beacon Press, 1985), pp. 162–68; Jerry Spangler, "A More Comfortable Image" (see note 1).

4. In the remainder of this chapter, unless otherwise noted, quotes, accusations, claims, and descriptions come primarily from three sources. The first source consists of legal documents, particularly a class-action suit filed January 14, 1987, in the United States District Court for the Western District of Texas, El Paso Division, entitled *BERNARDO M. PEREZ, on behalf of himself and all others similarly situated, Plaintiffs, V. Federal Bureau of Investigation, Department of Justice, EDWIN MEESE, III, Attorney General of the United States, WILLIAM H. WEBSTER, Director, Federal Bureau of Investigation.* In addition I have drawn upon legal documents, including a *Transcript of Proceedings,* covering the inclusive dates August 15–25, 1988 (9 vols.), for the above court hearings before the Honorable Lucius D. Bunton, III, and a transcript of Judge Bunton's *Findings of Fact and Conclusions of Law* on the *Perez V. FBI* case dated September 30, 1988. The second source is a series of journalistic articles covering not only the Richard Miller espionage case but also the events of the class-action suit of the Hispanic FBI agents during 1987 and 1988. In particular, two El Paso, Texas, newspapers covered the court proceedings and general lawsuit stories extensively. Many of the observations and opinions attributed to major actors in the drama, if not taken from court proceedings, originated in the local newspaper coverage. In particular, several journalists deserve credit for their extensive coverage: Teresa Kramer, Leon Lynn, Peter Brock, Raul Hernandes, and Leticia Zamarripa of the *El Paso Herald-Post,* and Ramon Bracamontes of the *El Paso Times.* The third source consists of several Hispanic FBI agents who reviewed and constructively criticized an earlier draft of a manuscript of this chapter and corrected inaccuracies.

5. Author's telephone interview with Bernardo M. Perez, Deputy Assistant Director of the Main Laboratory, Federal Bureau of Investigation, March 1, 1989; see also Frank Ahlgren, Jr., "FBI Agent Shoots Down Stereotypical Image of Lawman." *El Paso Herald-Post,* February 26, 1987.

6. Joe Old, "FBI Agent's Lawyer Says El Paso Assignment 'Retaliation' for suit," *El Paso Herald-Post,* January 15, 1987.

176   NOTES

7. Author's telephone interview with Bernardo M. Perez, (see note 5); March 1, 1989; see also Teresa Kramer and Leon Lynn, "Agent Says Bosses Jealous," *El Paso Herald-Post,* August 17, 1988.

8. Ahlgren, "FBI Agent Shoots Down Stereotypical Image" (see note 5).

9. "Ex-agent Had Problems, Officials Say," *Dallas Morning News,* October 5, 1984. See also Judith Cummings, "U.S. Agent Accused of Espionage, Reportedly Had Work Problems," *New York Times,* October 5, 1984.

10. An FBI agent quoted in "Probe of L.A. FBI Office," *Los Angeles Times,* October 18, 1984.

11. See, for example, Linda Deutsch, "FBI Arrests Own Agent for Spying," *Salt Lake Tribune,* October 4, 1984.

12. "Files Show LDS Supervisor Urged an Alleged FBI Spy to 'Repent,' " *Salt Lake Tribune,* January 1, 1984.

13. Judith Cummings, "U.S. Agent Accused of Espionage" (see note 9).

14. "FBI to Evaluate Its L.A. Offices in Wake of Espionage Arrest," *Deseret News,* October 18, 1984.

15. Jose Antonio Lopez, U.S. Marshal Liaison in Organized Crime (Miami, Florida) in *Testimony,* vol. 9, pp. 140–145.

16. See, for example, statements made in *Testimony* (vol. 4, pp. 191–197; vol. 7, pp. 42–44) by FBI Special Agent John Hoos and John Otto, Executive Assistant Director of Law Enforcement Services, respectively.

17. FBI Special Agent John Hoos, *Testimony,* vol. 4, p. 195.

18. A report of trial testimony by Teresa Kramer, "Former Boss Faults Perez's Work," *El Paso Herald-Post,* August 25, 1988.

19. FBI Special Agent John Hoos, in *Testimony,* vol. 4, p. 192.

20. FBI Special agent John Hoos, in *Testimony,* vol. 4, p. 193.

21. Frank Ahlgren, Jr., "Hispanic FBI Agents Testify About Bias," *El Paso Herald-Post,* June 23, 1987.

22. FBI Special Agent John Hoos, in *Testimony,* vol. 4, pp. 196-197.

23. Berta Rodriguez, "Agents Tell Horror Stories in FBI Discrimination Trial," *El Paso Times,* August 17, 1988.

24. FBI Special Agent John Hoos, in *Testimony,* vol. 4, pp. 198ff.

25. "Hispanic FBI Agents Testify About Discrimination," *El Paso Herald-Post,* August 17, 1988.

26. FBI Special Agent Samuel Carlos Martinez, in *Testimony,* vol. 3, p. 116.

27. FBI Special Agent John Hoos, in *Testimony,* vol. 4, p. 201.

28. Teresa Kramer and Leon Lynn.

29. FBI Special Agent John Hoos, in *Testimony,* vol. 4, p. 198.

30. FBI Special Agent John Hoos, in *Testimony,* vol. 4, pp. 204–205.

31. FBI Special Agent John Hoos, in *Testimony,* vol. 4, pp. 204–205.

32. Jim Bole, "Agent Seeks Injunction Against FBI," *El Paso Herald-Post,* November 20, 1987.

33. "Hispanic FBI Agents Take on the 'Mormon Mafia,' " *In These Times,* April 27, 1988.

34. Ibid.

35. David Rarity, FBI Personnel Officer, in *Testimony,* vol. 1, p. 64.

36. Berta Rodriguez.

37. FBI Special Agent Samuel Carlos Martinez, in *Testimony,* vol. 3, pp. 93–111.

38. FBI Special Agent Samuel Carlos Martinez, in *Testimony,* vol. 3, p. 116.

39. "Ex-FBI Chief Knew of Some Bias, Lawyer Says," *El Paso Times,* August 18, 1988.

40. Berta Rodriguez.

41. See, for example, Teresa Kramer, "Paper on Perez Withheld," *El Paso Herald-Post,* August 24, 1988; Teresa Kramer, "Squabble Erupts at FBI Trial," *El Paso Herald-Post,* August 26, 1988.

42. FBI Special Agent in Charge Richard T. Bretzing, in *Testimony,* vol. 8, p. 76.

43. See Lucius D. Bunton, Chief Judge, United States District Court for the Western District of Texas, El Paso Division. *Order* handed down in the matter of *Bernardo M. Perez v. Federal Bureau of Investigation et al.* (Court document EP-87-CA-10), September 28, 1988.

44. Raul Hernandez, "Decision Hits Hard for FBI," *El Paso Herald-Post,* October 1, 1988.

45. Leticia Zamarripa, "Various Meanings Read into FBi Pledge on Bias," *El Paso Herald-Post,* March 2, 1989; "New Position Will Counter Discrimination in the FBI," *El Paso Herald-Post,* March 1, 1989.

46. Leticia Zamarripa.

47. For a discussion of this concept in relation to both military and intelligence communities, see Heinerman and Shupe, *The Mormon Corporate Empire* (see note 3), pp. 176–8.

48. Bernardo M. Perez, in *Testimony,* vol. 9, p. 106.

49. "FBI Agent Will Retire to Head Church Security," *Church News,* April 2, 1988.

Chapter 7: The Challenger Shuttle Disaster

1. Chuck Gates, "Morton Thiokol After Challenger," *Deseret News,* January 25, 1987.

2. Malcolm McConnell, *Challenger: A Major Malfunction* (Garden City, N.Y.: Doubleday, 1987), p. 7.

3. Ibid., p. 7.

4. Eric Naider and Peter Lewis, "Beyond Challenger: Is the Shuttle Safe?" *Seattle Times,* May 22, 1986.

5. Malcolm McConnell, *Challenger* (see note 2), p. 5.

6. Eric Naider and Peter Lewis, "Beyond Challenger" (see note 4).

7. Malcolm McConnell, *Challenger* (see note 2), p. 6.

8. Eric Naider and Peter Lewis, "Beyond Challenger" (see note 4).

9. "Senator Orders Fletcher-Thiokol Probe," *Salt Lake Tribune,* December 19, 1986.

10. Jim Rowley, "Slush Fund at Thiokol Is Alleged," *Salt Lake Tribune,* April 17, 1987.

11. Philip M. Boffey, "Engineer Who Opposed Launching Sues Thiokol for $1 Billion," *New York Times,* January 29, 1987.

12. Robert Gottlieb and Peter Wiley, *America's Saints* (New York: G. P. Putnam, 1984), p. 127.

13. Ibid., p. 123.

14. Author's interview with former Utah Governor Calvin L. Rampton, Salt Lake City, January 21, 1988.

15. Author's interview with Milton Weilemann, Salt Lake City, January 21, 1988.

16. G. Homer Durham, *N. Eldon Tanner: His Life and Service* (Salt Lake City: Deseret Books, 1982), pp. 240–241.

17. "University of Utah Aide Gets Helm of Pro-Utah," *Salt Lake Tribune,* November 16, 1972.

18. Author's interviews with former Utah Governor Calvin L. Rampton (see note 14) and with Milton Weilemann (see note 15).

19. Malcolm McConnell, *Challenger* (see note 2), p. 53.

20. Ibid., pp. 52-53.

21. Memorandum to Senator Frank E. Moss from Bob Allnutt re Comptroller General Meeting with William L. Waller, Governor of Mississippi, on Lockheed Protest of NASA Selection of Thiokol for Space Shuttle Solid Rocket Motor Contract, June 12, 1974; in Frank E. Moss Collection, University of Utah library, Salt Lake City.

22. Malcolm McConnell, *Challenger* (see note 2), p. 57.

23. Ibid., p. 59.

24. "Senator Orders Fletcher-Thiokol Probe" (see note 9).

25. Letter of James C. Fletcher to U.S. Senator Frank E. Moss, Chairman, Committee on Aeronautical and Space Sciences, United States Senate, Washington, D.C., January 12, 1973, in Frank E. Moss Collection, University of Utah library, Salt Lake City.

26. Letter of James C. Fletcher to U.S. Senator Frank E. Moss, Chairman, Committee on Aeronautical and Space Sciences, United States Senate, Washington, D.C., February 23, 1973, in Frank E. Moss Collection, University of Utah library, Salt Lake City.

27. Malcolm McConnell, *Challenger* (see note 2), p. 54.

28. Ibid.

29. "Senator Orders Fletcher-Thiokol Probe" (see note 9).

30. Both men quoted in William J. Broad, "NASA Chief Might Not Take Part in Decisions on Booster Contracts," *New York Times,* December 7, 1986.

31. Author's interview with William Wright, investigator for the U.S. General Accounting Office, April 3, 1987, at Salt Lake City.

32. William J. Broad, "NASA Chief" (see note 30).

33. Ibid.

34. *NASA Procurement: The 1973 Space Shuttle Solid Rocket Motor Contractor Selection* (Washington, D.C.: United States General Accounting Office Report to the Honorable Albert Gore, Jr., U.S. Senate), p. 14.

35. Executive Order 11222 (signed by President Lyndon B. Johnson, May 8,

1965): "Prescribing Standards of Ethical Conduct for Government Officers and Employees," in Title 3, Chapter 2, pp. 306–311.

36. Eric Naider and Peter Lewis, "Beyond Challenger" (see note 4).

37. See "Thiokol Given Low Safety Rating in '86," *Salt Lake Tribune,* January 23, 1988; "Thiokol Under GAO Probe," *Salt Lake Tribune,* February 18, 1988.

38. "Air Force Blames Static Electricity for Thiokol's Deadly Fire," *Standard-Examiner,* Ogden, Utah, March 17, 1988.

39. Peter Lewis and Eric Naider, "Subpoenas Are Issued for Shuttle Booster Maker," *Seattle Times,* June 8, 1988.

40. See "Morton Thiokol, Inc. Battles to Remain Sole Maker of Shuttle's Booster Rocket," *Wall Street Journal,* January 23, 1987; William J. Broad, "NASA Chief" (see note 30); Guy Bawlton, "Suspicion Still Stalks Fletcher," *Salt Lake Tribune,* December 10, 1986; "Fletcher Won't Bow Out of Rocket Talks," *Salt Lake Tribune,* January 23, 1987.

41. "NASA Wants to Build Shuttle Engine Plant Closer to the Cape," *Deseret News,* February 19, 1988.

42. "Fletcher Will Quit NASA Job When Reagan Term Ends," *Salt Lake Tribune,* February 21, 1988.

43. "Interview: James Fletcher," *Omni,* December 1987, p. 122.

44. John Heinerman and Anson Shupe, *The Mormon Corporate Empire* (Boston: Beacon Press, 1985). See, e.g., on the FCC, pp. 46–55; on the Foreign Service, pp. 137–138; on Congress, pp. 139–142; on the CIA/FBI, pp. 162–168; on the Pentagon, pp. 168–176.

45. Letter of Gregory C. Thompson, Assistant Director for Special Collections, Marriott Library, University of Utah, to Anson Shupe, Indiana-Purdue University at Fort Wayne, November 22, 1989.

Chapter 8: The Shadow of Mormonism

1. See Jeffrey K. Hadden and Anson Shupe, *Televangelism: Power and Politics on God's Frontier* (New York: Henry Holt, 1988); Joe E. Barnhart, *Jim and Tammy: Charismatic Intrigue Inside PTL* (Buffalo, N.Y.: Prometheus Books, 1988); Larry Martz, *Ministry of Greed: The Inside Story of the Televangelists and Their Holy Wars* (New York: Weidenfeld and Nicolson, 1988); and John Stewart, *Holy War* (Enid, Okla.: Fireside, 1987).

2. This somewhat cryptic statement would require an entire essay to elaborate, but it refers to various investigative journalists and independent writers in the Intermountain West, personally known to this author, who are attempting to pursue lines of research similar to those presented here. Their various stories of intimidation, break-ins, and thefts of materials during their investigations, and other harassments, would make a fascinating volume. It is hoped that such data will see publication in the future.

3. See John A. Sanford, *Evil: The Shadow Side of Reality* (New York: Crossroad, 1984).

4. "Elder Decries Criticism of LDS Leaders," *Salt Lake Tribune,* August 18, 1985.

5. See "Sustaining the General Authorities," *Ward Teacher's Message,* June 1945, Church of Jesus Christ of Latter-Day Saints, Salt Lake City.

6. "Priesthood," an editorial in the *Millennial Star,* November 13, 1852, Liverpool, England.

7. See "Mormon Financial Scams," a recorded panel discussion moderated by Dr. D. James Craft, Executive Vice President of the Federal Home Loan Mortgage Company (Tape No. 895-048), and "Crooks, Con-Artists, and Crackpots," a recorded panel discussion moderated by Dr. Warner Woodworth, Professor of Organizational Behavior, Brigham Young University (Tape No. 895-011), both featured at the annual Sunstone Symposium sponsored by the Sunstone Foundation, Salt Lake City, at the University of Utah, August 23–26, 1989.

Index

Rendell, Kenneth, 102
Reorganized Church of Jesus Christ of
Latter-day Saints, 89–91
Roby, Dr. C. Y., 112
Roberts, Oral, 162
Rockwell, Norman, 1
Rogers Commission, 142, 144–145, 156
Romney, Marion G., 87
Rust, Alvin, 94–97, 99–100, 103–104

Salamander Letter, 85, 92–94, 99, 102
Salt Lake County Child Abuse Coordi-
nating Committee, 113
Sanchez, Aaron (FBI Special Agent),
132
Sanders, Colonel, 67
Saudi Arabia. See Missionary efforts of
the LDS Church
Schick, George, 156
Schiller-Wapner Galleries of New York,
98
Schmidt, Don, 89, 91, 95
Schwein, Richard, 139
Sheets, Gary, 78
Sheets, Kathy Webb, 77–78, 98, 101
Shirts, Morris A., 60
Sill, Sterling W. See NAVSAT scandal
Silva, Antonio, 136
Simmonds, Jeff, 86
Smart, William B. (Deseret News edi-
tor), 67
Smith, Alvin, 93
Smith, George Albert, 35
Smith, Joseph, 9–15, 23, 80–81, 85–87,
89, 92–93, 164
Smith, Lucy Mack, 95
Snow, Dr. Barbara, 107–109, 115–123
Somalia. See Missionary efforts of the
LDS Church
Sorensen, David E., 100
Soviet Life, 37
Soviet Union. See Missionary efforts of
the LDS Church
Stark, Rodney, 24–25
Stott, Robert, 102, 105

Stowell, Josiah, 92–93
Sunday Evening From Temple Square,
66
Sutter, John, 144
Swaggart, Jimmy, 13, 161

Tanner, Debbie. See Texas baby-mill
scandal
Tanner, N. Eldon, 147–149, 152–153.
See also NAVSAT scandal, 65–72,
87
Tanner, Sandra and Jerald, 94
"Telephone Tree" of LDS members, 10,
108
Texas baby-mill scandal, 61–65
Thiokal Company, 145–146, 149–151,
155–159, 162
Thomas, Barbara, 113
Throckmorton, George, 102
Tobler, Douglas, 37
Triad America, 31
Turley, Walter, 62–63

Utah Division of Family Services, 114–
115
Utah Light Ministry, 93–94
Utah War of 1857, 17

Valadez, Rudolph (FBI Special Agent),
134–135f.

Walker, Earl and Cindy, 108
Ward, Brent (US Attorney), 45
Warner, Paul (Utah Deputy Attorney
General), 109
Watson, Wayne, 116
Weilemann, Milton, 147–148
White, Jr., O. Kendall, 39
White-collar-crime problem in Utah,
44–50
Whitehead, Dr. Paul L., 109, 116, 119
White Salamander Letter, 85–89
Wilding, Thomas, 98–102
Wright, Michael Drew, 74
Wright, William, 154, 159